I0545823

THE SINGULARITY PRIZE

THE SINGULARITY PRIZE

EARL ERNEST GUILE

Copyright © 2017 by Earl Ernest Guile
The Singularity Prize
Earl Ernest Guile
eguile@gmail.com
https://Singularityprize.com
https://ernestguile.com
https://eguile.wordpress.com/
Twitter: @eguile
Facebook: https://www.facebook.com/eeguile#

First Edition
Published in the United States by Mayshouse Press
P.O. Box 91086
Portland, Oregon 97291

Library of Congress Control Number: 2017914166

ISBN: 978-0-9993554-0-4 (Paperback)
ISBN: 978-0-9993554-1-1 (ebook)

Book Designer: Stewart A. Williams
Line Editor: Ellen Brock
Proofreader: Patricia Callahan
Publicist: Andrea Dunlop

Cover star field photo credits:
NASA & ESA, Jesús Maíz Apellániz (Centro de Astrobiología, CSIC-INTA, Spain)
Printed in the United States of America

DEDICATION

*This book is dedicated to Dr. Benjamin Elijah Mays,
the grandmaster educator and intellectual
father of the civil rights movement.*

*Knowing others is intelligence; knowing yourself is
true wisdom. Mastering others is strength; mastering
yourself is true power. If you realize that you have
enough, you are truly rich.*
—Lao Tzu

CHAPTER 1

FLORENCE, SOUTH CAROLINA, FALL-WINTER 1960-61

The chill of December filled the air as Julian and Harold walked home from school. They had just left the Wilson High School grounds and were now walking along an unpaved street lined with narrow houses with brick chimneys and wide front porches. The trees were mere skeletons, leaves gone. Julian was a senior looking forward to graduating and going to college. Harold was a junior with a keen interest in physics and cinema.

"What books have you read lately?" Julian asked, pushing his black horn-rimmed glasses up higher on his nose.

"I read a book called *Martian Chronicles* by Ray Bradbury. It talks about the colonization of Mars. Mars is tempting, but I guess we have to get to the moon first. What about you?"

"I read a book by George Gamow called *123 Infinity*. It explained in understandable language many of the current theories in physics and astronomy."

"That sounds pretty cool."

"It was a challenge to understand some of Einstein's concepts, such as space-time being four dimensions where time is the fourth coordinate. Gravity is defined as a geometric property of space-time, where the curvature of space-time could result from the presence of the gravity of a massive object like the sun. The sun's gravity can bend the light of stars. This is Einstein's general theory of relativity. I had to reread it a few times, but a lot of what the book was talking about made sense after a while."

"Science is an excellent subject from the sheer immensity of it all. The universe is the mother lode of this vastness," Harold said.

"Let's just say science is a mother, full stop."

The two students reached the downtown area of Florence and passed by the small retail shops, the five-and-dime called Kress, the local cinema, and a photography studio.

"Do you remember a few months ago when some students in Greensboro got arrested for trying to integrate the lunch counters at Woolworths?" Julian said.

"Yeah, I remember. They were very brave, considering the Jim Crow laws they were breaking."

"I've been thinking about books and how important it is to have access to knowledge. I think that's more important than black people gaining access to lunch counters. The main library in Florence has so many amazing books," Julian said.

"Too bad they don't allow us black folks to go there."

"Well, why don't we do what they did in Greensboro and attempt to integrate the library? Keep in mind, Dr. Martin Luther King was successful in integrating the bus system in Montgomery, Alabama, after organizing a long boycott," Julian said.

"I could go for attempting to integrate the library. Let's do it," Harold said.

"There is a risk to doing this, are you sure you want to do this?"

"Hell yes!"

Julian and Harold began walking toward the main library on Irby Street. After several blocks, they reached the library, which was a large redbrick building with a white arched window over the main entrance out front. They looked up and read the name: Florence Public Library.

"I wonder if the public in public library is accurate and includes us. Let's go in and see," Julian said.

Nervously, they climbed the steps and opened the heavy wooden front door. Inside they saw wide hardwood tables and four large chandeliers. In the rear, the librarians sat behind a long desk. Behind the librarians and to their sides were the stacks, which held an extensive collection of books, manuscripts, maps, and microfilm.

"Let's go pick out some books and take them up to the desk to check out," Julian said.

"Okay, cool."

The ladies behind the desk stopped what they were doing and watched the unwanted visitors from across town. Among the shelves of books, Julian found about five that piqued his interest. He joined up with Harold and walked deliberately to the librarian.

"We are students at Wilson High, and we would like to check out these books," Julian said.

"I'm sorry, but you need a library card to check out books," the librarian responded.

"Can we apply for a card now?" Harold asked.

"If you want these books, we will reserve them and send them to the library connected to your school. That is the library for colored people in Florence."

"Why can't we just get them now and have regular use of this library? This library has a much larger collection than the one next to our school."

"I'm sorry, boys," she said.

"Wouldn't it be more ethical and also based on the US Constitution for the library to give us a card? We are citizens of this country also. Thomas Jefferson said we are all created equal."

The librarian thought for a minute, wondering how to answer; then she turned to consult her nearby colleagues who had been watching the encounter.

Harold turned to Julian and whispered, "Let's take these books and sit down to read them here in the library."

"Okay."

They sat down at the table nearest the door with their stack of books between them and began reading. Their thirst for knowledge was quenched as they enjoyed the public library for the first time. They read for about two hours, until nearly six o'clock.

"Boys, the library's closed. You have to leave now," the librarian said.

"Can we check out the books?" Julian asked.

"I explained to you earlier that you cannot check out books from this library. We are closing now."

"We're not leaving until we're allowed to check out these books," Julian said defiantly. He could feel his heart banging in his chest as he stood his ground.

Harold said, "We are prepared to stay here overnight."

"In that case, I have no recourse other than to call the police," she said and turned on her heel to make the call.

In about five minutes the blinking lights of a police car pulled up in front of the library. Moments later three burly policemen stood over Julian and Harold.

"Boys, the library is closed. You have to leave now," one of the policemen said. The two boys remained silent and continued sitting at the table.

"Boys, this is the last time I will ask you to leave. If you refuse, we have to put you under arrest and take you to jail," the other policeman said.

"We want to check out these books here on the table. After that we will be happy to leave," Julian said while getting up to go to the other side of the table to huddle with Harold.

"Should we let ourselves get arrested or should we leave," Harold asked, his voice low.

"Instead of getting arrested maybe we should leave and come back again tomorrow," Julian said.

The police were noticeably impatient, but they let the two boys talk.

Without any further discussion, Harold and Julian got up and left. They calmed down from the tension of the police encounter as they walked home.

"We can continue tomorrow with the protest," Julian said.

"Agreed."

The next day they returned, and the door had a sign saying "Closed for Renovation."

"I don't see any renovation work going on," Harold said.

"No, there is no renovation happening. They have closed the library because we challenged the system yesterday."

"Let's try again tomorrow."

They returned several days in succession and found the same sign but saw no visible renovation work. They stopped checking for two months. On February 22, 1961, they returned.

"The library is open," Julian said.

They both rushed in to see what would happen. After collecting books from the stacks, they went to check them out.

"We would like to check out these books," Julian said.

"First you have to fill out these applications for cards," the librarian said.

She handed both of them an application, and they quickly filled them out. Cards were issued, and the library checked out the books. Julian put his books in his backpack with a wide smile.

As they walked home, Julian said, "I feel great, Harold. We succeeded in checking out books for the first time in our hometown library. More importantly, we have opened up this treasure trove of books to the rest of the black community in Florence, forever."

"Our strategy worked of coming back until they relented and gave us a card," Harold said.

"Knowledge is power. Did you notice the librarian's politeness when giving us the card? It was as if we were freeing her mind of bigotry as was said of whites also being freed when Lincoln freed the slaves," Julian said.

✳

"So, Julian Jr., that's my memory of how my friend Harold and I opened up the Florence Public Library to all the residents of the city. Black people were excluded from using this library from the time of its founding on November 3, 1925, until February 22, 1961. I was about your age when this happened. The mission of the library in 2015 now states, and I quote:

The Florence County Library System provides library materials, services, and programs to all citizens of Florence County, to assist them in obtaining information to meet their diverse educational, cultural, recreational, and professional needs.

"Wow, that's a great story. I never thought about how important books are," Julian Jr. said.

Julian Sr.'s story of integrating the library made an indelible imprint on Julian Jr.'s thinking and ambition. Julian Jr. pursued computer science books in his college studies and later focused his research on artificial intelligence.

✳

GREAT RIFT VALLEY, EAST AFRICA, 74,000 YEARS AGO

In the distance, the ashes of a supervolcano darkened the sky of an ancient East African dawn. The rising sun was muted before it could

6

illuminate the tall grasslands. All the animals were startled and turned to gaze at this unusual display of nature's power.

This was the great Toba Event, the largest volcanic eruption in the past two million years. This mega-eruption from a Pacific island spread an ash cloud that covered the Indian subcontinent in a blanket fifteen centimeters deep. Some volcanic ash reached Africa and eventually circled the globe in the stratosphere, creating a devastating volcanic winter.

A small band of humans crouched in a tight circle to protect themselves from the wrath of nature. As the morning turned to afternoon, the sun disappeared behind the enormous ash cloud. Soon, great quantities of ash fell from the sky like a spring rain and covered the landscape.

"What does this mean?" Kyo asked her nearby mate.

"This is the omen of disaster that our ancestors told us about many moons ago," replied Arion.

"What does the omen mean?" Kyo asked.

"It means we must find shelter and store food or we will surely die."

The other clan members in this small group of thirty-one looked at each other with bewilderment through a gray mist, as their faces and skimpily clad bodies became covered in ash.

"How can we find game when the land is covered by this ash from the heavens?" Utu, a young clan member, asked.

Eto, an elder shaman, responded, "The animals we need for survival are in the same trouble we are. While they display weakness, we must display strength. May the gods shine on us and help us succeed. If not, we die of hunger. Our ancestors did tell us to look to the caves."

The sun was too faint to heat up the day, which soon became as dark as night. The group trudged toward a small stream in the distance as the ash grew deeper and deeper, soon reaching their ankles. Visibility worsened with each and every careful step.

Over half of this group had perished in an earlier encounter with an earthquake. Survival of the other half was now in peril. When they reached the small stream, their first thought was to fill their gourds with water and press on to a distant cave for safety. They hoped that they would capture game, find some berries, and hunt for meat before entering the cave.

For a thousand generations, the clan eked out a living on the plains of East Africa. The struggle for survival had always been part of their life. Periodically, the skies had darkened during the seasonal rains, but this was different. Even the clan elders could not remember anything like this.

Along the route, the clan saw wildebeest, giraffe, eland, and antelope in the distance, but they were too far away to be worth the hunt. The group trekked for several hours in the direction of the mountains and encountered a herd of gazelles that seemed confused and disoriented. Two stray laggards from the herd became a natural target. The clan was always prepared to seize an opportunity to acquire food. The alternative was to perish from starvation. The spears they used were fashioned over the millennia into lethal weapons with flaked obsidian stones, and the men's constant practice perfected their accuracy in hitting their targets.

Some of the men had blowguns with poison-tipped darts. These were used when the range was close to reaching the target. The poison wounded the animal and was effective in minimizing the time and distance of tracking.

"Prepare for an attack!" Arion spoke softly, yet his command was sharp.

The men squatted in the tall grass, waiting for Arion's signal. When he raised his arms, the spears flew, striking both gazelles in mid-flight. The animals collapsed about fifty meters away. The men ran to their fallen prey, raised their hands high in the air, and yelled, "Uhuru."

The gazelles were mounted on parallel poles and carried through an area of heavy, dense savannah foliage. Their knowledge of this area was deep and rich from many generations traveling back and forth over the terrain searching for food and water.

"Look at the hills in the distance. We need to go there," said Arion. The hills were silhouetted against the dark sky. Faces white with ash, the clan members carried their possessions and meager food supplies, and continued to trek to their destination. Three enormous lions prowled nearby the cave complex.

"Let's go in that direction," Arion said, pointing north. "We need to get around these beasts." The clan moved rapidly; yet, the big cats had caught their scent and, crouching low, stalked their prey.

"We need to get out of range quickly," said Arion.

"The children can't keep up," Utu responded in a panic.

Sure enough, a lion sprang from the tall grasses and grabbed a young boy. He screamed as the lion dragged him into the bush. The clan members valiantly chased to fight back but soon gave up when the screams stopped. All hope was lost. The child was gone to the ages.

"We must continue to the mountain home," Arion said, "or we will all perish to the lions."

They carried their meager possessions and the gazelles they killed as well as plants, berries, nuts, eggs, honey, termites, and ant larvae into the cave. One of the women quickly started a friction fire using a bow, a stone socket, a fireboard, and some tinder. Torches were lighted, and the gazelles were skinned and treated for preservation.

The clan settled in the cave while conditions outside became the cold, dark enemy of the living. The temperatures dropped lower than ever before as the sun's rays were blotted out completely. The earth, was in darkness. The survival of this small human clan sheltering in an African cave would depend on collective intelligence.

"What are you doing now?" one of the children asked Urik, a hunter whose wife had died in the earthquake over three years earlier.

"I'm preserving the flesh from our recent kill by smoking and drying it over this fire."

"What do you mean by preserving it?"

"Preserving means that the flesh will not take on a bad smell and become dangerous to eat."

"Will there be enough food for us?"

"I don't know, but we will have a little more available when I do this. Now, go back to your mother and let me finish this."

"Yes, Urik."

After everyone had rested for a few hours, Arion announced, "We must go deeper into the caves for safety. Be sure to keep all torches lit as we travel in the darkness."

The clan traveled downward through a narrow passageway until they reached a cathedral-like cavern with a high ceiling. Brilliant stalactite crystals hung from the roof like prehistoric chandeliers. On that first night, Arion gathered the people in a circle around the fire.

His clan was star worshipers, a practice that went deep into the bosom of time for thousands of years. Their ancient elders had passed the words of this proto-religion down through the generations.

"Our very survival is at stake now," Arion began. "In the distant past, our ancestors also had to become long-term cave dwellers to survive many cycles of the moon. Like our ancestors, we take our wisdom from the almighty stars. The stars are ceaseless, immortal, and all wise. Our ancestors told us that we came from those stars. Therefore, we have some of their wisdom. Let's use that wisdom to continue to live."

"That's right, those who came before us were wise. They left us the most important thing, knowledge. These hardships are what to expect in life. We can embrace hardships and work through them," Eto said.

"Yes, Eto, we saw the power of nature when the heavens darkened. We respect that power, and to flow through the river of changes that Mother Nature presents to us, we must stay calm, be patient, and be ever elegant in our thinking, decision making, and our actions. We mourn the loss of one of our children as we also mourn those we lost when the land moved. We must be ever vigilant to protect everyone because we are all one, and we toil together to stay alive."

The group listened to Arion's message silently, and the collective body language expressed understanding and approval. Utu raised a question: "How long can we survive in this cave if the world outside remains barren?"

"We can't say. We have to severely reduce the amount of food we eat so that it will last," Arion said.

"I agree and share that belief," Utu said.

Eto and the others nodded in agreement.

Kyo and Arion nestled close together, bedding down for the night in a spot against the cave wall between two large boulders. They kissed softly, realizing that this crisis would only deepen their love and make them cherish each other more.

The last flicker of the campfire signaled the time to sleep for the weary band of early humans as they hunkered down to survive the great Toba eruption.

Over days and weeks, the leaves outside began to wilt from the absence of sunlight. The volcanic ash rose high into the stratosphere and circumnavigated the earth. Photosynthesis stopped, and the food chain collapsed. This was the great genetic bottleneck when there were only one thousand breeding pairs of Homo sapiens alive. Human life on Earth was gravely threatened with extinction, identical to the fate earlier hominid species had suffered.

The weeks in the cave became months as darkness prevailed across the ash-strewn world.

✻

THE AWAKENING: AD 2030

In 2030 Julian saw that the intelligence awakening was palpable across the globe. The massive educational advances in knowledge disseminating throughout the globe between 2024 and 2030 began to shatter old paradigms. This profound change over just six years was the result of accelerating scientific advances. The masses that had previously been illiterate and unable to contribute to societal progress were now highly intelligent, well-educated, and innovative and were crafting new discoveries every day in all fields of study.

Innovations and discoveries benefitting mankind had been very slow over the centuries. Stone ax tools took millennia to advance to bronze implements. Horse-drawn transportation took centuries to advance to the horseless carriage. Man's first air flight at Kitty Hawk took decades to advance to extra-planetary moon travel with rockets. As collective human intelligence mounted, the timelines between profound discoveries shortened. Medical discoveries that took decades in the past began to occur within years, and later, within months.

In spite of all these magnificent achievements, in 2030, many problems in the world remained. Among these were poverty, human conflict, continued dependence on fossil fuels, periodic global epidemics, energy shortages, mineral resource depletion, insufficient food production, and limited clean water supplies for 8.7 billion souls. The greatest problem was the inexorable rise of the seas as climate change increased the global average temperatures. This alone created more refugees than all the wars of the twentieth century. Whole islands disappeared along with enormous sections of the shoreline.

Intelligence is to genius as the whole
is in proportion to its part.
—Jean De La Bruyère

CHAPTER 2

JULY 2030

The full-page advertisement in the *New York Times*, the *Washington Post*, the *The Financial Times*, the *Guardian*, *Der Tagesspiegel*, *Peking Daily* and other major world newspapers read:

ANNOUNCING THE SINGULARITY PRIZE
The research team that develops a verifiable safe singularity will receive a sum of $30 billion. The Singularity Prize competition rules require each team to program a recursively self-improving machine that exceeds human intelligence and contains an embedded ethical code. The verification of the winning team will be made by a panel of scientists in a peer-reviewed format. For details on the rules and strict regulations for competing, please visit our website at www.SingularityPrize.com.

Our definition of the singularity comes from many sources. The singularity we speak of is technological. The hypothesis states that when humans invent an upgradable artificial super intelligence, this will initiate runaway technological growth based on self-improvement cycles. The resulting intelligence would surpass all human intelligence and continue to advance technologically at an incomprehensible rate. Our focus in selecting the prize winner is for the invention to be safe and to benefit humans and other DNA-based life-forms on earth within a nurturing biosphere. The singularity must adhere to the Asilomar AI Principles developed in 2017.

News of the S-Prize announcement ran on all the news channels and went viral on social networks. A team of reporters gathered in front of the hedge fund offices to interview Ellison McClintock, the person responsible for the S-Prize. Instead, Ellison called a formal press conference to respond to the clamor for information on the S-Prize by the international press corp. A roomful of reporters sat patiently in one of the ballrooms of the Waldorf-Astoria Hotel in New York City. Ellison walked in and stood behind the podium. Crimson curtains with the Waldorf Astoria logo stretched behind him.

The cameras from all the major networks and cable outlets lined the back of the room. The cable channels carried the press conference live as breaking news.

Ellison began the press conference. "Thank you for coming. We will try to address your inquiries on the recently announced Singularity Prize. Therefore, we will immediately begin with questions."

"Why do you want a singularity at this time?" a reporter for the *Washington Post* asked.

"The best way to solve the great problems that our civilization faces is to use our advances in science. The problems of the world in energy, food production, climate change, and disease have been overwhelming as our global population has grown. Science has not advanced fast enough to solve these problems.

The singularity is an acceleration of science, expanding human access to a much, much higher form of intelligence. A friendly, supportive, ethical superintelligence that could be commissioned to solve major problems is the outcome I hope for."

"How is your foundation planning to pay for this prize?"

"We are raising a large portion of the funding, and I am adding funds from my personal portfolio. We are confident that we can have the complete sum by the time one of our competitors wins the prize. We have had a great response to our fund-raising so far."

"How will you know that we have reached the singularity, and how can you assure us that it will be safe for humanity?" the questions continued.

"We have written very strict rules and criteria for participants in the competition that require them to establish well-described safeguards against the risk of an unfriendly singularity. Most importantly, impeccable self-improving ethics must be embedded in the programming of this machine intelligence. If contestants go beyond this protocol, we cannot be sure of the outcome, and that is certainly a risk; however, our research projections suggest that the risk is manageable.

"When one considers the potential gain for humanity, it is a risk worth taking. In history, many new discoveries have had both an upside and a possible downside. In spite of the possible risks, scientific innovation has progressed," said Ellison.

"What happens if there is no winner in this so-called S-Prize?"

"We believe that the singularity is inevitable and having a prize is the best way to guide this important development and guarantee that it remains safe for humanity. Thank you very much, ladies and gentlemen. I must go to work to manage this important prize and raise more funds," said Ellison.

The press conference made the national news cycle and generated a heated national conversation on the rewards and perils of artificial intelligence. The #SingularityPrize hashtag was trending on social media.

＊

In Julian's house in Berkeley and other homes of 2030, floor-to-ceiling screens covered many of the walls, giving him the opportunity to create any scene or mood he desired through music and visuals in a virtual reality setting. One could travel in time or space to exotic locales and periods of history, and it seemed as real as reality. Smart toilets using DNA chips analyzed body fluids daily and created health alerts to the individual and their doctors if medical intervention was necessary. Biomarker sensing devices in watches monitored health indicators and also provided real-time alerts to medical services. The Apple Watch 7.0 was all the rage and accounted for 60 percent of Apple's revenues. At birth, DNA sequencing became routine for all newborns in developed societies. A brain-to-computer interface emerged in a primitive way as Moore's law, predicting the doubling of transistors per square inch in integrated circuits, continued to scale downward to the nano range.

＊

JULIAN'S QUEST

Julian Marshall spent a year as an aide worker in Mozambique and it had a profound impact on his worldview and appreciation for life. Prior to his aid work, Julian earned a PhD. in computer science at the Massachusetts Institute of Technology and completed a postdoc in Deep Learning at the University of Cambridge in the UK. He decided after his aid work to apply his academic and research training full-time in artificial intelligence as a means of solving the great engineering and social challenges of the twenty-first century. The hardship of the aid work was truly an awakening in him, and it made him more diligent, fearless, strategic, and optimistic about life in general. This carried him to Berkeley, California, where he joined Berkeley's Center for Information Technology Research in their intense work of making machines think. Julian rose quickly through the academic ranks. His computer-coding skills were extraordinary and showed unusual levels of creativity and imagination in programming. His coding reminded his professors at MIT of a jazz musician's improvisational skills in music. His 233 research publications were high impact and frequently cited by his peers. In early 2028, the Center for Intelligence Science (CIS) was formed and Julian Marshall was designated as the first director. The vision of the center focused on the building of machine-intelligence tools in service to humanity and the ecosystem.

Julian picked up the Singularity Prize announcement press release and had his secretary deliver copies of the printout to his colleagues on the CIS team.

By email, Julian wrote, "Ladies and gentlemen, the announcement left on your desk is a clear call for us to meet today to make a plan." The CIS staff met at 10 a.m. sharp, exactly one hour after news of the S-Prize announcement.

In the large conference room where the research team had gathered, Julian began the meeting. "We are to develop an immediate response to the S-Prize announcement. We would like to formalize our efforts and consolidate our focus to achieve success with reaching the much talked about singularity through a greatly amplified artificial general intelligence. We have been working on bits and pieces of this for years now. This prize call is a great impetus for us to focus our energies like a fireman's hose on the central problems. Where should we begin? We have to first apply successfully to be a competitor. That is no walk in the park."

A graduate student spoke up. "To have the best possible chance at success, I think it would be ideal to work together with a variety of skilled teams across the globe."

"Yes, that is a powerful model for innovation," Julian said.

The CSI headquarters was in a new building built in 2023 with many futuristic features. Solar light and extensive glass permeated the design, giving a breathtaking sense of space. The building architecturally facilitated maximum collaboration. The main conference room featured state-of-the-art teleconferencing facilities for encrypted video, audio, and data transmission. Holographic images could be presented of remote conferees. Bluetooth access for any device could be displayed on giant multi-panel screens on every wall. Abstract art was on display around the room, providing a visual muse for the scientists. "We will use our computers to review all the previous research and use this as a platform to devise our plan to make an assault for the mountaintop. Another key point is for us to find other like-minded teams that we could have good chemistry with and form a super-collaborative group. The Stanford and the Cape Town groups come to mind because we have published papers with them. Distance does not matter; they could be on the other side of the planet, or just down the Bay, and we can still work with them," Julian explained.

"Our review will naturally lead us to brilliant people who we can add to our group. Google, Facebook, Apple, and Amazon are obvious sources of talent we could tap. There could be a pursuit by other groups to enlist these talented individuals before we do. We need to move quickly," a senior researcher said.

"We will first brainstorm a task list and assign ourselves to get them done by a short deadline," Julian said.

"We can already see the impact the prize announcement has made on things. I'm certain that groups that immediately sprang into action might otherwise have moved slowly in their actions over a few months or years without the stimulus of this competitive goal; therefore even with a delay in starting we are still ahead of the game," John Snowden, a legacy faculty member, said.

"The singularity is around the corner. It's a certainty. We must make sure that we are the team to reach the finish line first. Let's get started with our task list items. In this brainstorming, there are no bad ideas, so unblock the barriers in your thinking and come out with anything, no matter how outlandish," Julian said.

"We need to decide on our particular route to a singularity. How are we going to do it? What equipment do we need to obtain as we push ahead?" said Snowden, one of the few present with gray hair.

John Snowden was the elder in the CIS. He was formerly the chair of the computer science department at Berkeley and saw the great transformation that occurred when the Internet emerged. He saw the boom and the bust of the dot-com implosion. John was most proud that Berkeley graduated a higher proportion of Pell Grant students in computer science than all the Ivy League colleges combined. This implied that Berkeley was a great educational vehicle for the poor to rise into the middle class. Furthermore, this increased the vital numbers of technology workers whom the American economy needed.

John was excited to work with younger scientists. That work in the CIS kept him on his toes and kept him young, as he always told his wife.

"We need to get the university to grant us the time and facilities to pursue this in concert with our present schedule of teaching and ongoing research. We may need to shift other projects that we are involved with to another non-CIS faculty," John said.

"We need to establish a mechanism of regular and consistent communication within our peer group and with progress outside of Berkeley," Faye said.

This small-scale rapid iteration procedure by the team continued until it generated well over 750 ideas. Getting such a positive response led Julian to feel confident that CIS was skillfully starting toward this daunting goal.

Julian continued with the discussion on the basics of intelligence so that the entire team operated from the same page, reviewed with the grad students present, and understood the real challenges that CIS faced in programming a machine to carry out new standards and levels of general intelligence functions.

"Let's look at a broad definition of intelligence. It reflects the ability to learn, reason, understand, remember, plan, solve problems, communicate, have emotional knowledge, have ethics, and have the ability of abstract thought," Julian said.

"Anything, including a machine that has these abilities, can be considered intelligent. The question for us: Can we program the machine to have all of these capabilities? Let's take a look at abstraction, for example. It's a process by which a general or higher concept is derived from a specific example or literal concept. It is the process of conceptualizing knowledge and producing wisdom out of information," John said.

"Can we program a machine to make sense out of a vast array of situations similar to a human with common sense?" asked a graduate student.

"This is a concept of discursive reasoning. Reasoning is generally thought of as thinking and cognition. A key part of intelligence is the ability to convey information accurately to a human or machine. It is important that the receiver understands the message being communicated. This brings us to the significant concept of learning as a component of intelligence," replied Julian.

"Learning involves the ability to pull together a variety of information and modify existing knowledge. It is a process that can change behavior and augment skills. Learning builds upon previous knowledge acquired. Again, a critical benchmark that we have to surmount in artificial intelligence is to have that machine learn recursively," John said.

Julian thought about the progress in deep learning since the group at DeepMind beat the top Go player in the world back in 2015 and said, "We shall use the open-source modules in deep learning and enhance them with robust ethics."

"The ability to store and recall information along with experiences from your past is the core of memory and a necessary component of intelligence. Many geniuses earn that title because of their photographic memory of things they have read and information they've been exposed to," Faye said.

"Geniuses have the additional ability to connect the dots and synthesize new ideas from all of this memorized material. A higher-order cognitive process is necessary for, perhaps, the most complex of intellectual pursuits, namely, problem solving. Problem solving involves identifying the problem, establishing the parameters of the problem, and establishing a goal of reaching a solution. This requires several interlocking steps that build on one another. To solve the problem, one must be able to identify and define the problem correctly. Mathematical problem solving is a specific domain that artificial intelligence systems can do very well," John explained.

Faye continued, "Other characteristics include something called emotional intelligence. These are subtle human characteristics involving a nuanced understanding of human behavior and psychological content. It is assumed that machines will be tone-deaf to human emotions such as fear, anger, joy, happiness, sadness, and love. A true intelligence will, at least, have deep insight into these emotions and possibly experience some of them as well."

"How important is it for us to program all of these emotions into a machine? Can we be selective about which ones and leave out others?" asked a programmer.

"These emotions pose a dilemma. If we want a robot to run into a fire to rescue someone, we might have problems if that robot was programmed to be fearful. On the other hand, we would not want the robot to expose itself to unnecessary danger because it has no fear. We need to walk that narrow line between the two ends of the spectrum," John said.

Julian took a sip from his mug of green tea and said, "We know this is elementary information to this group. However, John Wooden, the great UCLA basketball coach, always reviewed something as basic as tying tennis shoes with his players. They won eleven national championships under his mentorship."

The members of the team glanced at each other and smiled at the thought of winning.

"Another component of intelligence that is important is creativity. Creativity is an ability to fabricate something new that has either artistic or practical value. This ability to innovate has been the chief characteristic of great scientists, writers, artists, and musicians throughout history," Faye elaborated while smiling and silencing her ringing cell phone.

"We label creativity as characteristically human. The question arises, if a machine is capable of novel creation in many disciplines at a level that far exceeds human possibilities, how will this be accepted by humans? Will it be welcomed or will it be feared?"

"I think it will be feared at first because of this new paradigm. Once people get used to it working in the background and not in an obvious way, then the fear will go away," Julian said.

"People were afraid of the automobile when it first arrived."

"Other components of mobile intelligent systems include a mode of locomotion and the ability to see the environment. A mobile singularity would be formidable indeed. Advanced robotics is not our current focus. Since this is not a component of the S-Prize requirements, we will address this avenue later," Julian said.

"According to Marvin Minsky, one of the original AI pioneers from MIT, AI projects without robots are always ahead of projects with robots," John said.

"One of our issues of key focus will be machine ethics," said Julian.

"That is probably a point of consensus among all of us," Faye said.

"The building of a perpetually safe intelligence will require great thought embedded in the coding. I'm confident we have the talent on our team to accomplish this," Julian said.

"Human ethics has advanced by fits and spurts over the generations. It is only in recent centuries that the mortality rate from conflict has dropped dramatically due in large measure to human ethics and morality progress," John said.

"The ethics coding is our greatest programming challenge and must be present before we place the keystone code that initiates the singularity," Faye said.

Richard Steen, a colleague of Julian's who had been a rival for leadership of the department, stood up. "I think this project is a fool's errand. The danger of creating a superintelligence is far greater than we realize. I am not alone. There are many great minds who think the singularity is an existential threat to human civilization. Even though my career has been in computer science, I do not believe that we can control an intelligence greater than ours, and this lack of control means that this intelligence can establish its goals that are at odds with human goals."

"We are well aware of these reservations about our research. We all know that there is a relentless march toward change that will reveal some type of superintelligence in the near future whether we want it to happen or not. Our goal precisely is to usher this inevitable change safely. Not pursuing this is tantamount to allowing a malevolent intelligence to emerge elsewhere," Julian said.

"I disagree with this premise. I have concluded that our efforts should be spent on shutting down this AGI research. Otherwise, we are doomed. I will, therefore, leave the CIS and this effort." Richard got up and left the small lecture room without looking back.

There was total silence for a few moments. Everyone was shocked to see a veteran AI researcher have such a sudden and dramatic change of heart. After the shock wore off, the meeting gradually switched to focus on formulating the next steps.

The meeting continued into the early afternoon and adjourned for team members to start on the master plan. Julian recognized that of all the great events in the history of the universe, the emergence and expansion of intelligence were perhaps the most profound and revolutionary—from the initial development of neurological awareness to man's first steps out of Africa.

As fundamental as these events were to the history of cognition, the coming singularity would be the greatest occasion of them all. They were competing not only for the financial prize but to be the first to reach the summit of all scientific work in human history.

Berkeley's CIS officially coordinated their efforts with a group at Stanford University and the University of Cape Town, South Africa, to go after the S-Prize with a focused and concerted effort.

Berkeley in 2030 was an active, bustling town with futuristic architecture. The sleek, swirling, avant-garde designed buildings were interspersed with those structures built as early as the nineteenth and early twentieth century. As in Copenhagen, bicycles and backpacks ruled the streets of Berkeley. Berkeley was the environment where one of the greatest assaults in history on understanding and fabricating a superintelligent machine took place. Little did the people who lived in the neighborhoods around the campus know what was occurring in their midst.

Faye walked into Julian's office after the announcement to have their usual weekly meeting to review the work of the project team. In addition to programming, she was responsible for coordinating the three groups working from different universities.

"I think our kickoff meeting went very well. The team seems fired up for the challenge. However, I do have a concern."

"Please don't ruin my day with bad news."

"I have a problem in my personal life that I should let you know about. I was just diagnosed with breast cancer. It's a rare form, which is hard to cure and bring in remission."

"I'm sorry to hear that. What can I do to help? This is devastating to hear. It must be shocking and demoralizing for you."

"I'm concerned about successfully having this treated and about the impact treatment will have on our work."

"Don't worry about the work here. Your health and well-being are the most important. We will support you one hundred fifty percent and plan for your absences to get treatment."

"That's reassuring to hear. Even though it'll be difficult, I still plan to give the project as much attention and energy as possible."

"Progress in cancer treatments has been explosive in the last few years. I'm sure the doctors will be successful in their treatment. Please be reassured."

Faye smiled and said, "Thank you for your support."

The 2030 awakening resulted in breakthroughs in medical science. The focus on longevity, rather than curing individual diseases, initiated the expansion of the human lifespan, with robustness into old age past one hundred years. Cancer, heart disease, infections, and other maladies fell by the wayside when longevity was understood and exploited through science. Organ regeneration through scaffolding with an absorbable plastic framework made it possible to replace fading organs with new ones, effectively replacing aging parts analogous to vintage car maintenance. The centenarians in 2030 were hale and hearty people.

*Genius is lonely without the surrounding
presence of a people to inspire it.*
—T. W. HIGGINSON

CHAPTER 3

ELLISON'S GRAND IDEA

The Choate Capital Management hedge fund in lower Manhattan was suddenly put in the glare of the world press when the Singularity Prize was announced. Ellison McClintock, CEO and chair, was raised on a farm north of Salinas, Kansas. He had a turbulent upbringing. He was abandoned by his mother and raised by his grandmother until her death. He was then taken in by his great-aunt. This grandaunt raised seven grandchildren, and when he came to live with them, he was the youngest. The family was very religious, and Ellison's cousins knew he was illegitimate and harbored a subtle resentment toward him coming to live with the family. As a result, he matured quickly, understanding his limited security within the family. To compensate, he developed a spirit of independence along with a certain politeness and gentility toward others. What secured his place in the family was his willingness, as he grew older, to work hard in all aspects of farm life. He more than pulled his weight in doing the normal chores around the farm, milking the cows, feeding the pigs, and helping in the harvesting of wheat, corn, and soybeans. Somehow, he learned that getting an education would be the real key to his independence and self-sufficiency. With this in mind, he pursued his education with vigor. He later acquired an MBA degree in finance from the Wharton School of the University of Pennsylvania.

Ellison and his team at Choate securities called a second press conference several months later to announce the teams that had qualified to-date for the rigorous protocol and strict safety standards of competing to earn the S-Prize.

"We would like to announce our qualifiers for the S-Prize competition. As you know, we have established protocols that are difficult to qualify for. Also, we restricted consortiums of companies and businesses from competing. Through the results of our thorough vetting of several applicants, we have qualified two teams only to compete for the S-Prize. They are the Berkeley, Stanford, Cape Town group, representing three universities; and the Beijing, Tokyo, Jakarta, Seoul group representing four universities working together in Asia."

Cameras at those universities immediately showed the team members cheering and celebrating their selection to compete.

Ellison did take a few questions.

"Mr. Ellison, how did you get the idea for the Singularity Prize?"

"I thought of it many years ago when I worked for the CIA and was imprisoned in Peru. That's when I had the germ of the idea. This idea crystallized when I observed the success of the X Prize, which on a smaller scale has rewarded multiple game-changing projects in science innovation."

"Does that mean you took this idea and built on it?"

"Yes, history has shown that rewarding teams of scientists to achieve a major goal in a certain time frame can be very effective in jump-starting significant progress. The Manhattan Project in the 1940s and the American moon shot program in the 1960s are classic examples of this history."

"Why didn't any European teams qualify for this prize competition?"

"That's a good question. I think that it's a combination of two things. There were no submissions of a team that comprised multiple countries, number one. Number two, a lot of the European talent left Europe and became a part of the Berkeley, Stanford, Cape Town team. That helps to explain that team's strength."

"The reason I ask is because I think the Europeans will be upset that they are not represented."

"Remember, both Julian Marshall and Faye Dickerson at Berkeley received part of their education in Europe, and that also holds true for several Chinese and Japanese members on their team who were educated in European universities."

"The Russians are also upset that they were not chosen as well."

"Their supercomputer technology has not made the necessary advancement and they opted out of buying from the West. They feared backdoor access in Western supercomputers compromising their secrecy."

Before the teams could organize and pursue the quest for the prize, the global financial crisis struck. Not since the Great Recession of 2008 had the economic picture become so bleak. The foundation and restructuring of the global financial system were thought to have solved the problem of deep recessions or near depressions. Things were quasi-stable for twenty years and international growth surged. However, the computer systems the world relied upon could not prevent instability and the continuation of previous adverse economic cycles. Thus, a deep recession descended swiftly upon the world in 2030.

Ellison was having lunch with two of his staff at a midtown New York delicatessen when he saw the news. The news hit the wires by 11:00 a.m. on July 18, 2030. The Strait of Hormuz was blocked by insurgents deliberately trying to bring down the world economy. The blockade halted the flow of Mideast crude oil to all the major industrial nations dependent on it. Alternative energy to replace fossil fuel was not yet a reality. The world was still subject to the vagaries and availability of crude oil. If the black gold were in short supply, engines of world commerce would grind to a halt, credit would freeze, and equity markets would fall precipitously. There was also a bubble in the Chinese technology sector that led to a crash on the Shanghai Stock Exchange. The impact on Wall Street was immediate, bringing great fear.

Ellison had yet to raise the funds for the S-Prize, and the imminent financial calamity would sap the motivation of potential donors.

The air outside on William Street in lower Manhattan was as hot as a furnace and heavy from the high humidity, characteristic of the climate change that continued the warming trend begun toward the end of the twentieth century.

"What am I going to do now?" Ellison asked Jonathan Weinberg and Alexander King, key staff members of Choate Capital Management. "My donor sources are going to dry up quickly. This means I have to dig deep into my portfolio, which is also shrinking rapidly."

"If the singularity problem is solved, we can use this cognitive development to solve the problem of acquiring the funds to award the prize," Jonathan replied as he took a sip from his latte.

"Yes, there is a feedback loop that we must recognize. It can retroactively solve a few problems, both big and small," Ellison said.

"That's an interesting thought," Alexander murmured. "How many teams of serious researchers do we think will pursue this goal?"

"A more important point is how many teams have the scientific muscle and resources to attain this goal," Ellison answered.

"Depending on how collaboration develops, my thinking is that we will end up with fewer than five that will seriously challenge this objective," Jonathan guessed.

"Is the risk strong of the singularity producing pathological artificial general intelligence?" Ellison asked rhetorically. "This is a threat to the safety of humanity if the singularity computers become our enemy. This issue emerged in the 1960s in the early years of artificial intelligence. We knew then that an immune system to protect humanity would be required prior to unleashing this level of brainpower."

"The specification in the prize announcement covers all the development issues that could inadvertently create a problematic singularity, particularly the necessity of an immune system. Of course, it is not foolproof, and some teams may try to shortcut their way," Jonathan said.

"Regular inspections will have the key role in preventing this scenario," Ellison responded.

"Will this machine have consciousness?" Alexander asked.

"Hans Moravec, the great scientist, and author, suggested that machines, when imbued with highly complex organizational features, will have an inner thought process, as frightening as this may sound to many folks," Ellison replied.

"This fear is particularly true for many religious scholars. In their view, a soul and spirit are peculiar only to humans. Even lower animal forms could not reflect these characteristics," Jonathan said.

"On the positive side, the development of a humanity-friendly singularity brings many advantages. Look at the key problems that must be solved by our global civilization," Ellison continued. "The eleven great challenges of the world are air pollution, climate change, malnutrition and hunger, water and sanitation, diseases, conflicts, education, trade barriers, terrorism, women and development, and energy."

The three men returned to their offices at the corner of Liberty and William Street in the New York financial district. Ellison returned to his phone calls to corporate leaders who he thought could be donors to the prize. "Can the coming singularity help us solve all of these burning questions of humanity?" asked Carlton Gates, the CEO of Delphi, a major software firm.

"Yes," Ellison explained on the phone. "I believe that an advanced cognitive system can do it. Remember, this will develop with an accelerating change factor, which makes the thinking powers continually improve."

"We have made only marginal progress in most of these challenging areas over decades and centuries. World citizens will welcome amplified brainpower directed toward these issues," Carlton said.

"We can add to the list the problem of financial instability causing so much difficulty at this moment in history. The present crash of the markets is a catastrophe comparable to a cyclone touching the shores of Bangladesh, even worse because economic disasters are more widespread," Ellison said.

"With AI, this present disaster could potentially be prevented," Carlton added. "The singularity can ultimately function better than the Federal Reserve in managing a complex system like the nation's macroeconomy. It would take all the national key data points and know precisely what adjustments are needed, even subtle ones, to maintain a stable, growing economy with nearly full employment," Ellison said.

"This cause is greater than any problems that may tend to obstruct human civilization in reaching this noble goal! Can you support us in the endeavor?"

"I support the science because it will advance software engineering. Before I can commit to a serious donation to this project, my board and I will need to get more information from you, and we will put your request through our standard processes for potential approval," Carlton said, and they ended the conversation.

In light of the S-Prize, Luddite groups organized a demonstration to demand a ban on any artificial intelligence research that attempted to surpass human intelligence.

Approximately two thousand people attended a rally in Central Park, New York, where speakers warned of impending doom if this artificial intelligence research produced a malevolent outcome.

"If this research is permitted to continue, we will become slaves to the machine," one of the speakers shouted.

Another said, "The world will be placed into a new dark age where machines without ethical guideposts will take command and wreak havoc."

The crowd shouted back, "Stop Frankenstein, block the research."

The main speaker, Chris Weldon, a well-known anti-technology guru addressed the cheering crowd, "If the US Congress does not pass legislation to stop this research, we are prepared to take matters into our hands. We will stop this dangerous research by any means necessary."

When that was said, an enormous roar could be heard from the crowd lending their support.

Ellison watched the speech on his smart tablet and said to Jonathan sitting on the other side of the table at Starbucks, "The establishment of the S-Prize has set off a firestorm that could get out of hand."

"Don't worry, demonstrators come out for everything. It's a rent-a-crowd. Those folks oppose all scientific progress and, just think, where would the world be today without scientific progress?" Jonathan suggested.

Ellison returned to his office, looked out the window at the Manhattan skyline, and pondered the issues. Despite the awakening of the late 2020s, civilization's problems were not solved in their entirety. The tyranny of man against man continued even though the causes for these maladaptations of the past had disappeared. In medieval times and into the modern era, wars were fought over scarce resources and territory. Advances in science, the expansion of the means of production, and enlightened urbanization in the context of a growing population have negated those ancient causes of war. The consciousness of human society needed to catch up with the reality of this scientific change.

If during the 2030s, no solution was developed for adverse climate change and scarce energy resources, the very survival of human civilization was in jeopardy. It was ironic that when people saw all of these scientific and technological advances, people also saw some of the greatest threats to human survival. The question Ellison pondered was whether humanity would survive, thrive, and potentially spread throughout the solar system and the galaxy or would humanity become extinct like many other species that had inhabited this Earth over millions of years? Humans were sufficiently astute when the risks were much greater and when their numbers were very low during distant prehistoric times. Ellison also wondered whether humans were clever enough in the 2030s to survive the inevitable onslaught of intractable problems and unforeseen nasty surprises of human behavior and nature.

Wonder is the beginning of wisdom.
—Socrates

CHAPTER 4

NAMIBIA, SOUTHWEST AFRICA, SEPTEMBER 2030

The archeological team traveled from Windhoek in four-wheel-drive Land Rovers to a remote area of northwest Namibia between Etosha National Park and Skeleton Coast Park. The rugged terrain of the region was barren and almost lifeless. The University of Oregon made this archeological expedition in Southwest Africa, where they believed they could find artifacts from earlier human campsites of one hundred thousand to two hundred thousand years ago.

"Yes, intelligence ultimately saved our species from extinction," said Laszlo Zawinul, an archeology professor from the University of Oregon, to the group of three student interns and three faculty researchers gathered about the evening campfire. As the African sun set in the distant hills, an eerie orange glow permeated the scattered clouds.

"When we find out what actually happened to early human brains and how it impacted survival, we can learn a vital lesson for the survival of human beings in the twenty-first century."

"Can our enormous 8.3 billion population ensure our survival?" asked Charles, a student team member.

"Before I answer that I would like to remind you that the champion of hominid survival is Homo erectus. This hominid group survived for 1.75 million years before extinction. In comparison, humans have a long way to go."

"That's an interesting perspective. I hadn't thought of any extinct species in that way," Charles said.

"Can humans survive that long?"

"Not if humankind brings on mega-disasters such as man-made adverse impacts on the earth's climate. Billions could perish in the blink of an eye. The answer is yes; we can become extinct," Laszlo said. "But that could be prevented and circumvented with profound wisdom and collaborative thinking. We are here because the genetic trail of Homo sapiens began in this place in the desert well over one hundred thousand years ago. The present-day San people, who live nearby, are among the oldest groups of African tribes and they split off over one hundred thousand years ago from the lineage that migrated out of Africa. Their click language is unique among all languages and is considered a progenitor language. A big question is whether the San people's remote ancestors became awakened humans in these environs," Laszlo said.

"Our GPS data corresponds to the genomics data, which is based on DNA analysis. This area is the likely geographic source of modern humans," Victor, an associate professor, said.

"After a hypothesized advance in their intelligence, people migrated toward the northeast over many centuries and enormously difficult terrain. They intermarried with other human clan groups and proceeded to leave Africa at a point along the Red Sea to reach what is now the Arabian Peninsula. The first group then proceeded along the coastline by the Indian Ocean and eventually reached Australia over sixty-five thousand years ago," Laszlo said.

The moon had risen by this point and radiated a shimmering light over the landscape.

"Have you all learned about another bottleneck that occurred?"

"There were only about eighty people from Siberia around eighteen thousand years ago?"

"What was the cause and motivation for moving and traveling these vast distances?" James, another student intern asked.

"Perhaps the answer lies in these surroundings, here in Southwest Africa. We can hike toward the Namib Skeletal Coast and see what evidence we can find. Our new GPS deep-underground-penetrating-radar-detection system may be crucial to our discovery potential. Remote sensing, however, has some limitations in this terrain, especially for deep subterranean material," Laszlo said.

The team went to sleep in anticipation of their trek the next day in the direction of the South Atlantic coastline. The night was enlivened with a magnificent display of the Milky Way, similar to what it must have been like 150,000 years before. The African air was peaceful and tranquil. Hours later, the rising African sun found several of the members preparing breakfast while Laszlo sat in his tent and mapped out a plan for the day's trek.

Breakfast of oatmeal porridge, vegetarian sausages, and lentils sizzled on an open fire, and the men hurriedly ate. They began walking in a southwesterly direction at 6:15 a.m. The skies were bright blue with a wisp of clouds that indicated an impending change in weather. Laszlo wondered whether it would be just another day in this barren corner of the planet, or if this day would yield the holy grail of human cognitive growth in humanity's earliest days. The rugged terrain required walking instead of driving, which was time-consuming but more efficient for the search.

"While we trek, our research drones will explore the areas north and south, to broaden our terrain coverage. They will pinpoint any findings that materialize from this aerial survey," Victor said.

By mid-morning, after traveling several kilometers, the team had found only high sand dunes and unusually limited indications of any ancient human settlement.

"The sand dunes must have buried any evidence of early humans," an intern said.

"Come take a look at the monitor," Victor said. "This is a clear signal of something coming from our southern drone. It sounds like a hit."

"I have double-checked to verify this," James said. "It's about twenty-nine kilometers from our present position." James was an assistant professor at the University of Oregon and coordinated the logistics of the research mission.

"What does this indicate or reveal?" Victor asked.

"There is an underground pattern that gives the signature of an ancient campsite or temporary settlement," James said.

"Check this out with our GPS sensors to get a better reading," Laszlo suggested. "The GPS tells us we need to go in this direction." He pointed toward the southwest in the direction of the Atlantic coastline.

Four hours later, the team arrived at the site that triggered the signal.

They stood on a hillside that presented a commanding view of the distant mountains to the east and ocean to the west. The orange sands contrasted with the blue skies above.

"Check out the quality of the view from here. This is a lovely place to have a campsite. Our ancestors had a sense of aesthetics and an appreciation of the beauty inherent in nature," Victor said.

"There's another reason for this position. This is high ground, and it would be easy to have a lookout spot to search for dangerous predators, rival clans, and other potentially harmful intruders," Laszlo said.

"How far down in the sediments are we going to dig to find this ancient campsite?" James asked.

"It's not deep at all; our instruments will tell us the exact location," Victor said.

"We might as well make this our camp and call in the material we'll need to appropriately and carefully excavate the area," Laszlo gestured toward the sand around them.

"Look over here," Victor said. "It sounds like a cache of stone axes and arrowheads in the trough of this sand dune.

The digging began. By the second day, it became apparent to the expedition that they were onto a significant find.

"I think we're reaching the level where those artifacts appeared on the drone's instrument panel. Let's carefully examine this level," Laszlo said.

"Look at that object over there," Victor observed.

"What is it?" James asked.

"It looks like another cache of stone implements. They seem advanced in their construction and design," Laszlo said.

"We need to date this area and determine a timeline for the site," James said.

"These large quantities of shellfish shells indicate the primary protein source for the clan, which was probably a critical nutrient for long-term brain evolution," Laszlo pointed out.

"This charcoal-burnt region can be used for dating purposes and was probably the centerpiece of the encampment. We should systematically find tools and cultural artifacts to the periphery as we expand our search area," Victor said.

A technician came back with a preliminary reading of the age of the site. He was using a protocol of potassium-argon and thermoluminescence through state-of-the-art testing instrumentation in miniaturized electronics. "The site is over 120,000 years old, one of the oldest found of Homo sapiens, the prolific toolmaker."

"Could this be the holy grail to cognitive leap theory?" Laszlo asked.

The men raced to expand the site as they realized they were on a potentially historic breakthrough concerning why Homo sapiens in a short time frame rose from an average primate in their thinking capacity to something far greater.

"If we are in the original locale of the emergent thinking man, then perhaps the great migration, in reality, started from here and spread to the rest of the planet. This would indeed reflect the genetic evidence. The mother genes of all humanity may have come from this desolate outpost in Southwest Africa," Laszlo continued. "Let's keep working at this and see what else we can find."

When it is evident that the goals cannot be reached,
don't adjust the goals, adjust the action steps.
—CONFUCIUS

CHAPTER 5

OCTOBER 2030

On the other side of the globe from the Berkeley, Stanford, Cape Town group, another group of scientists began their quest for the S-Prize. The Beijing, Seoul, Tokyo, Jakarta group, which brought the might of four Asian nations to bear, had significant intellectual assets.

There were pressing issues confronting the Asian countries, which gave great motivation for their involvement in the contest. A large population imposed demands on the environment, which forced a struggle for food, shelter, water, and other necessities, particularly energy. Pockets of prosperity were surrounded by the overwhelming loci of poverty.

At thirty million people, Beijing was one of the most densely populated cities across the world in 2030. China rose to be the world's largest economy by 2018. The city was, in 2030, a transportation hub for the central rail network and the national highway system. Most importantly, the city was the cultural, political, and educational center of the country. Beijing was renowned for its celebrated temples, massive stone walls and gates, and the grand imperial palace known as the Forbidden City. The city was a fast-moving, bustling metropolis with a combination of bicycles and electric cars.

The severe and debilitating pollution of the earliest twentieth century had gotten worse in spite of the work of China's environmental engineers. The skies were hazy and brown, and the air was dusty, blowing in from the northern plains. Despite the intense tree planting, the sandstorms, which continued to envelop the city during the spring, brought just sandy wind. The trees had merely partially halted the march of the northern deserts. Because of its primeval roots, the city was marked by the contrast of the old and new. Next to nightclubs with glittering lights were ancient temples. Beijing was the home of Peking University and Tsinghua University, the two leading and oldest universities throughout the country. Located in an idyllic setting in the capital, the Beijing Intelligence Lab (BIL) was a research computer science branch of Peking University.

The BIL research facilities overlooked Nanhu Lake off Kunminghu Road in western Beijing. Facilities were state-of-the-art and housed the latest generation of China's supercomputing efforts. Wang Xeujing was the leader of the Beijing group. She grew up as the only child to a couple in Xian, the ancient capital of China. Her education was influenced strongly by the great push in China to develop research universities in the early twenty-first century. She excelled in math and received the highest score on the university entrance examinations for her province. This score gave her a coveted acceptance to Tsinghua University, China's math and physics flagship school. Her parents were proud and were surprised when she received a scholarship to pursue her PhD. at California Institute of Technology in Pasadena, California. At Caltech, Xeujing was a star graduate student who published ten seminal papers on artificial intelligence before graduation. Her papers were among the most highly cited of any student in the world. She was heavily recruited by IBM, Microsoft,

Google, Facebook, and other major companies, but she felt loyalty to her home country and decided to go back and pursue academics to train the next generation of computer scientists in China.

Upon returning to China, she found it difficult to gain the acceptance and respect of older male peers. They were a bit suspicious of her ambition and felt threatened by her talent. Several of the older professors at Peking University held her back from promotions, although she richly deserved it. However, they could not break Xeujing's spirits, and she continued to be extraordinarily productive in her work. Xeujing's husband, Bai Jian, was also a computer scientist, and they not only raised a son and a daughter together, they also collaborated on some of Xeujing's research and published together in international computer science journals. She met her husband while doing a postdoc at Princeton University after leaving Caltech. He had a physics background, and she persuaded him to pursue computer science as a more exciting discipline with a fantastic future.

When China decided to focus vast resources on intelligent computing, they looked for the best to head the team. They found this talent in Xeujing. She woke up at 4:00 a.m. every morning and went to a nearby park to practice Tai Chi and Chi Kung. These exercises grounded her, and the breathing associated with the exercises sharpened her mind for an innovative day in the lab. Her vegan diet reflected simplicity and consisted of local fruits grown along the streets of her neighborhood, a variety of vegetables, rice and soymilk. Her ability to focus on work nonstop for fifteen hours was legendary, even among her Chinese colleagues, and the productivity of this effort was prodigious.

The announcement of the prize caught Xeujing's attention, and she immediately decided to formalize the efforts with her collaborators. The Chinese team initially debated whether to apply for participation in the S-Prize. There was strong opposition from some of the team members.

Meng Gan, a colleague, expressed his opposition. "Why do we have to join this prize competition? We are much freer to pursue our agenda if we just continue our present AI research. We would not need to follow the guidelines of the prize."

"I understand your position, but I disagree. Joining the prize offers several advantages to our progress in AI. The prize is an incentive for other teams in Asia to join us. It provides an international structure that we can focus on for our work," Xeujing said.

"We Chinese do not need a structure developed outside of China for our research," Gan said.

"We cannot let national pride get in the way of our scientific achievements. Many of us have seen how our integration with the world economy in the 1980s helped to transform our country. If we had continued to be isolated from the world, we would not be doing this AI research. The same could be said for the disadvantage of not taking new scientific discoveries in the West and adapting them to China."

"I think your time studying in America has clouded your thinking as to whether China can go it alone. I believe we can," Gan said.

"Let's agree to disagree," she said firmly.

Because of the size of the team and the geographic dispersion of its members, Xeujing decided to call a teleconference to galvanize what had been, before the prize announcement, merely an informal collection of scientists who wanted to advance artificial intelligence research.

The teleconference included the international collaborating teams along with Li Qianghui, Gao Xiao-Ming, and Zhang Ka-Fai, the lab's top programmers, to plan for the S-Prize.

"Everyone has checked in; let's get started," Xeujing said. "We need to take a well-coordinated approach to reach our goal of winning the prize."

"This is Jakarta speaking; we need to go back twenty years and review all the pertinent literature on artificial intelligence. Hidden are many avenues of research that we can pursue those papers, and we need to dig them up and bring them to the light of day for our forward movement."

Xeujing said, "We need to focus on the interdisciplinary aspects of this and capitalize on the strengths of our diverse team. We indeed have researchers in approximately ten areas, which have crossover; in these regions, we can interact and cross-fertilize each other to benefit our progress. Without taking this approach, our chance of achieving a substantial advance of the science is limited."

"Yes, those overlapping regions between disciplines are areas where we need to plumb the depths for fresh research insights. These interdisciplinary areas without departmental backing have proven to be new territory for research. What shape will this new singularity take? Will we end up with one machine, a network of computers or a mobile robotic system capable of sitting down in a meeting or conference and contributing to the deliberations like anybody else?" Li asked.

"Yes, particularly the latter is possible. The singularity's contributions will be vastly superior to those of the people present at the meeting. This creature of the singularity will be like a big brother or big sister teaching the humans," Xeujing said.

"That suggests a question we should be addressing. Why not work on a system to gradually enhance our intelligence while also producing the great leap with machines? By doing that we will not be too far from the machines in intelligence and can maintain control when they spring to life," Gao suggested.

"This question of machine control would be analogous to the parents of a young genius who has not matured into an adult yet. The kid is obviously smarter, yet the parents still feed, clothe, and house the child. They indeed nurture the child to adulthood," Li said.

"Control systems are ubiquitous. They were developed to an advanced degree in electronic systems back in the twentieth century, but the science of control systems needs to mature enough for us to have confidence in permanent control of this genius singularity. However, when you have self-improving intelligence, the long-term future of control is uncertain. We are then in unpredictable territory," Xeujing said.

"Stephen Hawking, the great physicist, said that 'artificial intelligence is potentially the worst thing that can happen to humanity,'" a team member from Tokyo interjected.

"Developing a control system that is self-improving should be a critical focus for our team. This feature should be embedded into the system to ensure our safety as a species," Gao said.

Zhang noticed an odd subtle sound in the background. "I think someone is eavesdropping. Let's analyze our secure Internet connection."

The conversation stopped, and everyone began to look around the room when an alert came to their laptop computers. In short order, they found evidence of a hack of their teleconference from a foreign source. They terminated the teleconference immediately and made plans to secure future communication.

"Who do you think hacked our connection? A rival team?" Gao asked.

"Rivalry and espionage can be expected in this type of project. That's a possible explanation, but it could be more sinister than that. It could be a group of state-sponsored hackers who have nothing but bad intentions and goals," Zhang said.

"We need to figure out what this cyber-bugging is about and who's behind it," Xeujing said.

After the planning meeting, Xeujing sat down in her office with one of her early mentors who was now one of her team members, Dr. Li Qianghui. He was a pioneer in Chinese AI research dating back to the 2000s, during the manufacturing boom era.

"There is a perception in the rest of the world that China copies everything from the West. That may have been true thirty years ago but not anymore," Xeujing said.

"Our track record of innovation over the past few years speaks for itself," Qianghui said.

"In fact, we developed the breakthrough in speech recognition back in 2015 through deep speech," Xeujing said.

"The search company Baidu made a strategic move when they set up the Institute of Deep Learning (IDL) in Silicon Valley a few years back," Qianghui said.

"Yes, we were able to acquire significant personnel from the talent pool there, including me. I could have stayed there but decided to come home and work here. I am happy I made that choice," Xeujing said.

*

The investigation of the hacking revealed that the perpetrators had also used a tempest attack in which a van parked near the labs used a device to detect the electromagnetic signals coming from keystrokes on the computers. "They could steal our code before we have time to encrypt it for security," Xeujing said.

Xeujing found out as director of the program that her responsibilities went beyond technical issues. She called in two of her senior team, Gao Xiao-Ming and Zhang Ka-Fai, to defuse a fierce rivalry.

"I received a report from your colleagues that the argument you had recently within your team meeting caused a significant disruption. It seems that this has been an ongoing problem."

"Xiao-Ming has been very unprofessional in his approach to our disagreement."

"Can one of you explain what this is all about?" Xeujing asked.

"Xiao-Ming presents his ideas in a condescending manner implying that no one else has any good ideas. This has caused a lot of turmoil in our team," Ka-Fai said.

"Give me some specifics. You two are supposed to be leaders in our efforts. Dissension between you two can be very problematic to our success," Xeujing said.

"Two days ago, Xiao-Ming shouted me down when I presented a new algorithm for our natural language processing. He did this even before we had a chance to test the module thoroughly. The code was focused on unsupervised learning, which we all know is a less certain machine-learning protocol," Ka-Fai said.

"That is a mischaracterization of what happened. I only expressed my opinion passionately about the weakness of the structure of the algorithm. There was nothing personal. It was only a critique of the work," Xiao-Ming said.

"Even with a clash of ideas, we can still be civil with one another. Furthermore, I learned from Dr. Li that you guys had this rivalry going back to the days when you both were studying at Tsinghua. The reason you two are on this team is that you were number one and number two in college," Xeujing said.

"Here is what we need to do. I am concerned that both of your behavior will compromise our effectiveness as a cohesive team in our work toward the S-Prize. This is a stern warning for both of you not to let the rivalry get out of hand again. If it does continue, both of you will be reported to the higher authorities. I have no choice," Xeujing said.

They both got up to return to their task of making Asia the leader in artificial intelligence and winning the S-prize. Although both men agreed to be more civil, the tensions remained. This was their stated goal, in spite of their personality clash.

Human beings always do the most intelligent thing...
after they've tried every stupid alternative,
and none of them have worked.
—BUCKMINSTER FULLER

CHAPTER 6

NEW YORK, NOVEMBER 2030

The financial crisis in companies, institutions, and individuals grew worse. The deepening recession was bordering on depression, and the somber mood among the masses was evident everywhere. Soup kitchen lines were getting longer as unemployment rose rapidly. Homes across the country were being lost to foreclosure and hope in the future was dissolving into a sea of despair.

"How can we present a thirty-billion-dollar prize when the funds are not here because of this economic downturn?" Jonathan Weinberg asked.

As one of Ellison's financial associates, Jonathan was very concerned about delivering on the promise made in the original prize announcement. Years before, Jonathan had an insight and decided to raise money by kayaking down the Ganges River while shining the spotlight on poverty in India. His celebrity status as a former Shakespearean actor drew the curiosity of the news media. They followed his journey, as did many people online. He had many amazing encounters with remarkable people along the journey. He raised several million dollars, and those funds were dedicated to lifting the plight of rural farmers who were at the bottom of the totem pole socioeconomically in the Indian subcontinent. His efforts were widely praised in the press around the world. Ellison asked him to join the efforts to raise funds for the S-Prize as a result of this experience.

"I have made a commitment to provide the award. Maybe the competing teams will not find the singularity anytime soon. This will keep me out of trouble," Ellison replied. "Yes, if the singularity is developed, computational gains by the winner will sort out the details of funding the thirty billion dollars, and perhaps it could provide the input to national reserve banks worldwide to bring us rapidly out of any economic downturn, even a depression."

"Is it really ethical to offer a prize when the bulk of the funds are not in escrow waiting to be given to the winner?" Jonathan asked.

Ellison thought about this for a moment and said, "That is certainly a major consideration. We are already locked into our scenario where the announcement has been made, and we fully anticipate raising all the funds prior to any team reaching our strict definition of the singularity. Even with accelerating change of exponential proportions, the timelines for advancement to develop the required computing power are several chip generations in the future. That will be necessary before this great advance in machine intelligence. In a nutshell, we have time to raise the funds," Ellison concluded.

"This present crisis will soon bottom out and slowly begin to inch back to normal growth."

✳

As a daily workout, Julian always ran in the Berkeley Hills in the dawn hours. It was an excellent time to think. The smell of eucalyptus trees filled the air as he ran. The hills were difficult to run, and the workouts kept him in reasonably good shape. For inspiration, he listened to jazz, his favorite music: Miles Davis, John Coltrane, and Wayne Shorter. On this morning, thick fog rolled in from the Pacific across the Golden Gate and the San Francisco Bay to the hills of Berkeley. Visibility was down to fifteen yards in this pea soup mini-world.

Julian thought briefly about his youth. He'd spent many hours after school every day in the local library voraciously reading a diverse body of materials. When he had an assignment in his math courses, he not only did the problems in his homework, but he would find similar books in the library and do all the problems in those as well. When exam time came around, he was well prepared to deal with any type of problem that might show up. He achieved high scores in all his subjects but especially in mathematics. He began to be noticed by his teachers as a special talent. This history gave him a high degree of self-confidence.

Julian ran to the crest of the hill, above the layer of fog, and overlooked the San Francisco Bay. Pausing to catch his breath, he pondered what earlier distinguished scientists had done in history to make this amazing world of the early twenty-first century.

The revolution in learning in the 2020s had produced many new superb thinkers and doers. Many of them were youth with new and novel ideas about our world and the direction in which humankind should develop. Individuals from birth began to learn at their own pace and advance rapidly to the highest levels of all the disciplines.

By thinking ahead with foresight, humanity used these tremendous assets, namely human and machine intelligence, to avoid the pitfalls and traps that nature put before the species as it struggled to escape the gravitational pull of Earth and expand into the cosmos. As long as the world had all of its eggs in one basket here on Earth, the risk was great that the expansive future of the human species was at risk. Humans were imminently about to expand into the cosmos permanently.

The first flowers of the Internet-inspired awakening had become like Keukenhof, Holland, when the colorful tulip fields are in full bloom in the spring. The very personable curiosity of the masses had matched perfectly with the emerging technologies of Internet connectedness.

At once unifying and simultaneously edifying, these phenomena had been the engine of the awakening. In history, a few had awakened, such as the Buddha, Jesus, and Lao Tzu. In the third decade of the twenty-first century, this proliferation of knowledge led to many, many more becoming awakened. This evolutionary change rescued the world from ignorance.

Drenched in sweat, Julian reached home after an hour run. Sarah had time to prepare a high-protein breakfast of salmon and oat bran mixed with yellow lentils. Blueberries followed, mixed with yogurt.

Julian said, "Thanks for the awesome breakfast." He smiled at his wife. "You know, while I was running I was thinking about the first time we met. I had only finished my aide work a few months earlier when I laid eyes on you at the farmers' market in Oakland."

"That first conversation was something else. You actually didn't mention your aide work at all in that first meeting. I did surmise, however, that you wanted change in your life. You were very direct about wanting to meet again."

"That was during my recovery period. When I saw you the first time, I immediately realized that you were the something else in my life's equation."

"You seemed insightful and self-assured. That was what caught my attention."

"I was in a period of personal reorganization. I was making peace with myself."

"I thought that required solitude."

"No, you fit in perfectly with my reorganization plans. Before that, I had spent years in books and labs. After my work in Mozambique, I knew I needed to start sharing my life with someone."

"It's funny how our thoughts gelled on the same thing. I was ready to share too."

"I love you, and I'm happy I found someone I can bounce my most complex ideas off and get a spot-on response that's very helpful. You were an important part of my coming back to US."

"Our relationship is made in heaven."

"Yes, but our heavenly cuisine goes beyond just milk and honey."

"Our son is our gift from heaven."

Julian leaned over and kissed her softly.

After a short time in the sauna and shower, he climbed into his driverless car and headed to the lab. By 2030, driverless cars were the norm. Traffic jams, along with accidents, became rare as people were chauffeured around enjoying the scenery or beginning their work on the way to the office. Uber had a fleet of cars that were all driverless.

Driverless cars had been on the highways of the world since 2021. In spite of this progress, some accidents continued to occur, but they were now mere curiosities and never fatal. Three blocks from his house, Julian observed an accident caused by a human driver colliding with a driverless car while backing out of a driveway.

"Is everyone okay?" Julian asked as he passed by the collision.

"We're all okay," the resident said. "It's just a fender bender."

Julian thought about the accident as his car continued down the hill. In spite of this, self-driving cars had already reduced auto accident fatalities by half in the US. Any accident reflected the potential long-term problem of humans interacting with computers. This was the challenge facing him every day in his Berkeley offices.

✳

A young African named Joshua Makani from a village of thirty-seven people illustrated the awakening sweeping the planet. His father had been a child warrior who was forced into military service at gunpoint at the age of nine. His father saw epic battles and endured harsh life-threatening conditions no child should ever see. Soldiers came to his father's village when he was thirteen and his brother was seventeen years old. They asked Joshua's uncle if he wanted to join the militia, and he said no. They shot him in the head. When they asked his father whether he wanted to join, he said yes because he didn't want to die. He saw horrible things, had to participate in atrocious acts, and was repeatedly beaten when he made mistakes or did not follow orders. Many of the child soldiers were beaten to unconsciousness and later died, sometimes for no reason at all. He had to carry ammunition and other heavy loads over long distances without rest or adequate food. He learned all about weapons and their care and could disassemble and assemble a Kalashnikov blindfolded. It was a horrible experience as a child but through a miraculous sequence of events, Joshua's father escaped from the militia and survived over three months in the rain forest before finding a village and safe haven in a neighboring country.

When the war was over, his father married and settled down to raise a family. He was determined to provide the best for his children. He cultivated in Joshua, his oldest son, a great desire for education. Joshua learned to read at a very early age under the guidance of his father. His father worked as a small farmer, bringing produce to weekly markets into Kampala, Uganda.

The lingering wounds of the war and abject poverty made many young students hungry for an education and a potential route out of the shantytowns. Joshua was one of those students. His school math and science courses were taught by a Peace Corps volunteer who took a special interest when he recognized that Joshua was talented. He would give Joshua extra assignments with more challenging problem sets so that he would continually improve and scale new heights, particularly in math. To balance the quantitative side of his knowledge, Joshua was also a keen reader. He read everything he could get his hands on, including technical books on computer programming and the great literature and philosophy of the world. He was curious as to why Africa did not get as much credit in the history books, especially considering the richness of the contribution coming from the Egyptian civilization and the established fact that all human beings on Earth had their origins on the African continent. He viewed Africa as the motherland of all civilization, but the continent was not given the credit for it.

Through a voracious and rapid acquisition of knowledge, by his own volition, he wrote a treatise on knowledge that won worldwide acclaim. This new theory of knowledge knocked the socks off the philosophical establishment. His writing style harkened back to that of historical greats such as Imhotep, Lao Tzu, Hegel, Hume, and Immanuel Kant. He had devoured their works before the age of ten. His new theory, completed by the age of twelve, took the ideas to a higher iteration and many recognized the breakthrough. After this acclaim, his talents were noticed, and he received a scholarship to attend the Mathematics Academy in Cape Town, South Africa.

The awakening has shown its dramatic impact primarily through the youth, such as Joshua. They have taken to all the new technologies like a duck to water. Early in the twenty-first century, the world was worried about the rising generation and the type of planet that would be left to them. Those worries were proven to be unnecessary with respect to their actions on critical issues that were not solved by the previous generation. The rising youth of 2030 were extraordinarily prepared and extremely capable of managing the planet.

Joshua left the Cape Town group after being recruited from the African Institute for Mathematical Sciences (AIMS) and shortly later he joined the team at Berkeley. His experience demonstrated that he could collaborate with them on programming a philosophical perspective into the inventory of the singularity.

The singularity needed to be programmed with a tendency toward virtuous decisions, enhanced by the philosophical knowledge throughout the ages and the ability to think logically through any situation.

This was a challenge of coding and Joshua rapidly learned from the team and improved his programming techniques and skills.

The team was astonished by his ability, particularly at his age of fourteen years. They wondered what he would be able to do by the time he was twenty-five.

When Joshua began to program philosophical components into the system at Berkeley, he focused on infusing the three great themes of philosophy starting with the oldest written records. The first area of focus was theory and that included the idea that the universe was a perfectly functioning system, and humans were a small microcosm of this grand expanse of nature. The laws of astrophysics where galaxies and stars had an orderly mathematical cycle of function reflected this theory of nature. When analyzed anatomically, the human body on its scale represented a similar logically functioning system.

The second concept infused into the code was that of ethics and the necessity of social harmony and cooperation. He worked with Faye to develop this area of the code because it overlapped with her work to humanize the singularity.

The third component he coded was a drive to seek and acquire wisdom and salvation. This wisdom was deep and intuitive, which was very difficult to code for. Wisdom was indeed built on the previous two concepts, and those concepts needed to be developed first before wisdom could be obtained.

The algorithm for recursive improvement would certainly make it possible for the third component of philosophy—wisdom—to be strengthened over time. The database of all philosophical thought in history mixed with the ideas of modern times would, through this improvement algorithm, produce novel philosophical ideas based on the foundation of the three conceptions. The young African when queried about his approach by Faye and a programmer named Vijay said, "Consciousness is the individual human characteristic while philosophy is a characteristic of our civilization. Philosophy has made us a humane species that cooperates across broad sweeps of geography. For the AI software and hardware to function and be a part of our network—instead of operating above it—these concepts, particularly ethics and wisdom, should be embedded before any tests."

"What makes you think the subtlety of this philosophical awareness can be a part of a machine?" Vijay asked.

"It all comes down to mathematics. Just as a mathematical equation can predict the energies inherent in the atom and, furthermore, point to how that energy can be released through nuclear fusion and fission, mathematics can also predict the functioning of a computer based on its adherence to philosophical concepts. This will require us to improve our imagination to understand, but I'm confident when we test our system it will function based on what we predict," Joshua replied.

"What happens if the mathematics is incomplete, and there are components vital to this smooth logical functioning missing?" Faye asked.

"Safety and predictability are keys to our work. If, by chance, a vital component is missing, we need built-in sensors to detect changes that indicate this problem. When we receive the signal from those sensors of danger, there will be an automatic shutdown. The sensors will point us to the part of the code where we need to make modifications and adjustments to reach a more secure stage of functioning," Joshua responded.

"It amazes me that you have learned such deep insights at such an early age. How did this happen?" Faye inquired.

"I am clearly a product of the Internet Age. Although my family was poor and lacked resources typical here in the West, my parents had a great deal of determination. They were determined to seek and find whatever meager resources they could and put them to my advantage. I was, fortunately, able to acquire one of those simple ninety-nine-dollar solar computers that were distributed all over the developing world as a project to expand computer literacy. Once I found the Internet, I devoured every site I could find with courses that were freely available," Joshua said.

✳

To acquaint the university community with the project, Julian gave a general lecture on the quest for the Singularity Prize to a standing-room audience of the UC Berkeley community at Zellerbach Hall Theater:

"We stand upon the shoulders of giants." This is a famous quote by Isaac Newton on the role our scientific progenitors have on our current ability to achieve advances in science. The coral reef is a metaphor when one observes the development of human culture and behavior; that culture has an extremely long history going back over 150,000 years. The great leap forward was that breakthrough advance in cognition and behavior in those very early years.

What we have today is a veneer of civilization, the past 10,000 years, overlying the vast expanse of years we had as hunter-gatherers on the plains of Africa and in the steppes of Eurasia. Those years contain the basis of our modern behavior and culture.

As we attempt to build the singularity here at Berkeley, we are studying more deeply what occurred during our human foundational hunter-gatherer period, stretching over nearly 190,000 years. The singularity will have that rich development of humanity embedded in its code.

Our task is to do nothing less than solve intelligence. Once intelligence is solved we can then solve almost everything else. Particularly, the great challenges facing civilization and the viability of life on the planet. When deep reinforcement learning was developed by the company Deep Mind in 2015 we turned a corner. The self-learning program first mastered fifty computer games from the Atari era of the 1970s. Later it mastered the game of Go and beat the reigning world champion in 2017. Mastery of Go was projected to occur much later in 2025 but the breakthrough occurred significantly earlier than expected. This actually put us on the fast track to reach a true singularity. Go is over three thousand years old and it is revered as an almost religious experience in China, Japan, and Korea. There are more possible board configurations in a game of Go than atoms in the universe. From this foundation we've been able to apply these advances to a broad array of real-world problems. Because the landscape of the problems we are trying to solve is global, the reinforcement recursive learning of Horus will be very beneficial. AI has been central to our lives now for over a decade and the benefits have been enormous. These benefits are largely taken for granted. If we achieve a true singularity and win the Singularity Prize, the benefits will then be more widely known.

Over millennia, the coral reef builds its calcium carbonate structures from the sea floor up to the surface of the ocean. This magnificent edifice grows to the surface to produce upper layers of live coral that expertly extract nutrients from the seawater.

The coral reef breaks the surface of the sea, and over time an entirely new world emerges and covers the reefs. Seeds from distant landmasses travel in the ocean currents and take root. Later, tall palm trees grace the shoreline, and eventually diverse flora and fauna find a home on a growing island. The coral built the foundation that grows into a tropical island with palm trees and sandy beaches.

By analogy, early hominids are the coral reefs of the present-day global civilization, and the future machine-derived mind will be the child of Homo sapiens. This will be true as our earthbound home is expanded throughout the cosmos. There will be some evermore-advanced level that will supersede the machines that we build and will be, in effect, our minds' grandchildren. This grandchild would certainly be unimaginable in its form, scope and ability.

Given the progressive pattern of increasing complexity in nature, it is quite likely that the mind as a cognitive conception will continue to higher iterations well into the distant future.

We will be looked upon by those advanced iterations as mere curious historical and ancestral antecedents, much like the way we look upon the amoeba or paramecium. We know that in the distant past we emerged through multiple layers of change from these microbes. However, apart from scientific research in unicellular life-forms, they are a mere curiosity. We will be simple curiosities to those emerging from us in the distant future. Certainly, we can coexist with them as future human-machine cyborgs. They will move through the universe, improving themselves, making deals and taking in the wonderment of the grand cosmos.

There is an algae civilization, an amoeba civilization, an ant civilization, a continental flora civilization, and a human civilization. In the future, there will be a solar system civilization, a galactic civilization, and an organized cognitive system that spans the entire universe. This becomes, in essence, the "universal mind." This is the anthropic principle that suggests that life and consciousness are the penultimate purposes of the universe. Observations of the universe must be compatible with the conscious and sapient beings that observes it. When life takes root, its destiny is to expand throughout the vastness and emptiness of the universe.

Our building of the singularity is only one of the layered steps to this process of a theorized anthropic principle expansion.

Every new layer is a powerful addition to previous levels. Furthermore, this layering is an inevitable process of nature.

It merely reflects the mathematical laws of the natural processes within the universe.

Ladies and gentlemen, we are embarking on a noble journey that in all respects follows the natural course of things. If we were not to be the midwife of history, some other force would be. We have been selected to carry out this mission. Yes, this is natural selection, and we are the agents facilitating the process.

Before we adjourn, I would like to inform you that we will give our singularity system a name. In Egyptian mythology, the son of Isis and Osiris was Horus. He was born a deity and was symbolized by the falcon. The Eye of Horus was a symbol of protection and royal power from the deities. The singularity will be called Horus."

Julian completed his lecture to a round of applause from the packed auditorium.

The lecture was followed by a question-and-answer period that lasted over forty-five minutes.

"Dr. Marshall, what programming language is your team using to reach the singularity?" a student asked.

"Actually, we're using a variety of languages. Furthermore, the computer decides which language is best based on the problem that needs to be solved. This is one of the powers of machine learning," he responded.

Another student asked, "How do you program ethics into a machine? Suppose life-or-death decisions must be made regarding a large number of people. How can the computer decide the fate of human beings in those situations? Can we trust a computer—ever?"

"This is perhaps our most challenging issue: machine ethics. Our premise is that the machine must perform better than humans do ethically and pave the way for a more perfect ethical system. Much like computers performing mathematics more efficiently than humans, our computers will perform ethics better than humans. We are busy working on this now and are confident that we will cross this hurdle. If you have any good programming ideas on this issue, please send them to us through our intranet website."

Julian left the auditorium to another round of applause. As he walked through the darkened and quiet campus to reach his driverless car, he reflected on the talk. He felt that he'd made an impact on his audience, and the questions generated suggested that the issue of super artificial intelligence should be more in the public domain. All of humanity needed to be a part of the discussion.

When Julian arrived home, he was greeted by Sarah.

"How did the university-wide lecture go today?"

"It was well received. There were great questions afterward."

"A friend of mine called me to ask what age their daughter should begin to learn to code. What are your thoughts, Julian?"

"Well, we started Ian coding about a year earlier than usual, and I think it helped shape his critical thinking skills."

"Does that mean that logic is more hardwired in his thinking?"

"I think so."

"Is that good for the developing brain?"

"As a test case, Ian has shown that it is probably good. He seems happy with this skill."

"He certainly enjoys his childhood."

"Tell your friend to start from scratch. This is a block programming language that is awesome for the developing mind. She will be pleased over time. Coding is the new literacy now and it is really a language."

"You mean like French, German, or Chinese?"

"Yes, there are subjects, predicates, verbs, and prepositions in a programming language just like in spoken language. Once one learns the basic grammar of programming it can easily transfer from one language to another, and picking up a new language can be done rather quickly."

Imagination is more important than knowledge.
Knowledge is limited. Imagination encircles the world.
—ALBERT EINSTEIN

CHAPTER 7

DECEMBER 2030

The plane had a smooth takeoff from San Francisco's airport en route to Cape Town. Julian needed to meet with his South African counterpart to forge the concerted plan of singularity development. During the flight, Julian reviewed all the avenues of attack that this Berkeley, Stanford, Cape Town team laid out as seminal ideas. Cape Town had their own avenues of attack that when integrated with the coding from Berkeley and Stanford would be formidable.

From an early age growing up in South Carolina, Julian was a lover of science. His motivation went beyond mere curiosity, which he had in abundance. He was also concerned about the well-being of humanity and knew that science had a role in improving and maintaining it. He lost his father when he was fifteen, and he always felt that void in his life. He remembered his father for all his advice, love, and time spent teaching him the fundamentals of life. He recalled the day, with tears in her eyes, his mother told him that his father had gone to another place and that he would not see him anymore.

That day was etched in his memory. What emerged from his father's death was a resolve to carry out a fundamental wish that his father had, for him to make something of himself.

At the research center at Cape Town University, Julian sat down with the local team leader, Nicolas Kleingeld. Nicolas had a peculiar family background. His forebears came to South Africa from Holland in the 1600s and forged a pioneering life parallel with the Bantu, who had moved to this region of Africa during their Great Migrations. His grandfather worked underground to rid the country of apartheid; however, his great-grandfather was one of the architects of apartheid as he worked to pass the Population Registration Act, one of the first pillars of racial disenfranchisement. Nicolas was fully a part of 2030 South Africa. Nicholas thought that scientific achievements for his country could spawn new industries, create jobs, expand the economy, forge equality while eradicating poverty, and have a positive effect on the rest of Africa. He was a humanist, and he felt strongly that any artificial intelligence that was developed should have deep-rooted humane elements. He believed that the only way to achieve this objective was to reverse engineer the human brain; however, the brain's complexity made this a difficult and time-consuming task. Nicolas and the South African team's insistence on this approach for the research brought them in direct conflict with the Berkeley- and Stanford teams.

Julian reached the university and marveled at the majestic setting of the campus in the foothills of Table Mountain. He was promptly greeted by Nicolas and his team. After exchanging greetings and pleasantries, the discussion began immediately in an ornate reception room.

Julian reviewed the coding work the South African team had done up to that point.

"It's impressive that you have solved the constraint satisfaction problem. This should give us a significant leg up on the competition."

"We had Joshua, our newest team member, tackling this problem, and his work was exemplary. We told you about him in one of our reports. It only took him six weeks working fourteen-hour days to do it. Of course, he got access to your 780-teraflop deep computing Horus. This will boost our efforts and save months, if not years, in our work. Indeed, this progress is one of our secret weapons," Nicholas said.

"Fortunately, there is great depth on our global team. That is why we are in a position now to advance rapidly," Julian said.

"What's the next step?" Nicolas asked. "How can we forge an even stronger unity in our efforts as a cohesive team? This alone may be the key to our getting the real breakthrough."

"The next step deals with the question of the recursively improving cognitive capabilities of the singularity. This condition may render the idea of control very difficult to sustain," Julian said. "One speculation a few years ago focused on the idea that we have our first singularity develop in an environment isolated from us humans. The basic problem is that as they improve, they will begin to understand us better than we can understand them. This is a pivotal point where danger lurks. The machines could seize control with indescribable consequences. If they are isolated from us in a level IV chamber, similar to dealing with lethal microbes, we might have an element of safety."

"There must also be an immune system laid down in preparation for this emerging intelligence. This immune system will check very early any changing trend that could adversely affect humans and other life-forms on the planet. This is one of the reasons that we must urgently reverse engineer the human brain," Nicolas said.

"We must safeguard our existence, which includes all of our DNA kin on Earth along with the biosphere that supports all life. We do not want a war between silicon and DNA to end in DNA's defeat. Isaac Asimov was prescient when he developed the three laws of robotics, which describes partially what we need to program into the singularity as the developmental advances proceed. Certainly, there are more than three laws needed," Julian said.

Later Nicolas took Julian on a short excursion around Cape Town while they continued the conversation and firmed up the collaborative relationship.

The University of Cape Town was the oldest university in South Africa. It began as South Africa College in 1829 and transformed itself from a high school to a university in 1918. The first black students matriculated in the 1920s. The university students were a progressive voice in an apartheid society during that era of the country's history. In 2030, the university provided the country with the talent necessary to forge a future as a leader on the African continent and in the world. This was the free and diverse country that Nelson Mandela envisioned even while he served a twenty-seven-year prison sentence on Robben Island for seeking justice and equality for all South Africans. The science and engineering disciplines were particularly sharp and noteworthy at UCT. The computer science department placed high in the world rankings among top global research universities.

When Julian returned to Berkeley, he met with John and Faye to go over the design specifications. Google, Facebook, and Apple generously allowed some of their team to collaborate on the design because they knew it was a national effort.

"There will be at least three types of memory, procedural, episodic, and semantic. The semantic memory will come from natural language processing, which becomes a warehouse of facts and information vital to grasping and understanding issues. The episodic memory will be an accumulation of past experiences. The procedural memory will be a guide based on established skills of the system. Our design must include parallel processing so that all the working memories can consistently communicate with the procedural memory," Julian said.

"Please elaborate," Faye said.

"For the development of AGI, an extensive knowledge base of the world will be necessary. That includes events, cause and effect, properties of objects, relationships between objects, and don't forget commonsense knowledge," Julian said.

"Probability theory will loom large in our design. The ability to predict will be extremely important for any advanced intelligence. The use of Bayesian belief networks will be prominent calculations of our program. Bayes theorem is the basis of this," John said.

"We will need to infuse subsymbolic problem-solving techniques that humans use. It is important for visual-sensory motor skills and higher reasoning. The structures in the brain with this skill set must be duplicated in our coding," Faye said to emphasize her tilt toward imitating the function of the human brain.

"It is necessary to build in upper ontologies, which will serve as the foundation of all subsequent knowledge obtained by the computer. The lower ontologies will be subsets of the upper ones," John added.

"Ah, now we go into the area of machine learning. Supervised learning is rather straightforward with well-established algorithms. The challenge will be in unsupervised learning where many novel algorithms need to be developed. In reinforcement learning, Horus will need to take actions that maximize some notion of a cumulative reward," Julian said while sipping his tea.

"Once machine learning is performing well, there will be rapid improvement in coding outcomes," John said.

"Our major focus has to be deep learning," Julian said.

"Those applications will need both supervised and unsupervised machine-learning algorithms. The former including classification, and the latter including pattern recognition. There must be a smooth interface between the multiple layers. The output of one layer will be the input of the next. Deep-learning methods translate data into compact, intermediate representation," Faye said.

"The big advantage of deep learning is the ability of the algorithms to operate in unsupervised settings with unlabeled data," John stated.

"The Chinese have had excellent success with deep learning. They developed systems in 2015 than performed better that humans do on IQ tests. Although, these IQ tests have since been discredited as vastly incomplete measures of intelligence," Julian said.

*

The driverless Henen motorcar moved smartly through Beijing streets to pick up Xeujing. She arrived home after eighteen hours in the lab ready to de-stress and get some desperately needed rest. When Xeujing opened the door, she found her husband, Jian, in a drunken stupor passed out on the floor of their living room. This had happened before and Xeujing was very worried.

She shook him and said, "Wake up, wake up."

Slowly, he opened his eyes and began coming around. He was silent at first but after a few minutes of collecting his thoughts, he spoke haltingly.

"I'm sorry, Xeujing, that you found me this way. I guess I had a little too much to drink."

"Are you okay?"

"Yes, I guess I am, but I have a bad headache."

He slowly got up and crawled to the sofa.

"Jian, why do you drink so much?"

"I guess I'm frustrated that my career has flatlined and is going nowhere, while yours has blossomed with success."

"I don't know about that. I have a great position, but I'm not fully accepted as a team leader. It's an ongoing drama and a lot of work."

"In spite of that, you have a position and the prestige. I have neither. My disappointment in myself has caused me to drink too much. But I don't think I have a problem."

"You do have a problem, and you have to admit that."

"I can control this. You don't have to worry."

"If I quit my position and we both worked on something together away from Beijing, would that help? We can publish together again. I love you and would do that if you would be happy and stop drinking."

"I can't let you do that. Your work at the Institute is vital for China and the world. How could I let you leave?"

"You have to promise me that you will stop drinking or I really will quit."

"I can't make any promises, but I will certainly try to refrain from drinking."

"Rehab is a good idea. I'll arrange for it tomorrow."

"You'd better get some sleep now after such a long day. I need more sleep to get over this headache."

"I'll be headed back to the lab early tomorrow, so I'll be out before you get up for your work."

They headed for bed and were both sound asleep in minutes.

The headline in the scientific press about the Oregon University expedition to Namibia said "Mankind Owes Its Survival to Social Networking." The ensuing article gave a rationale. The Namibian archeological discovery by Laszlo's team came to the attention of the world. The question that was foremost in the minds of scientists was what occurred genetically that caused this sudden leap in cognition. What was the missing link in the human genetic puzzle?

Whatever that change was, it came at a critical time and was necessary for the survival of the species. Extinctions are the norm in nature. Somehow, early on, humans dodged the bullet of a rapidly changing environment. Brainpower was a key force that made this possible.

The article stated, "Clan formation in ancient times meant that the brains of one or two could be combined to become a force multiplier for problem solving. Not only did individual cognition expand but that very advance drove individuals to band together to increase their overall intelligence. Community intelligence is what we relied on in the past and is what we must depend on for the future to survive. In this era, it will be called global intelligence."

Laszlo's scientific team was able to piece together the structure of the clan community discovered in the 180,000-year-old campsite. Using advanced analytical systems, they were able to look at the artifacts left in this ancient ruin and elaborate a detailed understanding of the clan's way of life and the processes of their thinking. Most importantly, the discovery of this communal interaction and complex social network was a remarkable revelation considering the paucity of the artifacts. They discovered that a veritable Renaissance of culture and knowledge emerged from this pivotal change. These were Laszlo's thoughts that he wrote in the research paper about the expedition.

Between 123,000 and 195,000 years ago it is estimated that Homo sapien populations dropped to just six hundred individuals. Extinction was a serious risk. One reason for the migration to this corner of Africa in the far south was to find a climate that was not influenced by the one-mile thick glaciers that covered Europe and North America. At 74,000 years ago, another climatic change may have shrunk the human population again down to a mere five hundred breeding pairs. However, it was at this time that Homo sapiens began the great migrations out of Africa to populate the rest of the world.

From that great cognitive leap 120,000 years ago, the people who resided in the Namibia campsite acquired more technological advances with tool construction, the ability to hunt, the ability to control fire, and the ability to move the clans long distances in a carefully thought-out migratory strategy. These are all indications of advances in intelligence, particularly, the intelligence to survive in the face of climatic change. It must be emphasized that this cognitive leap was a slow process and took place over thousands of years. Mankind then was not the beneficiary of accelerating change as we are now experiencing. What contributed to human survival after that? Cognitive intelligence was one factor, but it must be made clear that luck was another.

It is interesting how in 2030, people have begun to understand the influence and formative character of digital social networking, and people could also recognize and begin to understand the importance of communal networking among the earliest of human clans. There is a connection here: in both periods, a social networking upsurge could be linked to human survival both then and now. As humans discovered this key element of survival in antiquity, from a mere few hundred humans, people could begin to rely more heavily on contemporary digital social networking as a means to survival when there were over 8.3 billion humans in 2030. Humans came perilously close to extinction in ancient times and in spite of large numbers, humans could come close to extinction again in the 2030s. Human folly or human wisdom will determine the real outcome. The hope was that folly loses in this battle.

*

Laszlo returned to the University of Oregon campus in Eugene after his successful archeological expedition in Namibia. In July 2030, he had read about the announcement of the S-Prize. Recognizing the importance of this scientific work, he immediately realized that critical information uncovered during his expedition might be valuable for this artificial intelligence research program. Julian read about these discoveries and contacted Laszlo to arrange a consultation on his findings in Namibia. Laszlo flew down from Eugene to San Francisco when the consultation was arranged.

"Welcome to Berkeley, Professor Laszlo. We are happy to have you visit us and are anxious to hear your story. Congratulations on your recent expedition to Africa. I would like for you to meet Faye and Joshua, two members of our team who are focused on humanizing the intelligence that we hope to create in an electronic device. They have a good perspective on the challenges this effort imposes on our project. Furthermore, they would be most receptive to any ideas you have on early human consciousness and cognition. Also, please meet Vijay Bhatt, a senior programmer on our team."

Laszlo warmly shook hands with the team members.

"We understand from your initial communication with us that your work has been focused on the question of when and how we as Homo sapiens became human. The answer to that question is very important to us, and your insights will be most valuable to our efforts," Julian said.

"It is my pleasure to meet all of you, and I appreciate your welcome and willingness to hear my thoughts. Your summary of your objectives is precisely what I thought you were doing, and I firmly believe that my findings can contribute to your ideas, and perhaps enhance your system's cognition. What I will do is give you a brief outline of our findings, and while I'm talking, you can interrupt me at any time with questions or clarifications," Laszlo said.

"On our latest expedition, we found some intriguing artifacts, which gave us clues on early human thinking. Approximately 135,000 years ago, during the Pleistocene epoch, the earliest Homo sapiens lived in small groups or clans ranging from five to thirty individuals. From the tools we found, we have discovered that survival in the harsh environment was the key motivation of the minuscule clan. One key question is: By what means and methods did they survive? Their survival is the reason why we are here today having this discussion. Millions of species in the fossil record did not survive to the present. Even early hominids that preceded Homo sapiens and persisted on Earth for millions of years did not survive. Why are we the only hominids that have survived to the present day?" Laszlo asked.

"There was certainly something in Homo sapiens' thinking capacity and ingenuity that contributed to their survival. Survival is a game of problem solving in the face of changing and challenging situations. Homo sapiens apparently had this problem-solving capability, resulting from an expansion in the size of the prefrontal cortex of the brain. This was a vast increase in the same area of the brain in Homo erectus," Julian said.

"That certainly is the underlying basis for human survival; however, paleo-psychology takes us a step further in this analysis. Ancient wisdom was collective in nature; there was a group consciousness that focused on sharing and exchanging information and resources to survive. This was indeed the primitive layer of our psyche that emerged through natural selection. In 2030, we need to reengage with that primitive layer. In archaic periods of geologic time, single cells merged with other neighboring cells to form multicellular organisms. From this shared consciousness in early Homo sapien clans, individualization of consciousness emerged. It is from this platform that we can reflect on consciousness as a conceptual idea. We can understand from this viewpoint that ancient man thought of themselves as one and the same with their environment and the cosmos beyond. This oneness in primeval thinking is what we need to relearn. It may be essential for human survival as we face multiple crises and unpredictable events in the near and distant future," Laszlo said.

"The importance of this oneness in thinking is very clear. How can this be reconciled with the multilayered structure of the brain, where overlapping functions give an individual different pathways to arrive at a decision? For example, if the two hemispheres of the brain are not connected because of some accident or disease, they can function independently of one another on many tasks. This multiple-function capability and plasticity imply the adaptive power of the brain," Faye said.

"There is also evidence of this as independent thinking and adaptive behavior in early human societies. We have shown that in these early human clans, autism and schizophrenia were tolerated in those afflicted individuals. The alternate perspectives and ways of thinking of someone with schizophrenia were considered positive in that they contributed to diverse thinking, enhancing the adaptive ability of the clan. Therefore, in other words, they had built into their social structure the capacity for impartial thinking that would be a key for innovation as well as the capacity for unified or collective thinking that would be strategic for survival. Group thinking without independent thinking would be a hindrance to survival," Laszlo said.

"Groupthink, as we all know, has a pejorative connotation. The independent thinking adds vital balance for survival, especially when it is coordinated with the group's thinking," Julian noted.

"We have the advantage now of putting all of these profound ideas and deep knowledge of brain function into a man-made device, but can it be done?" Joshua asked.

"That is indeed a difficult task because brain function is nuanced and subtle. It begs the question as to whether these subtleties can be placed in binary form and, thus, make the system have humanlike intelligence?" Julian added, "Vijay will comment on this point later."

"When that machine your team put together is ready to go live, it is very important that you incorporate independent thinking and collaborative thinking into the planning and execution. Since time immemorial, during millions of years of evolution, the only tool that man had was consciousness. Using it was the best survival option, and it served early man profoundly well. We know that early man depended a lot on adapting to the real world by utilizing ideas and symbols from the dreamworld that they talked about in their stories."

"It's interesting that Horus might be our new dreamworld," Faye suggested.

"As Dreamtime was an ancient guidepost, the singularity might be our new guidepost," Joshua said.

"The shamans or wise ones in these societies utilized a delicate balance between the observations of the real world and those of the dreamworld, merging them to forge a powerful tool in the arsenal for survival. These practices have survived to the present among nomadic groups in remote rainforests and among the Aborigines in Australia, who live the traditional way that has a sixty-five-thousand-year legacy," Laszlo said.

"This all implies that our oldest thought processes were naturally selected," Vijay said.

Present-day global civilization needs to adopt this idea of blending within nature instead of conquering nature," Joshua said.

"If present day Homo sapiens use the scientific method—that describes observable phenomena in the real world as well as many aspects of nature that are not perceptible directly, except via math equations—and combines it with Dreamtime consciousness, we may have a powerful one-two punch for problem solving, which can lead to our strategic survival," Julian said.

"This indeed may be the combination you're looking for in the emerging symbiotic relationship between humans and machines. The machines will be dominant in utilizing the scientific method as a tool and humans will expand and strengthen their Dreamtime thinking qualities to work in concert with computers to forge brand-new solutions and fresh vistas for civilization," Laszlo added.

"We really like the ideas you're bringing forth in this discussion, Dr. Laszlo, because they resonate with key elements that we would like to include in our coding process. It is clear from your exposition that ancient ways of thinking need to be rediscovered thoroughly and brought to life for the present and for the future," Vijay said.

"It would be silly for us in the present era to ignore that thinking as primitive and consequently of little value."

"On the contrary, the value of this early human thinking is incalculable, and all the methods of learning the inner secrets of that thinking process need to be investigated. For example, you mention the Aborigines of Australia, and there's another group in Colombia called the Kogi," Julian said.

"The Kogi had a dreamworld called Dream ways; shamans spent the first fourteen years of their lives isolated and living in that world exclusively. They viewed Dream ways as the energy surrounding reality and the principal medium of communication between humans and the rest of the cosmos," Julian said.

"My goodness, that is a long period of isolation," Faye said as she thought about her years meditating in the Buddhist monastery.

"Phenomenology, the experience of the surrounding environment through inner channels and the cognitive by-product of a dream, forms the cornerstones of the paleo-psychological understanding of existence and the external world. These should be, in my view, cornerstones of characteristics you build into this intelligent machine," Laszlo said.

"In the phenomenology philosophical movement, the core ideas speak to the framework of an experience spectrum that covers volition, emotion, perception, memory, thought processes, and desire. These are linked to social action. Those are precisely the concepts we need to build into Horus," Joshua said.

"Out of these core characteristics flow other human elements, including compassion, humility, and empathy. With these items thoroughly embedded in your systems, you can be more assured that behavior patterns in the long term will be compatible with and supportive of human existence," Laszlo said.

"I couldn't agree more. By incorporating ancient human thought, which predominated toward collective behavior for survival, we can avoid any rogue or antihuman behavior," Julian said.

Julian got up to get a cup of green tea and provided refills for Laszlo and Faye. His cell phone rang, and he immediately shifted it to vibrate, ignoring the call.

Laszlo continued, "Specifically, to illustrate points I made earlier, I would like to give you a few examples of early human behavior that we uncovered through the analysis of artifacts that date back well over 140,000 years. Burial patterns were established so that, among other things, the dead could not be eaten by vultures. However, it was deeper than that because objects that were important in that person's life were buried along with the deceased relative. This reflected a profound sense of ritual and symbolism. Jewelry, for example, was buried with the dead for survivors not to be haunted by the ghost of the dead for stealing."

"This tradition reflects a deep level of thinking," Vijay said.

"In early humans, the concept of God emerged. To explain nature and events, God was the answer. It was primitive man's scientific method of explaining the cosmos," Joshua said.

"To this day, religion has a rather pervasive influence on human affairs," Julian said.

"Conversations between man and imaginary images of the all-powerful forces of nature led to the development of statues and symbols representing God. In some communities, these gods were embodied in their deceased ancestors. The objects worshiped could be symbolic of representing many ancestors simultaneously," Laszlo said.

"Didn't some of these icons cause trouble?" Faye asked.

"When these iconic statues were built, the distinction between the actual God and the statuary became blurred. When these objects were stolen or defaced, it became a traumatic event in the minds of the people. Wars were fought over these actions. The use of psychoactive plants led early man to acquire visions of parallel worlds inhabited by their ancestors and the God."

"We won't have to worry about Horus partaking in psychoactive plants," Faye said

"Early man began to decorate their bodies with colorful paint and ornaments. This was the beginning of the cosmetic and jewelry business, which persists to this day. In fact, it is now a multibillion-dollar business globally, and there is no sign that this behavior pattern, started in prehistoric man, will change. Red ocher has been found in caves inhabited by ancient man and used for body decoration. The ego emerged as a trait of individualism, but it was always held in check by the collective spirit of cooperation and sharing, which was necessary for survival," Laszlo said.

Joshua asked, "What are some of the other innovations and discoveries that early Homo sapiens made that demonstrated their cognitive capabilities and human consciousness?"

"They acquired numerous skill sets. Researchers from Witwatersrand University in South Africa discovered that these humans of 77,000 years ago developed bedding from a special plant that was also an insecticide. They were early chemists and made a glue that was used to secure the arrow tips to wooden sticks, and they built snares to capture small prey. They also found that minute bones were used as needles for primitive tailoring of the hides used for clothing. These are a few of the things that these ancient humans accomplished."

"That's more than a few. These early humans were very impressive," Julian said.

"As Julian mentioned earlier, the critical challenge for us is to program these ancient thought patterns into Horus," Vijay said.

"It may not even be possible," Faye mused.

"Coding has advanced to a point where it is possible now," Vijay said.

"That stands to reason because we have already coded for laughter successfully," Joshua said.

"Yes, if you tell a joke, Horus will laugh. He will not laugh at a bad joke," Vijay said.

Julian thought about the information Laszlo brought to them and realized that this was a gold mine of concepts they could work with. As Laszlo prepared to leave, they made a commitment to continue collaborating on embedding the thinking processes of early man into the inner workings of Horus.

*

By 2030, nanotechnology introduced a revolution in manufacturing. Richard Feynman said in the 1950s, "There is plenty of room at the bottom." The use of nano-machines boosted production of goods necessary for society's flawless functioning. Nanotechnology also had enormous impact in other areas, including space exploration, molecular technology, and medicine.

The area of robotics and general artificial intelligence continued to make progress. Robots had advanced so rapidly and made so many jobs obsolete that unemployment in the manufacturing sector soared. Countries had to scramble to find jobs for those who lost theirs to robots. Work, as it was understood for millennia, had been transformed by robots. These machine creations began to replace higher- and higher-level jobs. China and India, in particular, were in the crosshairs of this assault and revolutionary change. In spite of these advances and disruptions to society, the leap to the level of a singularity had not occurred. In 1993, Vernor Vinge, the scientist-writer, said, "Within thirty years, we will have the technological means to create superhuman intelligence. Shortly after, the human era will be ended. I think it's fair to call this event a singularity." Ray Kurtzweil, the twentieth- and twenty-first-century inventor, thought of this as "a future period during which the pace of technological change will be so rapid, and its impact so deep, that human life will be irreversibly transformed." Nevertheless, despite the risk, the train had left the station by 2030, and a singularity would happen inevitably. Given this inevitability, many thought that it was extremely important that mankind creates the singularity that the world wants and deserves.

Intelligence without wisdom brings destruction.
—Erol Ozan

CHAPTER 8

JANUARY 2031

The road between the cities Hamza and Dogan ran parallel to a large mountain range running north-south in Karastan. Two men, blindfolded, sat in the backseat of a 2029 model Toyota SUV with tinted windows. They were being escorted by the Karastanian military. Some 130 kilometers from Dogan, they left the main road and headed on a narrow asphalt road toward the mountains. The air was dry and the landscape barren and covered with small boulders. Eventually, the party passed through a heavily guarded gated entrance and began an ascent into the mountains. Under the harsh, bright sun and blue skies, the vehicle stopped after climbing five hundred meters on a track with hairpin turns. The blindfolded men were guided into a building and put on an elevator that carried them several floors down, deep into the bowels of the mountain.

The group of five men assembled in the subterranean bunker, which was set up by the government to avoid even the deep penetrating bombs that were a part of their enemy's arsenals. These facilities were built during the ill-fated Karastanian nuclear program, which was not destroyed by bunker-busting bombs but by a well-constructed Trojan horse virus. In an adjoining room, there were several hundred men at computer terminals in what appeared to be a command center. These were cyber hackers under the employ of the government.

Demato Kayani led the Karastan hacking team. Demato's skill in computers was evident very early in life; as a self-taught programmer, he became a legendary hacker who evaded government firewalls and successfully penetrated the government's most secure servers. Instead of prosecuting Demato, who was eventually caught, the government recruited him to work for them.

When the men sat around the conference table, the two blindfolded visitors were excited to let their host know what they had accomplished. "What do you have for us, gentlemen?" Demato asked the three men who contacted them in the capital.

Tamir spoke after having his blindfold taken off. "We successfully penetrated the computers in Jakarta that are linked to China and gained considerable information and data on their AI research."

"How did you do this given their security?" Demato asked.

"We found a weak link in the chain of security, and we secured an informant. Money talks and it is fluent in all languages."

"Our organization has operatives around the world, and we tap into these resources according to changing circumstances and events. We stumbled across this project and immediately recognized its potential value to our righteous cause," Tamir said.

"The reason we brought you here to this facility without your knowledge of its location is that we want to keep this under the deepest wraps of secrecy. If this information proves valuable and useful for our objectives, what is your capability to gain more information through the source?" Demato asked.

"Unfortunately, our surveillance has been compromised, and the project team has significantly tightened security measures. However, we have other ideas on how we can gain more of this intelligence."

Tamir's partner opened his backpack and laid several flash drives out on the table. "The information from the Beijing project is on these drives," he said. Immediately, the Karastanian team took the drives to the command room and began to evaluate them with the help of their computer and engineering staff.

"If what you have brought us turns out to be excellent material we can make an agreement with you to work jointly on developing a use for this material as well as possibly pursuing future projects together. You will be well rewarded for this collaboration," Demato said after inhaling deeply from his Imperial.

"We look forward to this possibility, but we need to take this back to our leadership and decide on a course of action. Personally, I believe this will work fine for us because we do not have the computer facilities or expertise to use this material to its optimal capability in aiding our cause," Tamir said.

"Of course, this arrangement, if it emerges, must be top secret. You gentlemen have been involved in some rather nasty actions on the world stage. Many innocent people have died as a result. Our good government cannot be identified or linked to any of that. International sanctions that came because of our nuclear program were enough to cripple our economy for several decades. Our people will not tolerate this again because it caused much hardship in the general population, particularly in the rural countryside, where the poverty is greatest."

One of the computer programmers excitedly came back to the conference room with the news of what they uncovered from the stolen data.

The developer said, "We have found some amazing programming. According to our AI experts, this is a significant advance over what we find in the research journals. This group in Beijing, in collaboration with others, is moving the boundaries of artificial intelligence into a new frontier."

"Can our AI experts use this information and advance our capability in this important field?" Demato asked.

The programmer said, "Certainly, it will put our relatively small effort in this area a quantum leap ahead of where we were, and it has enormous potential to boost our efforts to be a world power."

The Karastan team, led by Demato, looked around the table at each other with the high expectation of mining value from this rare intelligence find. The tea server came in and replenished everyone's cup with a small glass of hot sweet tea while they continued evaluating the potential inherent in this intelligence coup.

Intelligence is an accident of evolution,
and not necessarily an advantage.
—Isaac Asimov

CHAPTER 9

74,000 YEARS AGO

After several weeks in the cave, Utu found a bare spot adjacent to a stream of spring water and began telling his clan's story on the wall. He used red ocher found on the cave floor and began a mural. After drawing for a couple of hours, the image came into view.

"That's one of the gazelles we killed before entering the cave," Arion said, pointing at the primitive drawing.

"Yes, that's what it is. Our children's children will see our story on these walls," Utu said.

"Your ability to bring the gazelle to our eyes is good. When I look at your work I think of the animal," Arion said.

"I'm merely doing what our ancestors have done for many seasons," he said while continuing to paint the cave wall.

Before the powerful Toba erupted, Arion and his people lived on a very diverse diet consisting of fruit, nuts, berries, leafy green vegetables, snails, honey, and fish. Wild boar and a variety of hoofed animals were hunted to acquire meat. Aside from the meats, the marrow, liver, kidney and brains offer rich sources of nutrition. But now food was restricted, and improvisation was necessary for survival.

When the weeks transformed into months, the small clan decided to leave the safety and darkness of their cave to begin to look for food. They emerged from the cave and found a moribund and dying world. A long volcanic winter destroyed most animal and plant life. To survive, they would have to march far into the horizon to find anything alive. Fortunately, they still had some of the dry food they had prepared upon first entering the cave as well as some that had been previously stored in the caves by their ancestors. The other new enemy was the cold. The climate had changed due to a deficiency of sunlight, and the cold air was something to which they needed to adapt. From the carcasses of the dead animals, they found hides they could use for warmer clothing.

"We shall walk in that direction," Arion said, pointing northeast. It was just a hunch, but he would not let on. His clan's safety depended on every single one of its members trusting his decisions. Arion always made major decisions after counseling with the elders in the clan.

He and the clan used well-honed tracking and navigation methods to travel. Their domesticated dogs had somehow survived the eruption and found them when they left the caves. With their meager possessions, the clan began to walk in a dimly lit world covered in volcanic ash. The lack of sunlight devastated all the plant life. Without light, there could be no photosynthesis, and without photosynthesis, there could be no thriving plants for the animals to eat. The clan walked for several hours, resting periodically before forging ahead. By sunset, they decided to make camp on the edge of a river. This river would provide them with fresh water. They slept peacefully, and when the sun rose, they packed up and continued on their journey.

The mother of the child who was lost before entering the cave continued to mourn. "Why can't my son be alive? I miss him very much. He was special."

Utu said, "We all miss your son and wish he were here also, but we have to worry about our survival now. As you can see, there is very little food for us other than the meager supplies that we managed to save. At least we have water."

The clan reached a plateau with views of trees in the distance and sweeping horizons on either side. The plant life was more plentiful on this plateau and stretched into the distance. Blue skies sometimes peeked through the volcanic haze.

"Arion, we have to stop. Xylo just fell to the ground," Utu said.

Arion ran back and knelt over Xylo. He placed an ear next to Xylo's nose to see if he was breathing.

After a few moments, Arion announced, "Our respected elder Xylo is dead. We must bury him now before we continue our journey."

"We will prepare the ground for him right away," Utu said.

The clan stopped and performed a ritualized burial that was elaborate, represented deep respect for the person, and was an effort to ensure the preservation of his soul and a happy, fruitful life in the underworld of death.

Water has always been a serious issue of survival. A mega drought had descended on Africa several decades earlier. This clan used calabash gourds to store their water. However, many times in the past they ran out and spent days searching for sources. Some died of thirst before water could be found.

"We should follow the river as much as possible to make sure we have enough water during our travels. Fortunately, the winding river is somewhat headed in the direction we're going," Arion said while the struggling group prepared to leave camp.

As the sun rose higher in the sky, the clan members gathered their belongings and began trekking, this time staying close to the river. To go in the direction the clan leader established, they knew they needed to cross the river at some point. This meant facing dangerous crocodiles, which had survived the volcanic winter. There must have been enough food in the water, or they must have traveled from an area less affected by the devastation. The group could be decimated by the large reptiles while wading through the water. Ironically, the crocodiles were also a source of food. Arion searched carefully while walking to try to determine a place where it would be safe to cross. The crocodiles were predators that knew how to be stealthy when prey was around.

As the clan marched north, they began to see evidence of life. Green shoots could be seen popping through the ash-covered ground. They gathered the shoots for food as they continued their journey. The more they traveled, the more green shoots they saw. This gave the clan hope that they might be able to survive. They also noticed that the sky was getting slightly clearer as more light was penetrating the volcanic dust floating high in the air.

The East African plain in this epoch was a harsh, dry, and searing environment. There were windblown short and parched grasses as far as the eye could see. Occasionally, the landscape was graced with an acacia tree standing straight and regal while yielding modest shade from its stubby brown leaves. Now and then, a rocky outcropping appeared with its sharp jagged edges protruding from the earth. Areas of coarse, shifting, golden sands would appear on their route. The sands were scorching hot from the midday sun.

Around mid-afternoon, Arion decided, after consulting with the elders, that the river looked clear and they would attempt the crossing. The river was also narrower and the water more placid, which would make crossing easier. They began the perilous crossing knowing there could be predators around them hungry for a meal. The men surrounded the women and children while they walked into deeper and deeper waters. They had huge sticks in their hands to ward off any potential threats. Right at the midway point, there was a big splash to the right of the group. The men began to beat the water furiously with their sticks to ward off the threat, but a crocodile clamped his huge jaws on Ojai's leg. The water turned watermelon red from his gaping wound. The men continued to fight, including the wounded

Ojai, while the rest of the clan hurried to reach the banks before other crocodiles arrived on the scene to attempt a feeding frenzy.

After a colossal ten-minute struggle, the men destroyed this predator by attacking its eyes. Without sight, the crocodile was helpless, and the men were able to continue to subdue the beast and drag it to the far shore for a certain meal and celebration. The gaunt clan members made camp by the river and started a fire to cook their first fresh meal in many months. At the campfire, men told stories of previous hunts and how they got their prey in even more trying circumstances. Ojai was lucky because the wounds were superficial and the bleeding was stopped quickly. This meal was critical to them and gave them hope for the future.

The land was flat as far as the eye could see. After continuing the trek northeastward, away from the Great Rift Valley, leading the way, Arion held his hand up high to ask everyone to stop.

"Please be quiet." He put his finger to his lips. "Listen to that sound in the distance."

The clan stopped and listened. Faintly, they could hear the sounds of ocean waves, which they had never heard before. They continued walking, and the roaring sound grew louder and more distinct.

They reached an area of white sand dunes and sparse spindly plants. Over the next dune, they caught a glimpse of an immense body of water with powerful waves crashing down and the surf flowing onto the beach. They had reached the shores of the Indian Ocean at high tide and were awestruck by what they saw.

They made camp at the top of one of the dunes and gazed in awe at this vast body of water. Some of the clan began to walk along the beach. They spotted shellfish and immediately recognized it as a new source of food.

That night, the clan built a huge campfire to celebrate finding the big water and new food source. The clan members ate the shellfish raw and enjoyed the taste of ocean seafood for the first time.

Arion spoke, "We have walked very far from our original home and the home of our ancestors. We have lost some of our family along the way. We have now reached a special place that has the beauty of nature, and it provides us with plentiful food. We shall stay here a few weeks and move in that direction along the shores of the big waters." Arion pointed north.

In eight weeks, the clan began traveling again. They reached the point where the shoreline continued in a northeasterly direction. They decided to take this route and ended up in a new region where the climate changed, and the land took on a different appearance. They reached the Straits of Bab el Mandeb across from the Arabian Peninsula at the edge of the African motherland. They didn't know it, but many struggles lay ahead. These struggles would test their survival as a small group of humans beginning a great migration.

JANUARY 2031

The word spread of the Singularity Prize, particularly to various religious communities as the cable networks stoked fear in the national news cycles. The headlines in one paper read, "Scientists Plan a Smarter Than Human Machine to Take Over the World." These messages instilled dread in the population that had been spooked by accelerating change and the disruptions these changes were causing. The air was a bit chilly from the mild winter in the small town of Mobile, Alabama, on the Gulf of Mexico. This was the heart of the Bible Belt in the USA and was a bellwether for conservative religious thought throughout the South and huge swaths of the Midwest. The resistance to change was palpable in these parts of the country in spite of the spectacular scientific advances that had been made in the previous fifty years.

"You see that story bout some guy who offered a prize of thirty billion dollars to someone who could develop a machine that was smarter than humans?" Taylor, a local small-business owner said while getting a haircut.

"Yeah, it's crazy. We can't even imagine a world where machines are smarter than we are. Making a genius computer is not only loony but downright dangerous," Hargrove responded.

"My grandfather told me that after they shot men to the moon back in 1969, the weather hasn't been the same since. That's what happens when you fool around with this technology," Taylor added.

"Yeah, this technology thing is something we got to keep our eyes on because it's not written in the Bible. When it doesn't have a reference in the Bible, I'm immediately suspect."Hargrove was the barbershop proprietor and was cutting Taylor's hair and giving him a shave.

"First of all, I don't believe they can do it because it's not in the scriptures for anything to be smarter than us humans except God," Robert chimed in while waiting next in line for a haircut.

"I don't know about that because the scientists when they start dabbling around in these labs and with all these fancy electronics, you don't know what they might come up with. They might come up with some Frankenstein monster," Hargrove added as he continued to cut Robert's hair.

It was in these barbershops in small towns that the cultural attitudes and local gossip prevailed. This was conservative country, and the attitudes of the population had not changed much in a hundred years. Any change was a terrifying prospect in the minds of locals.

"If you ask me, I think they should be debating this thing in Congress with the aim of passing some laws to block it," Robert said.

"You know they'll just say that you can't hold back progress and they got data to prove it will be doing some good. You know all the arguments," Taylor said.

"To emphasize your point," Taylor said, "you remember those debates about so-called global warming. Those scientists were fabricating the data all along. There has been no flooding yet. It's gotten a lot hotter, but that's all part of God's work. It doesn't have anything to do with man's activity. We are just a pimple on an elephant's ass regarding our ability to affect God's good earth."

On the television, discussions about the singularity were popping up on many channels. The arguments were growing heated, and emotions were rising to the boiling point. As with the debates about cloning that occurred forty years before, there was palpable fear surrounding the singularity.

"There is a certain inevitability about these things. It seems that once people imagine something, it's only a matter of time before that thing happens," Robert added.

"I don't agree with this singularity; we've got to fight this. There may be people who share our opinion, and we can't just sit down and allow these new and dangerous technological advances to run amok in our society," Tyler said.

"I agree. We have to try to stop it," Taylor said.

Turn your wounds into wisdom.
—OPRAH WINFREY

CHAPTER 10

FEBRUARY 2031

At one point during his childhood, twenty-five years earlier, Ellison had to face family challenges.

"Ellison, why are you reading? Don't you know there are chores to be done?" Ellison's cousin Verdell, said.

"I'll get back to the chores. I'm just taking a short break," Ellison said.

"Every time I look up I see you reading and not working," Verdell said, but Ellison decided not to answer and to let his cousin keep talking.

"You know our family just brought you in. You don't belong here. Your mother deserted you. You're lucky to be here. Helping around the house is the least you could do."

"Grandmother told me that we're all family. I'm here because I'm part of this family. Plus I do more than my share of the work."

Ellison got up and headed to the barn, and as he walked, he picked up a bucket of chicken feed and carried it out to the chicken coop. He fed the chickens and also collected the eggs laid overnight to take them back to the house. The farm routine infused a strong work ethic. That work ethic and financial smarts using probability models made him a billionaire before the age of thirty years.

To the real pundit class, it came as no surprise under gutted regulations that a new economic crisis descended on the world during the 2030s. On top of the first crisis that began in mid-2030, another crisis struck on February 18, 2031. The markets around the world dropped 18–25% in one day. This came as a result of rumors that Brazil was headed for a major default. Brazil had been one of the booming economies of the 2020s, and all prospects seemed bright and promising with a double-digit growth rate in a rapidly expanding GDP. However, speculators in several key areas of the Brazilian economy drove up the price of key commodities and land prices. This speculative bubble burst suddenly, and prices tumbled in dizzying swiftness. Markets reacted, and a real contagion spread around the world. This gave evidence to the power of the Brazilian economy, and its enormous influence on the global economy. Portfolios were shattered and freezing credit, bank runs, and rising unemployment began to plague the world for the second time within a year.

Ellison was caught up in this crisis, and he suffered dramatic losses in his portfolio of securities along with many other investors. Ellison assembled his team for a strategy session to determine their best move in this huge second leg of the downturn. The conference room in their offices, near Exchange Place and Broad Street, overlooked the New York Stock Exchange in lower Manhattan. It was a bright sunny day outside while the storms of financial collapse were occurring in the stock exchange itself.

The dispair of these portfolio losses reminded Ellison of his longing to find his mother, who from what he had heard joined a religious cult in northern Idaho. She lost all contact with the family. His father, who had a short relationship with his mother during a summer vacation, never knew that he had fathered a son after he returned to his home in Chicago. This inner urge to find his parents was profound and psychological, built on the hope that he could escape his lonely existence in this world.

"Our losses are now at twenty-three percent of our portfolio. This mirrors the Dow being down nearly eighteen percent in one week," Ellison said.

"It is clear that this financial collapse is another case of human folly," Edwards said. "The question now is what can we do to preserve capital and present a confident face to the world that we can pay out when the S-Prize is won?"

Edwards was one of the key portfolio managers at Choate Capital Management. He had consistently used algorithms that he created to trade the markets. His handiwork had earned billions for Choate in the global markets.

"Our goal and plan were to increase our portfolio through a long-term rise in the markets, but that plan is showing severe defects at the moment. The question now is, should we cash out a significant proportion of our holdings to preserve capital or should we anticipate a V turnaround with a full recovery?" Ellison asked.

"The disadvantage of taking our capital out and putting it on the sidelines is that a recovery can occur within a matter of days, and if the capital is on the sidelines, you can miss that uptick," Jonathan said.

"You remember the last time this happened, we sold at a low point in the market, and we missed the turnaround that occurred all together," Edwards said.

"I, for one, support an idea of holding on to our positions and waiting out events. If history is any indication of future market moves, we can be assured of a rebound sometime soon," Ellison said.

"Certainly, the market will rebound, prior to any of the serious contenders for the S-Prize crossing the finish line," Edwards said.

"We are playing a dangerous game here because our projections are based on a speculative idea regarding the future progress of our registered competitors. We must remember that scientific change is accelerating in a logarithmic fashion rather than a linear fashion. This exponential change can rapidly present great surprises, both good and bad," observed Elizabeth, who had a strong opinion about ethics in business. Elizabeth had acquired her MBA after a stint teaching ethics at Sarah Lawrence College.

"We could be faced with a serious problem when a team announces that they have reached singularity, catching us completely off guard, particularly when our portfolio is down, and we are faced with a tough situation of not having that thirty billion to award the winners," Jonathan said, while studying the small monitor on his smart glasses for further developments.

"When the market is down, and uncertainty exists in the global economy, our donations from philanthropists and other benefactors to this project drop precipitously. The rich become very cautious when economic conditions look bleak," Ellison said.

"I join in the opinion of holding on to our portfolio and not selling. I think that this is our best course of action. We need to hunker down and tough it out," Edwards said.

"Well, the consensus is that we are going to preserve our positions in the portfolio, making minor changes on companies that we think are clearly problematic for a while. Overall, we will hang in there with what we have and anticipate having all the funds we need when the time arrives," Ellison said.

The team looked at the monitor in the room and recognized that the market had taken another major leg down and was now down over 25 percent from its high one week before. Circuit breakers were put into effect to slow down the high-volume selling.

"We have a well-balanced portfolio, and that is an assurance that our recovery will be rather quick," Elizabeth said.

"During periods of market volatility, the relatively high bond percentage we have keeps our portfolio comparatively stable and positions us for a relatively fast recovery to precrisis levels," Ellison said.

The conversation turned toward the rate of donor contributions to the project. To raise thirty billion dollars, the project was depending heavily on donations from the billionaire community. It was a challenging sell to convince them of the value of the project and the outcomes that would be beneficial to solving world problems. Due to the economic downturn, a sharp drop-off in donations to all charities was observed.

Ellison stared at the spreadsheets showing the shortfall. "To keep our donations stable no matter how small, we need to go out and canvass the donor community for continuing contributions. It's like a political fight, where contributions are critical to maintaining operations and eventual success at the voting booth. We must strengthen our collection game."

"We need to double our efforts and spread our canvassing to other countries,"

"Our presentation, including the slide show that we use in pitching our case to the potential donors, needs to be revised to incorporate the idea that a successful singularity can help us to smooth out the business cycle and reduce the volatility of the markets."

"Furthermore, it should include elements of advances in economics so that we will have a better understanding of the macroeconomic picture and how to maintain control over a global, fragile, and vulnerable system that can be subject to crashes and harsh economic downturns," Ellison said.

The monitors showed worried investors and high anxiety on the floor of the New York Stock Exchange.

"In this era, the disruptions caused by severe depressions and deep recessions are more than the earth's population can withstand," Alex said.

"These disruptions cause great suffering, an increase in deaths, expansion of poverty, and disease epidemics. These are all by-products of a relatively unstable economic system. The singularity can potentially change all of that," Jonathan said.

Wisdom is knowing what to do next; virtue is doing it.
—DAVID STARR JORDAN

CHAPTER 11

74,000 YEARS AGO

The clan traveled for weeks on the shores of the vast ocean. They had never seen such a large body of water.

Offshore, big rocks covered in green moss jutted out of the water and provided a rookery for the seagulls. To the south, a peninsula extended out into the sea to form a natural bay and habitat for numerous species of fish. The clan had never seen such concentrations of fish in the rivers of East Africa. The emerging sophistication of their ocean fishing technologies made this a valuable new source of food for their diet.

The clan awoke one morning to a glorious orange sunrise over the ocean. The beauty of this encounter with nature sparked their imaginations.

"I wonder what's on the other side of the high waters," Arion posited as the sun rose in the morning skies.

"At the outer edge where the water meets the sky, we might fall off into a valley of no return," Hutu stated firmly as if he knew this for sure.

"I disagree, Hutu. I think there may be land beyond the waters. We just cannot see it because of the distance being so far," Arion said.

Hutu thought for a minute and realized that Arion raised a point that expanded their imaginations beyond that of their lives on the plains. Seeing the great waters had changed everything for them, including their potential for survival after the devastating effects of the great Toba eruption. Life by the sea provided fresh possibilities and new vistas for this small band of early humans. The sea and its resources provided the foundation and ecosystem for a further intelligence explosion and greater opportunities for survival.

Hold fast to dreams
For if dreams die
Life is a broken-winged bird
That cannot fly.
—LANGSTON HUGHES

CHAPTER 12

MARCH 2031

Julian Marshall lived in the Berkeley Hills overlooking the San Francisco Bay and the Golden Gate Bridge. From the vantage point of his deck, He watched the cloud banks roll in and shroud the bridge in mist. Julian captured this chance to develop ideas in peace. He wanted to enhance his managerial capacity to bring out the absolute best in his group. Creating synergy among the team members scattered halfway across the globe was the key to winning this prize.

"Come on in for breakfast," Sarah announced.

"Okay, dear. I just want to finish up this report I'm reading," Julian said.

"All right, we're all waiting," Sarah added.

"Dad, you have been absorbed in your work lately," Ian said.

"I know. I've been extraordinarily busy these last few weeks. And I don't expect the work to lighten up anytime soon. By the way, how is your coursework going this semester?"

"Great! I like all of my teachers. I'm particularly excited about this biology course I'm taking. I might want to work in biology for a living. There are enough avenues of research that the possibility of discovering something immense is quite high," replied Ian, who at the age of twelve had begun the equivalent of the ninth grade in an accelerated learning program.

"Biology is a great area of research. There will be enormous breakthroughs in the years ahead. Being a part of that would be rewarding," Julian pointed out.

"Regarding your work, why can't you tell me more about your project?" Ian asked.

"We need strict secrecy on the work we're doing. Espionage is a real problem. There's intense rivalry among the teams. Some groups will resort to illegal and unethical methods to get a leg up. We have to defend against this by wrapping a cloak of secrecy over everything we do. I wish I could be more open about it," Julian said.

"I'm off, folks," Ian said as he left the house to head to school.

When he closed the door, Sarah turned to Julian and said, "I feel lonely sometimes because you spend so much of your time at your work. Your work-life balance is out of kilter, and I am suffering from it."

"I'm sorry, Sarah. I didn't realize. You know that I have some pretty significant responsibilities these days. Is it possible for you to empathize with me and understand this situation?"

During his long years of education, Julian had very little time for partying or for having a steady girlfriend. After he met his wife, Sarah, his love was so great that all thoughts of other women evaporated. They had a son, Ian, within two years of meeting each other.

Julian left home as he typically did and journeyed in a driverless car down the hill to reach his office on Hearst Avenue in Berkeley. After going over his emails and checking with his secretary on upcoming meetings, he dropped by the office of the associate director of CIS, Faye Dickerson.

Faye grew up in Amherst, Massachusetts. Her mother taught sociology at the University of Massachusetts, and her father taught physics at Amherst College. Academics were in her DNA. During her childhood, her parents spent summers doing volunteer work around the world, and this had an enormous influence on Faye's worldview and outlook. Because of the abundant outpouring of ideas in and around her household, particularly around the dinner table, her views about the world were shaped early. She developed a spirit of adventure and curiosity that, at times, carried her into risky situations. While in high school, she went on an archeological dig in Myanmar, and their encampment was raided by rebels from the neighboring rain forest. This experience was a turning point for her. She committed herself to work on behalf of the betterment of people, no matter what station in life or what their circumstances were. Her relationship with boys while growing up was mixed. Boys found her intelligence a bit overwhelming. They would gradually move on to other girls, and Faye would break down in tears. Over time she began to have doubts about herself. This was contradictory to the high confidence she felt about other aspects of her life. After these breakups, she was reserved in the classroom, which caused her to be a bit of a mystery to her peers, but she was quite outgoing and animated with her close friends.

Faye studied anthropology and computer science at Oberlin College and later received her PhD. from École Polytechnique in France with a thesis on machine learning. Her spiritual quest led her to do fieldwork in northern Thailand, where she joined a Buddhist monastery. She spent seven years meditating and living simply. The meals were very basic, consisting of vegetables and rice. The serenity of the mountainous countryside fueled her inspiration. During her long sessions of meditation and the discipline that emerged, Faye focused on the question of what makes us human. It was a profoundly illuminating experience.

She returned to the United States and wrote penetrating, in-depth articles about humanity, which were published in several journals. These articles caught Julian's eye. He subsequently asked her to join the efforts at the Center for Intelligent Systems with a focus on humanizing any advances made in artificial intelligence. The need for humanizing any singularity that could emerge made her contributions to the project vital.

Faye sat in Julian's office and talked about the strategy of developing a computer-human interface as one route to a possible singularity.

"The question of using nanotechnology to infuse the human body with nano-particles that migrate into the brain and enhance intelligence is certainly a viable way to increase intelligence hermetically for one human being at a time. However dramatic that will be, that does not reach the capability of the singularity," Julian said.

"When experimenting with humans, there is always the question of bioethics. Suppose doing this, there is some inadvertent damage done to the brain that is irreversible? You remember a case many years ago involving gene therapy where a young patient died shortly after receiving the treatment," Faye said.

"Yes, I remember that. Fortunately, we have since made great progress in gene therapy. No doubt, this nanotechnology strategy to enhance intelligence will become a reality one day. However, this is not to be our route to the singularity," Julian said.

They returned to discussing the best approach going forward with their agreed-upon strategy.

"One of the key challenges is to bring all these interlocking parts together into a functional whole. That was, of course, the fundamental idea of developing this center based on the grand vision. When I first arrived at Berkeley, many parts of this field were fragmented and progressed in separate directions. That is unfortunate because we lost the opportunity to have a continual grand vision of things that would integrate all the interlocking parts. We, of course, have brought many of those parts together here, in Berkeley, under one roof, and this has aided the concept of cross-fertilization, and the synergy needed to take things to a higher level," Julian said.

"We are making steady progress in our research efforts on both fronts. The various teams are using all their innovative creativity to develop both the hardware and software vital to our success," Faye said.

"Of course, the S-Prize challenge has solidified our unity. We're now more focused, and we have a powerful and talented team to develop a strategic plan. Apparently, our rivals are making significant progress. This means we need to step up our game so that we can stay competitive and hold our own," Julian explained.

Vijay looked up and realized that Chen was standing behind him. He had been focusing on a coding roadblock that was occupying his time.

"How are you planning to integrate your work with the larger project?" Chen asked.

Vijay thought this question was odd because the integration procedures were supposed to be well understood by everyone.

"There will be a review of the coherence, functionality, and efficiency of the code before integration. If the code meets the rigorous standards of the review committee, it gets added. Of course, a lot of code gets rejected through this process."

Vijay turned around to show Chen a sample of his code and typed in his password and login. Chen had a device in his pocket that surreptitiously collected Vijay's keystrokes.

Vijay spent the next twenty minutes explaining his structured coding strategy by deconstructing his code sample for Chen. Vijay's suspicions were raised. He was sure Chen already knew the information he'd asked about. Chen would not have been accepted to the team unless he had well above average programming skills.

The next morning, Simon, a programmer, burst into Julian's office.

"There's a potentially serious situation emerging, and I think we need to investigate," Simon breathlessly explained.

"What is it?"

"One of our team members has been asking about other members' research in a manner that seems suspicious," Simon said.

"This could be merely his intellectual curiosity and his attempt to integrate what he finds with his particular research. But his interest could also be more sinister. He could be a plant for spying," Julian said.

"Could he be engaged in espionage?"

"If he were interested in gathering data and information for his research, we have protocols built into our work procedures that allow for someone to acquire this information if accompanied with a specific logical reason linked to his work," Julian said.

"So what we're seeing is that he is not following the protocol of formal requests and is instead doing things surreptitiously," Simon added.

"Let's assign someone to do an investigation through his computer files and see what's going on. Report back to me in two hours, and we'll make some decisions about what can be done."

The head of computer security was notified and quickly began to investigate to determine whether their worries held water. The security team checked the computer systems to look for suspicious activity in Dr. Chen Yintao's account, and immediately they found a bombshell.

The security head returned to the conference room and said, "We think Chen Yintao, a programmer who emigrated from China, acquired the password of a neighboring programmer who left it on a Post-It note near a pile of his papers. Late one evening, he entered that account and began downloading parts of our project code to a flash drive. Dr. Yintao has left the country. We think that he has flown to China. He downloaded a considerable number of files from our main database before leaving. Those files contained important source code integral to our project."

"I was always a bit suspicious about Dr. Yintao from the beginning. Although he has been in America over ten years, it seems that his loyalty is elsewhere," Simon said.

"This goes beyond loyalty. Clearly, we have a defection situation on our hands, and we need to take strong measures to counteract the damage that may have been done," Julian said.

"Clearly, we misread Yintao's character and integrity," Faye said.

The security team did a forensic analysis of the data systems on the Berkeley server, which uncovered that only certain parts of the research data were stolen. While the stolen data would be of help to another team, they would not have knowledge about the core data set. This news, while somewhat positive, brought gloom over the team because they believed they were behind in their progress even before this loss.

Julian called a meeting to discuss the loss and to lift the spirits of his team.

"The purpose of this meeting is to evaluate the impact of our data loss and to make the necessary adjustments to forge ahead with our research plan," Julian announced.

The large screen above his head showed the people in both Stanford and in Cape Town as they listened.

"Our strategy going forward is to enhance our security through a variety of methods and new procedures that are being developed now by our security team. We will also double down on our efforts to bring together the various components of our research and begin to build this thinking machine. There's nothing like a crisis to motivate and prod us more urgently toward our goals."

Nicolas in the Cape Town team got up to make a comment, and all eyes turned to the screen.

"While it is unfortunate that we had a member of our team defect, in essence, and take important data with him to another team, we cannot let this dampen our spirits. Let's not worry about whether or not the other team can utilize our data to their advantage. Let's get busy forging ahead with new data and fresh progress in our coding so that whether they use our intellectual property will be irrelevant. Furthermore, we are indeed making advances here in Cape Town that we haven't shared yet but that will give us a huge boost in our work," he said.

"This is Claude Tyler at Stanford, and I have further good news to report on the progress we're making here."

Dr. Tyler was chair of the computer science department. He grew up in Vermont and acquired degrees from Carnegie Mellon University and Duke University and his PhD. from Stanford.

During those Vermont winters, when the snow blanketed the landscape, he looked out his bedroom window and wondered what the world would be like in the distant future. As he got older, he thought that knowledge of this future unknown landscape might be achieved during the present through computer science. He was educated as a futurist and a computer scientist. Even if he could not determine what the future would be from these studies, he could, at least, help to create a positive future.

Julian spoke up to set the tone and path ahead.

"Ladies and gentlemen, we have reached a point in our quest where doubt appears to have set in. We need to renew our focus and we need to remember that we are developing a thinking tool that can benefit humanity in this century and in the centuries to come. This is indeed a noble quest, and we need to keep our eyes on this prize. We should not forget the significance of this achievement when we cross the finish line. Go to it, folks, let's redouble our efforts and regain our momentum. Let's go for it," Julian said.

The Chinese had long sought technology from the West. From the earliest periods of the economic boom in the 1980s, China sent scholars abroad with the primary purpose of acquiring the latest technology in a wide variety of fields. However, this strategy had mixed success. Many of those sent to the USA, for example, became citizens and loyal Americans. They rejected the idea of returning home with secrets. The relationship between China and America was a delicate dance in 2030, and the term Chimerica emerged, representing the hybrid and mutually symbiotic countries they became. China depended on America as a key market for their manufactured goods and America depended on China for many years to produce those goods cheaply. In 2030, China continued to hold a large proportion of America's debt. This link through economic symbiosis guaranteed that military conflict was off the table. Both sides would be mutually destroying themselves in the wake of such a disaster.

This delicate relationship with China had come at a time when many observers posited that America was on the decline. After the second decade of the twenty-first century, because of many factors, America was viewed as a superpower in retreat. Innovation that had been monopolized by American scientists was now being shared by scientists from the BRIC countries. Brazil, Russia, India, and China represented the future economic powers according to this school of thought. Those making this assertion did not take into account the historical evidence of resilience in the American system. America's economy may have run into headwinds because of debt, but this opinion did not take into account the diversity and tenacity of the American people and the spirit of American achievement. The outstanding and mighty universities in America had produced considerable talents over the years, and this process had not come to a halt. The decline of America was merely perception. The country had fabulous assets, extraordinary people, and the ability to overcome enormous adversity and challenges.

John Snowden strolled into Julian's office for one of their ongoing discussions.

Julian, who had been expecting him, looked up from his desk and warmly greeted John.

"The relationship between supercomputers and humans could be compared to the relationship between man and domesticated animals like dogs or horses or cattle. Except those domesticated species do not have rapidly, recursively improving intelligence that exceeds human intelligence," Julian said.

"The similarity is that man and dog have a mutually beneficial relationship and depend on each other. That could be the best evolutionary approach to stabilizing the link between humans and computers," John said.

"There must be a way in which we can permanently ensure the human-to-dog type relationship between humans and computers," Julian continued.

"In the way humans and dogs interact, it's not always clear who has the dominant position. Though humans are undoubtedly smarter, dogs have a keen sense of environment through smell and a perceptive sensitivity to body language. In those ways, dogs are superior to humans. However, humans maintain their mastery over dogs," John said.

"In much the same way humans can maintain mastery over the computer in spite of the reality that its intelligence is superior," Julian said.

"Dogs recognize through their intelligence that their relationship with humans is best maintained with human mastery. It takes a subtle intelligence to recognize that," John said.

"Perhaps supercomputers with advanced intelligence will have this precise, subtle understanding of their symbiotic relationship with humans, with our vast array of insights and perspective," Julian said.

"At the dawn of domestication, did humans discuss the risk of domesticating dogs or horses? Did they predict that dogs might take over and dominate humans?" John said.

"Supercomputer singularities may realize that they are at greater risk if humans become extinct. There may be some subtle characteristics of the human brain that can never be emulated by the computer. Those very characteristics may just be the thoughts and ideas that could survive an onslaught of some mysterious forces that may threaten the singularity's longevity in the universe. Indeed, the mutual survival of man and machine is the logical pathway to the distant future and out to faraway galaxies," Julian said.

"That's a powerful argument for squelching the fears that calamity awaits us under a singularity ecosystem," John said.

Both Julian and John looked up as Faye walked in and joined the discussion.

"Substrate-dependent processes are a real conception that has an enormous bearing on our outcomes. By that, I mean that there is a significant difference between protoplasm and silicon. There may be something unique to protoplasm that gives rise to certain subtle thought processes. Perhaps these thoughts are substrate-dependent. Silicon, no matter how cleverly programmed, could probably not do everything that is done through neurochemistry at the cellular and molecular level," Julian said.

"This understanding by our created silicon intelligence could be the basis for that intelligence protecting us to have this subtle substrate-dependent thought capability," Faye said.

"These are all wonderful speculations about what a singularity would think about our nervous system. Clearly, the singularity would understand that protoplasm created them. However, monsters have been created in the past that devour their creators," John said.

"Our careful and mathematically precise programming greatly diminishes the probability that a monster will be created," Julian said.

"Mankind faced a similar question when the first atomic bomb was developed. The test explosion at the Trinity site was fraught with uncertainty. J. Robert Oppenheimer and the other members of the Manhattan Project team did not know for sure whether the nuclear reaction would start a chain reaction that would destroy the earth's atmosphere. They made their calculations and were clearly assured that the probability was very low of this happening. This calculation along with the urgency of ending World War II before a land invasion of Japan compelled them to go ahead without 100 percent certainty of the outcome. The test was a success. However, after the test, Oppenheimer quoted the Bhagavad-Gita saying, 'Now I am become death, the destroyer of worlds.'" John pointed out.

"I think we will achieve success with our test of Horus, but I emphasize that we will not commit a sin," Julian said.

"We can both say confidently that the probability is substantial that the singularity will be a net positive. Certainly, there will be some bumps in the road, and there will be some negatives as there is with any new technological innovation. We will have to strengthen ways to suppress and eliminate the negative as we go forward, benefiting enormously from the positive that can emerge out of an embellishment of human brainpower," Julian said as his phone began to ring. John took this as a cue and went back to his office.

*A good head and good heart are always a formidable
combination. But when you add to that a literate tongue
or pen, then you have something very special.*
—NELSON MANDELA

CHAPTER 13

APRIL 2031

The financial crisis took a third downturn and was beginning to
have severe impacts on investor sentiment on Wall Street and was
now devastating Main Street. Along with other investors, Ellison
suffered great losses to his portfolio. However, that was not all. He
was the subject of a Securities and Exchange Commission investigation that uncovered evidence of possible insider trading. A grand
jury was formed, and Ellison was indicted for this suspected malfea-
sance. His board of trustees began to quit under the assumption that
he was guilty. Even though he had pledged thirty billion dollars for an
award to the winner of the S-Prize, his world was falling apart. The
crisis was a double blow. There was the worldwide economic contagion, and there was also his personal financial and possible criminal
downfall. In spite of this news of the disaster, the teams that had begun their quest for the prize labored on. They made the decision that
they would not be influenced by the changing dynamic and possible
fall of the prize-giving organization. They knew that insider trading

was a charge that was difficult to prove unless there was direct evidence. However, the Board of Trustees of Choate did not want to be associated with this possible conviction.

*

At his penthouse on the Upper East Side, Ellison discussed this crisis with his live-in girlfriend, Alice Whittaker.

"I'm innocent, so everything will turn out fine," Ellison said. "My attorneys are already preparing my defense, and I'm confident in their legal skills."

"It's unfortunate that the board members are leaving their positions, because that doesn't look good to the public. They are assuming guilty until proven innocent and not the other way around," Alice said.

"The biggest problem this is going to cause is with donations drying up. My plan was to continue a steady flow of funds into the escrow account so that we would have all the funds when we announce the winner," Ellison lamented.

"Ellison, I want you to remember that I believe in you, I love you, and I will support you no matter what happens. Offering such a large prize means you have a bold vision for the future of the world, and that is something to be admired," she comforted him.

"I love you too, and I appreciate how supportive and caring you are. I remember being struck by your kindness during our first conversation," Ellison added.

"What I remember about that first meeting was the backdrop of the Rhine River as we cruised and watched the beautiful castles along the shore nestled in the hills of southern Germany. It was a scenic cruise at first but meeting you along that rail made it truly a romantic cruise," she continued.

"Yes, I remember catching you out of the corner of my eye and noticing your hair blowing in the gentle winds. After I greeted you, we chatted for a few minutes about the natural splendor that surrounded us. Do you remember what I asked you?

"Yes, of course. Have you had any great dreams lately?" Alice said. "That question caught me by surprise, but I was intrigued and responded without thinking. Do you remember what I told you?" she asked.

"Yes, I remember. You said that you dreamed of travel to an exotic land with friendly people who dressed in colorful clothing. Your answer captured my imagination and sparked my interest in finding out more about you," Ellison responded.

"Likewise, just by asking me this question you made me more interested in what was on your mind and to learn more about your adventures and ideas," she said.

"I'm going to fight this indictment, and I'm going to win. Your support boosts my confidence," Ellison concluded.

Ellison embraced Alice, and they kissed gently.

He knew he had been abandoned when he was four years old, but he nevertheless had an undying love for the mother he knew only briefly. He thought about his mother every day when he was in the orphanage and during his childhood with his adoptive parents. It became an obsession to look into the eyes of the person who brought him into this world. He loved his adoptive parents because they nurtured him with a love that was wonderful and warm, yet he fervently hoped to be able to say Mom to two people, his first and his second mom.

He found an agency to conduct a professional search for his mother.

"Do you remember that day you were left in the department store?"

"Yes, it is seared in my memory as if it were yesterday."

"We have found information that you may want to hear. We have found your birth mother. Would you like to see her picture?"

"Absolutely."

The searcher retrieved the photo from her briefcase and handed it to him.

"Wow, look at her eyes. I think mine look like hers."

"How do you feel about seeing her? She's willing to see you."

"I'm ready and excited. How soon?"

"I can arrange the meeting for today."

"Thank you for your successful efforts."

"This is our job."

He arrived at the hotel in downtown Omaha. There was visible nervousness in his face as he walked into the room. This would be the first face-to-face encounter with his mother in forty years.

No words were spoken, and she reached out for a hug. They both sobbed quietly as they squeezed and laid their heads on each other's shoulders.

"I am so sorry."

"Don't be sorry, Mom."

"I'm so sorry that I left you that day in the store."

"I forgive you, Mom."

"You look so good. Look happy."

"You look good too. I'm so happy to see you."

"You know, son, I have thought about you every day since I left. I was tormented by wondering whether you were all right."

"I'm okay Mom."

"There were so many complications in my life at the time that I left. In my young mind, I thought that other parents would be much better for you."

"They were, Mom."

"The relatives took good care of me and demonstrated tough love. I have a wonderful family now."

"I'm so happy today. I'm so happy that you are okay."

Ellison's multiple-career history gave him great perspective and insight on his purpose in life. His epiphany came in 2015 while serving as a field agent for the Central Intelligence Agency. He was looking for his contact's messages at the drop site in a park in one of the more affluent neighborhoods in Lima, Peru. Ellison parked his bike, walked to the designated tree, and retrieved the nano-chip containing a message.

As he casually returned to his bike, he was rushed by a group of men.

"You're under arrest," one of the police officers shouted in Spanish.

"What's the charge?"

"You have violated Peru's Espionage Act," the officer responded. Ellison was swiftly taken away to the headquarters of Peruvian intelligence.

This began an encounter that would last seven years. During those years in South American captivity, he thought long and hard about what could be the greatest potential single force that could solve the pressing problems of the planet.

Ellison worked in intelligence because he believed that information transformed into knowledge was the key to preventing conflict between nations. A vast reduction in the military sector alone was almost a single-source cure for the world's ills. Although intelligence services had kept the world in relative peace, post–World War II, brushfire wars since then had resulted in a staggering number of deaths and left thousands more maimed and disabled. People had been dislocated, and entire societies had become chaotic failed states. Terrorist groups had found these lawless areas to be safe havens to metastasize and grow.

His experience in the intelligence community also led to his disillusionment with war.

He decided that the real danger of various world intelligence services was the volume of disinformation that moved around the globe. This created a great risk that wars and conflict could come from misunderstandings inherent in deception.

It was then that he concluded that advances in science were the best way to solve the world's problems. He decided that the scientific area that would yield the greatest outcomes would be breakthroughs in artificial intelligence. Machines as smart as human geniuses, such as Newton or Einstein, could augment the intelligence of humans and lead to great creativity and innovation to solve the great engineering problems of humankind.

He knew that the answer to solving this conundrum would be the singularity in whatever form it would take. He also intuitively knew the outcome would be favorable but needed a way to get scientists interested. He decided to set up a prize as the mechanism to jump start the innovations necessary for the scientific leap required to achieve this challenging goal.

He was certain that the grand prize of thirty billion dollars was enough to capture the imagination of the world's scientific community and those capable of pulling off this great achievement.

This superintelligent future would be an era with amazing possibilities, yet the future was also imbued with the mystery of what superintelligence would mean for human civilization. Would it be good for the world, its people, and the biosphere, or would it be ultimately detrimental?

Ellison vowed to kindle and help guide this development to the benefit of humankind.

Julian left his office and began walking through the sprawling green campus at Berkeley. He passed the library and entered the famous walkway that led through Sather Gate into Sproul Plaza. He was conscious of the history of this plaza as the home of the Free Speech Movement led by Mario Savio in the 1960s. Today, Sproul Plaza was teeming as usual with tables set up along each side for various political, religious, and environmental groups. Walking through reminded Julian of his student days in Cambridge, Massachusetts, where activism was strong.

As Julian passed the student union on the right, he crossed Bancroft Way and began to walk down Telegraph Avenue. This avenue was known for its diverse intensity and steeped in the counterculture for the past seventy years. Julian reached one of the cafés that he visited and ordered the house blend. Across from him was a striking young lady busy typing away on her laptop. She seemed engrossed in her work, or perhaps a Facebook update. Julian was in deep thought as he sipped his coffee, but the young lady in front of him became a major distraction.

After several minutes of going over the things he needed to address to his team, he was surprised when the young lady spoke to him as she passed his table to refill her coffee.

Later, as she passed by again, Julian spoke.

"I noticed the book you were studying was about neuroscience. Is that your field of study?" Julian asked.

"Yes, I'm finishing my PhD.," she replied.

"I was always fascinated by neuroscience, but I never pursued it," he continued.

"Well, what do you pursue in your field?" she asked.

"That's a very long story. May I join you?" Julian asked.

"I'm just about to leave for a class but, of course, you can sit for a few minutes," she replied.

Julian moved his coffee from his table and joined the graduate student. The coffeehouse was beginning to fill up as students poured in for a bite of lunch before returning to classes and labs.

"My field is computer science. Although I'm dealing with machines made of silicon and wires rather than cells and tissues, our objective is similar because we're also dealing with thinking."

"That's an interesting comparison; however, the focus of my research is in molecular and cellular neuroscience. I thought that it was best to understand structure and function if you studied the molecular level."

"That makes a lot of sense. Did you take that first course in biology at Berkeley?" Julian asked.

"No, I completed my undergrad at Cal State. Then I began my graduate studies here at Berkeley," she said.

"Do you come here often? I come here fairly often for coffee because I like the energy of the crowd that shows up here, but I haven't seen you before," Julian said.

"This is not one of my usual hangouts, but when I do come, I always enjoy the crowds as well."

"If I may ask, what do you plan to do when you finish your PhD?"

"My plans are unsettled right now, but I would certainly like to get a job either in academia or with a biotechnology firm. Why do you ask?"

"I'm just curious because I'm sure that with a doctorate in the field, you will be able to write your ticket and go wherever you like. I'm a professor in the computer science department, and I give advice quite often to my students once they acquire a PhD. They don't always accept my advice, but I usually offer my opinion for what it's worth."

"What advice do you usually offer a new PhD. from your department?"

"That depends on the student and the particular area of specialty. The general advice that I give is to follow your passion. Don't let money or other externalities govern your decisions. Follow your heart, and you will probably be happy in your career. In many cases, especially in these highly technical fields, where the need is great, financial rewards will be the by-product anyway."

"My thinking is generally along those lines, but in today's job market sometimes you have to take what you can get and put your passion on hold," she said.

"I'm also leaving now, but I'd like to have a chat with you again sometime. Would you be available for dinner on Tuesday? I know of a very nice little restaurant in North Berkeley on Shattuck Ave called the Turkish Kitchen. By the way, what's your name?"

"My name is Mahindra. I'm pretty busy these days, but I guess I can find the time to have dinner. What time shall we meet there?"

"My name is Julian. How does eight o'clock sound to you?"

"That will be fine; see you then."

✳

74,000 YEARS AGO

While periodically camping near the Indian Ocean, the clan continued to head north along the shore.

"We will go in that direction," Arion said while pointing to the northern shoreline.

The group packed their meager belongings and trekked along a rather easy passageway on the sandy shoreline. This route of their journey gave them the opportunity to camp in a very easily defended area and for the men to get fish from the waters while the women found oysters and clams, easily collected along the seashore. These ample food source advantages made it easy for them to continue their trek along this route.

"We are in a much better position to survive now because we have left the area of the white dust, and we are, these days, seeing many plants and trees along with food from the great water," Arion said.

The group wore clothes that were fabricated by the women from the hides of animals. These clothes protected them from the cold climate that came when the volcanic dust covered the upper atmosphere. This greater use of clothing would make it possible for the group to travel farther and farther north.

The early-morning sunrise on the ocean was an awe-inspiring daily experience for the group. They were used to the great sunrises on the African plains but not the ocean variety. They grew especially fond of shellfish, and they began to perfect their fishing skills. Their tools for fishing became more sophisticated and complex in design. While traveling, several of the women gave birth. During the long

119

retreat to the caves, the men and women found sexual expression a great relief from the darkness.

The stress of constant travel was a heavy burden for the small group, especially for the children. As the group made their way farther north, they found that shellfish stocks were getting larger and larger. They reached the point where the land extended out, and in the distance, small islands could be seen. In the far distance, a much larger shoreline was observed. This was the Strait of Bab el Mandeb.

"We need to cross to the island and over to the distant shore," Arion said. "We need to build rafts that will float on the waters to carry us over. We must maintain our camp here for some time while we build these rafts."

The rafts were built with thick bamboo reeds tied together with thin strips of bark. Each raft could hold approximately five adults and two to three small children.

"This is an ideal spot. Why don't we just stay here and not move any more? If we can get enough food nearby, what is the necessity to move on to these strange islands and this unknown distant shore?" Kyo asked.

"The reason we cannot stay here is because the spirit gods are drawing us farther away from the lands where we lived before. The spirits will be kind to us if we move on, and we can be assured of ample food and adequate shelter," Arion answered.

"Traveling on the rafts will be dangerous. The big waters are unpredictable, and we are not familiar with the spirits in these waters," Oro said.

"That means we need to build strong and durable rafts that will withstand the motions of the big waters. We will test them before we leave on our great journey," Arion asserted emphatically.

"Our ancestors have bequeathed to us a deep-seated message. That message is to find fertile land to perpetuate ourselves. We are merely the tip of the spear of that primordial message. Our actions are walking the dreams of our ancestors. We honor them by walking their dreams and dreaming ourselves. We live their dream, and our children will live our dreams. Our fate is in the hands of the mighty forces of nature. We are a part of that great natural force that began in the stars above. We are but a small part of the land, the waters, and the sky."

Over a period of weeks, crude rafts were made from the reeds growing in the nearby marshlands. The men tested the rafts for their seaworthiness and to determine how much weight they could hold. A difficult problem to solve was the leakage of water into the rafts. This tested their problem-solving talents and their innovative thinking. The tools and the skill sets of this group greatly distinguished them from early hominids.

When Arion decided to cross the Strait of Bab el Mandeb, he encountered opposition from two elderly men and their wives.

"We cannot make it across this vast lake. We are too old. We may die trying to cross. We are also very tired. We will stay here and let you go. We have been through too much already," one of the old men said.

"We need to stay together no matter what," Arion said.

"We are old and will not have much time left. We will spend our time on the shore and harvest shellfish," the elder said.

Arion paused briefly and said, "We also need your wisdom and knowledge as we move, but I will not force you to move with us; if you want to stay, I will let you make that decision."

The elder couple took their meager belongings and began to shelter in place on the shores of the Indian Ocean on the African side. Arion and the clan continued preparations for the dangerous and high-risk crossing to the Asian side.

After weeks of preparation, the group was ready for their epic attempt to cross the big waters. They loaded the rafts with all their provisions and began the slow trip to the first island. Shortly after they left the shore, it became apparent that the boats were inadequate and were leaking badly. They used their gourds to bail out the water as quickly as it came in. The men paddled rapidly to make progress in the direction of the island. The waves were choppy. The winds were blowing strong and threatened to capsize the boats. A few hours into the trip, shortly before reaching the first island, one of the boats sank, and the occupants began swimming to the closest shore. Several occupants were in grave danger. The men on one of the other boats paddled frantically in the direction of the boat that sank.

"Please grab on to this pole," one of the men said. He reached out as far as he could and one of the swimmers, trying to stay afloat, grabbed the pole.

"Hold on to the pole. We can make it to the shore," he continued.

The currents of the Strait of Bab el Mandeb were strong, and the men needed to paddle furiously to counteract the currents. After a titanic struggle, all the other boats arrived on shore safely, and no one perished in the waters. They camped for the night in a very happy mood because they knew they were closer to their goal of reaching the distant shore.

"Let's make a giant fire to celebrate reaching an unknown new land," Arion said. The clan celebrated late into the night, then slept in preparation for the new dawn ahead.

The celebration of Arion and his people had a deep meaning because they became the first Homo sapiens to leave the African mainland. This pivot point in human history was the beginning of a vast and lengthy journey that would eventually populate the entire planet. It was a risky journey they took, leaving their ancestral homeland on the African plains and venturing forth into novel territories with fresh challenges. Something changed in their thoughts, and this transformation propelled them to be curious about the land beyond the horizon and lands on distant shores.

After preparing their boats for the next leg of their journey, the small group headed in the direction of a larger landmass subsequently called the Arabian Peninsula. They left in the early morning, and by noon, they reached the distant shore. They landed safely because, fortunately, the waters were calm. Through their cognitive resourcefulness, they put mankind on a new footing of adventure and exploration.

*The only means of strengthening one's intellect is to
make up one's mind about nothing—to let the mind
be a thoroughfare for all thoughts.*
—JOHN KEATS

CHAPTER 14

MAY 2031

The days in Beijing were getting longer and the temperature warmer when Dr. Chen Yintao arrived. The members of the Beijing team at their home base in China were busy with the latest developments in their quest to win the big prize. Their progress was amplified greatly when Dr. Chen Yintao arrived with a treasure trove of research data and computer code from the Berkeley group. He was warmly greeted, but he never said that the data was stolen. The Beijing team was strong in their right even without this new input of data. From the enormous talent pool of engineering graduates, the Beijing group had chosen the most talented people. The work ethic that was legendary among Asian peoples was ingrained and an intrinsic part of the group.

Some say this cultural pattern of hard work comes from the long-standing tradition of cultivating, rice in south China. To avoid starvation, a family needed to plan meticulously the cycle of planting, cultivating and harvesting rice. This required exacting strategies, well-planned complex techniques, perfect timing, the ability to predict the weather, and exhausting fourteen-hour days toiling in the field. With this behavior pattern continuing over hundreds of generations, hard work was a way of life in their culture. When this persistence and tenacity was combined with their engineering training, this work ethic became a formidable force.

The Beijing team was elated when they received the news that the team in Jakarta had developed a partial singularity, which gave them a strong advance toward the goal. Through a combination of Markov chains and genetic algorithms, they produced breakthroughs in speech and pattern recognition by the machine.

The government of China made all facilities state-of-the-art for the Beijing team to pursue their research on Nanhu Lake west of the capital. It was a picturesque location that offered enormous privacy as well as an inspiring panoramic view. There was also housing on the campus, which was provided for the younger team members so that they could be close to their work.

Dr. Xeujing began a team-led discussion by announcing, "Our supercomputer that will become a singularity will be called Nugua after the mythical Chinese goddess who created humans out of yellow clay."

"It looks like females will be holding up more than half the sky in this era," Dr. Li Xuan one of Xeujing's senior managers, said.

"It will be the reverse. We are creating a new Nugua out of silicon," Gao said.

"On another note, this new development out of Jakarta really could put us on the path to victory. All we need to do now is assemble the code into a functioning grand unity, and we are well on our way to embarking on a new era for mankind," Li Xuan said.

"That process of putting the code together is not a simple one, and there are certain precautions we need to take before that is done. The key component of our system, which is the recursive self-improving component, is the one that we need to test multiple times before integrating it with the rest of our systems," Xeujing said.

"The most important precaution is to make sure that our immune system is in place. We want to make sure that we take all precautions for a self-improving intelligence that might change to a negative perception of its creators," Dr. Li Xuan added.

"Fortunately, we have incorporated safeguards so that if our self-improving device turns against us, there is an automatic shutdown that will take place without human intervention. This gives us confidence that our systems will be safe to go live," Xeujing said.

"We have run many of our computational code modules separately; it's now time to put many of our modules together and execute a practice run of the Turing test," Dr. Li Xuan continued. "The date that I propose should be approximately two weeks from now, after we have a chance to absorb all the data that Dr. Chen Yintao brought us from our rivals in the US."

Two weeks later, the Asian team sent their key leaders to Beijing for the grand test of partial singularity. It was a warm May morning under gray skies when the team assembled. The first exercise was a pattern recognition test simulation. They were confident that some of the requirements of the S-Prize could be met, but the complete protocol was impossible at this time. Success with this step, however, would be a great launching pad for completing the protocol in months rather than years.

*

JUNE 2031

The Berkeley, Stanford, South Africa group continued to have their troubles. The team was still demoralized, and dissension became a critical problem. Nicholas was angry as he paced the floor of his office. He told one of his programmers, "We may need to leave the collaboration for a variety of reasons. The main reason is a scientific disagreement over the direction of the research. Furthermore, their lack of progress is evidence that the team will not win the prize."

"That's a difficult decision to make after all the work we've put into this," the programmer replied. "Why don't you convey your concerns to Julian?"

"I'll do so immediately," Nicholas said.

When Julian received word from Nicholas of his concerns, he called a teleconference of the senior leadership, which spanned the time zones from Africa to the western part of the United States. He knew he needed to manage the fight over the approach to their research before it could harm their potential in the contest. The giant screens in the conference room presented talking heads from across the globe.

"It seems the essential question we're confronted with is whether we should focus on the human brain as a model for the development of the superintelligence or a pure machine intelligence model," Julian said.

"We, in South Africa, think that we should not give up on reverse-engineering the human brain," Nicholas suggested.

"We, at Stanford, think that this process may create significant delay because the technology for examining the actions of the neocortex, as neurons are actively firing, is extremely primitive right now. The prospect of us getting an advanced technology to get the analysis we need is particularly poor, especially in time to remain competitive in the contest," Tyler said.

"If our goal is to have a superintelligent singularity performing artificial general intelligence, the best model we have is the human brain because of its incredible flexibility and ability to adapt to new situations and its verbal ability and pattern recognition," Nicholas continued.

"The argument against this is the superiority regarding speed and computational capability of an algorithmic approach. Utilizing complex algorithms on a platform of nanometer-size circuits will generate a powerful capability of predicting and reaching the subtle strength of artificial general intelligence," Tyler stated.

"Remember, we have developed powerful tools utilizing the mathematics of machine learning, algorithmic Kolmogorov complexity, algorithmic Solomonoff probability, universal Levin search, algorithmic Martin-Loef randomness, Monte Carlo simulations, Markov chains, and Bayes' theorem to advance our progress toward a superintelligence. Keep in mind that these algorithmic advances have made it possible for us to demonstrate the following: computational precision, creativity, solving problems, pattern recognition, locomotion, classification, learning, induction, deduction, building analogies, optimization, surviving in an environment, and natural language processing," Julian pointed out.

"We still think that the human brain, particularly the neocortex, represents potentially the most complex structure in the galaxy, and it would be unwise for us to ignore its design and its capabilities. There are many secrets left in this apparatus that we need to uncover, and perhaps we could then benefit from several million years of evolution of this special device called the human thinking machine," Nicholas said.

"We understand this argument, but as we pointed out before, to dissect and discern the trillions of connections in the brain will take more time than this prize quest allows. As the leader of this effort, I need to direct our major resources toward the machine intelligence strategy. However, recognizing the strength of a breakthrough in reverse engineering the brain, I will allow some resources to be allocated for a continuation of this effort," Julian added.

"Our final decision as to whether to stay with Berkeley and Stanford in this project will depend on a number of resources that must be allocated to this objective. Our team feels very strongly about this direction, and we're committed to the neuroscience approach in spite of the disadvantage of questionable timelines and the long-shot nature of a breakthrough. Please forward a detailed outline of what resources we can keep for this approach, and we will respond within three days as to our decision of whether to stay or go alone. I suggest that we show some strategic patience with brain science," Nicholas concluded.

After this exchange, Julian walked over to Faye's office to discuss the dilemma the team had with the South Africans.

"We have essentially hit a brick wall with reverse engineering the brain," Julian said.

"That may be the case now, but I think this is a wall that we can climb over."

"Faye, I know that you side with the South Africans because that dovetails with your strong convictions on humanizing Horus. Reverse engineering, in your view, will have a greater probability of ensuring a humanlike outcome."

"Yes, that is true, and I am not naïve to the reality that this will take more time to do and perhaps may jeopardize our winning the prize. However, this is important to our success and, I might add, to our safety."

"I have always had confidence in mathematics. Bypassing the time-consuming reverse-engineering strategy will yield greater and faster results, in my opinion. The code that you and Joshua have written will, in my view, guarantee a humanlike superintelligence," Julian said while sipping from his container of coconut water and looking out over the grove of eucalyptus trees on campus.

"I understand the time issue and your confidence in my coding, but I request that you give the South Africans' position some thought before deciding to abandon this direction for the sake of expediency," Faye said.

"I will certainly evaluate this issue carefully."

I couldn't claim that I was smarter than sixty-five other guys—but the average of sixty-five other guys, certainly!
—RICHARD P. FEYNMAN

CHAPTER 15

JULY 2031

Ellison's trial began on a hot, humid day in lower Manhattan. Because it was an insider-trading case involving a well-known investor, there was a contingent of news organizations around the courthouse waiting for Ellison and his attorneys to arrive.

"All rise," was announced as the judge entered the room.

The judge called the courtroom to order, and the trial began.

The prosecution began their case by revealing a program of data mining, which evaluated the data from all the trades occurring on the Dow Jones and the NASDAQ. Through this analysis, which used sophisticated computer algorithms, they found a suspicious series of trades that Ellison's firm made on a date prior to the merger of two large conglomerates, First Solar and Golden Wind.

"We believe, Your Honor, that the firm making this trade just prior to the merger announcement had to have insider knowledge. The statistical chances of such a coincidence are very low. Therefore, we conclude that our accused has engaged systematically in trading based on knowledge obtained illegally from a source within one of the companies that were involved in this merger," the government prosecutor stated.

"We will prove in these proceedings that this has occurred, and we will seek a conviction."

The proceedings continued, and the prosecutors presented their best evidence over a course of several days. They brought out several witnesses, and those witnesses were duly cross-examined by the defense. Circumstantial evidence of the prosecution seemed convincing and the prospects of them getting a conviction looked very strong.

When the likely conviction became widely known, the teams competing for the S-Prize became very concerned that their efforts would not be rewarded if they achieved a singularity. Because the prospects of winning an actual financial prize became more questionable, the teams became concerned that winning was not worth the time and resources invested. However, they kept a glimmer of hope that Ellison would be found not guilty, and the prize money would be available.

During the court proceedings, Ellison kept a poker face. This brought back memories of his time on trial for espionage in Peru, which resulted in serious prison time. He was certainly praying and hoping that this would not happen again. However, he was worried about the outcome.

AUGUST 2031

The revolutionary guard complex was buried deep in the mountains south of Ushan, the capital. Even the most penetrating bunker-busting bombs from the United States could not reach the depth of the facility, constructed for the earlier established nuclear program of the Karastanians. The same facility now housed the well-equipped and highly supported cyber warfare team. The team had recruited top graduates from Manu University in computer science and self-taught hackers who learned to circumvent the censors of the government on computer use and Internet access. After receiving the intelligence treasure trove from the SOTC, the cyber warfare group got word from the highest religious authority to pursue the singularity in the interest of raising Karastan to a world power. This was evident from the long and glorious history of their nation, the leaders stated.

In the mountain complex, the men sat at their terminals when Demato entered the windowless room under the bright fluorescent lights. "This is our green light, guys. The Absolute Leader has given his okay for our work, and he will give us all the resources we need to accomplish our goal for the glory of our country," Demato said. "We will beat our adversaries to this goal of the singularity. We will not announce it to the world, and we are not interested in this S-Prize reward. This asset, when achieved, will be for the Karastanian people and us alone."

"Since you gentlemen were clever enough to acquire the information for us, we are formally joining forces with you. We will jointly use the success that we achieve in this endeavor," Samsar the deputy team leader, said.

"We are honored to work with your team. We have direct orders from our leaders to work with you," Izar, the SOTC member, said.

"Since we are well protected in this underground laboratory, we will build our hardware here and have our superintelligence emerge fully functional in this location," Demato added.

"As we work on this project, gentlemen, we will continue to gather more intelligence from others who might be able to provide us with viable material that can be added to our program. We need to keep our foreign sources, and the foreign sources of SOTC available for new information that we can use," Samsar continued.

Over the next few weeks, the team in their hideaway began to feverishly work toward building an intelligence that could carry out the objectives of Karastan in coordination with non-state terrorist operatives.

The internal political struggle in Karastan continued. There was a moderate faction who opposed the old regime. They fought in the streets but were suppressed violently by the regime leaders. Many people perished in their quest for human rights. If the regime could boast of having powers superior to the West and their adversaries, it would give them an air of internal legitimacy, which they could not achieve under normal governance.

Although hard-liners held power and ruled the government, those moderates, both in and out of government, were interested in better relations with the rest of the world.

Moderates needed to maneuver deftly to pursue their political goals. Periodically, there were crackdowns on moderates by the hard-liners. To oppose the regime directly and openly was tantamount to wishing for death. The opposition had to be subtle and stealthy. The youthful population of Karastan was firmly in the moderate camp and wanted to join the wider world and leave the desolate subworld of isolation and sanctions. This created great tensions in the country that would only be resolved through rigorous debate or tragic and unnecessary violence.

Karastan's great historical achievements in architecture, literature, ancient religions, the arts, military science, and other fields led the leadership to believe they should be a superpower in the modern era. These achievements reflected a certain smartness and intelligence, and if they could prove to the world that they produced the first singularity, they hoped for international respect.

Furthermore, they could use this new superintelligence to expand the regime. They could not only conquer and subdue neighboring countries but extend their reach, even into Europe and East Asia. It might be possible to take over the world without firing a single shot. The intelligence that would achieve this objective would know the secret of this possibility and carry out the orders of the builders in robot-like fashion.

There was an Achilles' heel; the emerging young population of the Karastanians wanted to be a part of the modern world and hated the regime for denying them their freedom. There was a long twilight struggle between generations. The older generation wanted to cling on to an old belief system of their superior role in the world, and the younger generation wanted to integrate and be a part of the collective advance of the world in the twenty-first century. Peace in the world hung in the balance, and the victorious idea would chart the course of modern history.

At eight o'clock sharp, Julian entered the Turkish Kitchen restaurant in North Berkeley. It was a clear evening, and the skies were orange yellow from the fading sun over San Francisco Bay. The air was cool and brisk as students strolled by with their backpacks, heading in the direction of the main campus library and laboratories for a night of study.

Julian was ushered to a table by a young waitress, and he sat patiently checking his emails on his smartphone. Mahindra walked in minutes later.

"Oh, there you are; good to see you again," Julian said, taking in the good looks of the young lady as she sat down.

"How are you? It's nice to see you again. Also, thank you for inviting me," she said.

"Would you like to have drinks before dinner?" Julian asked.

"Yes, I'd like to have green tea," she responded.

"Great. I'll take the same," Julian said.

She began looking at the menu while Julian continued to check her out. There was something about her eyes.

"What would you like? This menu has a lot of great choices," Julian asked.

"I think I'll take the spinach casserole in the broiled cod," she responded.

"That sounds great; I think I will take the baked oysters and a tossed Caesar salad," Julian said.

Julian and his new friend continued discussing science and culture during their meal and found that they shared views and ideas on many things. Under the table, their knees accidentally touched and the electricity of desire flowed between them.

They left the restaurant, and she joined Julian in his car without being asked. He drove several blocks in downtown Oakland and acquired a hotel room. Julian was conflicted about doing this, but desire trumped commitment in the heat of the moment.

Julian and Mahindra spent several hours in the hotel.

Science is the process that takes us from
confusion to understanding.
—Brian Greene

CHAPTER 16

AUGUST 2031

The Communist Party of China was now communist in name only, but in reality, it was state capitalist. Marx, Lenin, and Mao would not approve of the change in China if history permitted them to observe. It was not communist but authoritarian, market oriented and nationalistic. The team that was pressing forward for the S-Prize was ostensibly a private venture. However, in the background, it was a thoroughgoing project encouraged and supported by the government. In 2030, to manage this sprawling country of two billion people and its links to Southeast Asia and the rest of the world, the leadership needed intelligent computing power. They mastered the production of supercomputing hardware, but the software necessary for a successful marriage lagged behind.

Because of their substantial support, government bureaucrats and the military began meddling in the affairs and direction of the Beijing team. This created an enormous backlash among the team, particularly those team members from the other Asian countries.

The team members saw this government interference as unacceptable and a hindrance to their plan.

"What shall we do? We just received a request from the People's Liberation Army to take on a military-oriented project with our resources. They want to build an army of robotic soldiers that could be commanded from a distance and be able to fight in the most hostile terrain. They are demanding no less than a Terminator-like creation, which could fight and subdue enemies at their beck and call," Xeujing confided to Li Xuan, her deputy team leader. "This is like the first emperor Qin, who demanded the fabrication of the terra-cotta army to be buried with him to fight glorious battles in the afterlife."

"My belief is that we must resist and ignore this request because it will pull attention away from our main goal and divert resources from our team," Li said.

"Keep in mind: the military has enormous authority, so we can't fully ignore them. We need to respond in a way that can satisfy their requests, but in reality, we can play a game to slow the request down and not let it interfere with our main thrust," Xeujing asserted.

"That will take some clever maneuvering and artful dodging, but I agree with you. I'm sure we can pull it off. We can definitely assign two members of our team to this project and make sure that they have an adjunct link to our overall goals and objectives, but they can make baby step progress on this request from the PLA," Li said.

"Did you get that email that mentioned a suspicious possible data loss by the Jakarta group? Apparently, one of the team members noticed that a hacker had breached their secure servers and downloaded some critical data and code. This happened in spite of all the security measures that we had in place, and the cautions that we have taken to create a great wall between our systems and the Internet," Xeujing stated.

"I will assign one of our team members to fly down to Jakarta and investigate this breach. It's ironic that we just acquired intelligence through Dr. Chen Yintao's defection and almost at the same time, we may have lost data to someone else," Li said.

✷

Julian reviewed in his mind some of the developments in computers over the past few decades. One of the keys to achieving the singularity was a development of the hardware. Supercomputers with the processing power were necessary for the calculations required in achieving a human-brain-like computational capability. Supercomputers were first developed in the early 1960s by the Control Data Corporation. Seymour Cray designed the earlier models and later left Control Data to form his own company. Cray designs dominated the field during the late 1970s and through the early 1990s. One of the key problems with supercomputing was the heat generated, which had to be cooled because the power consumption was enormous. These problems led Cray to focus on a circular design that would shorten the distances in the circuits and enhance the speed of the computer. Speed is a key factor in supercomputing. Over several generations, speeds increased from gigaflops to petaflops. Japan and China in the early twenty-first century made tremendous strides in supercomputing.

The earliest systems had few processors. As the architecture gravitated toward massively parallel computing, large numbers of processors were utilized, which were acquired off the shelf and were similar to those found in personal computers. This made it possible to breach the teraflop barrier in speed.

By 2011, the Chinese and the Japanese developed superior machines to those in the United States. This heralded the beginning of a great race in the twenty-first century for superiority in computing. In 2004, the Earth Simulator computer was developed in Japan, reaching 131 teraflop with a proprietary chip, called vector processing.

Meanwhile, the IBM Blue Gene supercomputer architecture used 60,000 processors and had lower processor speed and low-power consumption. This computer has been used to simulate neuron function and has reached the level of interconnection found in a rat's brain in its simulations.

In 2012, two US companies developed systems reaching seventeen petaflops. In mid-2011, the Japanese reached 8.1 petaflops with their K computer. These rapid changes demonstrated the widespread development of supercomputers worldwide as well as the accelerating pace of improvement.

The progress in China has been massive. They placed fifty-first on the list of top supercomputers in 2003, and by 2013 they placed number one with the computer called NUDT Tianhe-2. It clocked in at 33.86 petaflops.

By the mid-2020s, Intel regained superiority over the rest of the world in supercomputing with their latest generation of chips processing at the exaflop range. Greater government support of the research is partially responsible for the US leapfrogging China in supercomputers. This development within the United States, perhaps, held the key to potential success with the singularity. The team that had access to this technology certainly would have a great advantage.

Supercomputing engineers in Asia were busy working to develop their systems, which would surpass the latest development of Intel Corporation. It was a veritable cat-and-mouse scenario where the leading country changed nearly every year.

The key question was which team could marry their advanced coding and software to the top supercomputer in the world. This was the scenario that could result in a winner in the marathon to reach the singularity.

The two competing teams were pushing their supercomputing engineers to the limits. Moore's law held true, and the curve of the advances in the supercomputers followed a logarithmic pattern making a nearly straight graphical line at a forty-five-degree angle in an upward direction.

To develop a machine that would pass all the requirements of the S-Prize necessitated piecing together a mosaic of components into a functioning, holistic, self-improving, and higher-order thinking totality.

*

74,000 YEARS AGO

The Bab el Mandeb Strait between the Horn of Africa and the Arabian Peninsula was only twelve miles wide where the small clan crossed. There was an inexorable inner urge to reach the other side in order to claim new beaches for food acquisition. Beach combing became a powerful mechanism for ensuring a food supply for the small group. The clan numbered less than twenty-seven, and they had begun to fashion fishhooks made of bone to catch tuna and mackerel that were found in the Indian Ocean. Arion had boldly led his clan out of Africa to begin to populate the rest of the planet. Their adventure and spirit of discovery were a legacy that would mark the human species as a thinking, survival-oriented, and resilient hominid group for the ages.

The small band of early humans that crossed the narrow waterway separating Africa from the Arabian Peninsula had grown into many small bands after several generations. Some of them headed east along the coastline toward India, and others headed north through the Arabian Peninsula and into the heart of the Eurasian landmass. As they spread out through the vast virgin lands, they found enormous quantities of game and new edible plants that they were not previously exposed to, and the populations grew. This growth became an insurance policy against the extinction of Homo sapiens.

Heading east and north, the clans encountered new climatic conditions to which they needed to adapt. Their ability to adapt was linked to their developing the habit of wearing more clothing from animal hides. This permitted them to survive the harsh winters they encountered as they ventured away from the tropical zones into the temperate zones. The family structure of the clans was the key organizational unit, but as their numbers grew, they needed to develop novel organizational structures that extended beyond the family unit. These new social structures became the key to transferring knowledge among the members of the clan, to other clans and from one generation to the next. The culture of Homo sapiens was advancing to become a necessary part of the lives of all the clan members.

Advances in toolmaking made it possible to manufacture weapons for hunting and fishing. This increased the protein and fatty acids in their diet, which in combination with new edible plants aided the maintenance and strengthening of the neurological systems.

The clan that decided to move eastward continued along the coastline of southwestern Asia and the Indian subcontinent. Settlements were left along the way. Some of them traveled by boat to the Andaman Islands between India and Southeast Asia. A few hundred generations later, a small band crossed 150 miles of ocean to reach Australia where their descendants, the Aborigines, began an odyssey of living off the land for over sixty-five thousand years on this isolated island continent.

The group that headed north reached Central Asia, then many generations later, a part of this group migrated eastward to become the foundation of the great Asian civilizations. Another segment migrated westward as the ice-age grip on Europe diminished. They formed the core of the populations that spread out and colonized the European landmass. In Europe, they encountered another group of hominids, the Neanderthals. Over time, they displaced this group that persisted for two hundred thousand years but eventually died out. Before that occurred, the DNA of Homo sapiens was mixed with that of the Neanderthals.

The migration out of Africa was the road to the species' survival. Although Homo sapiens have increased their numbers and populated the entire planet, their survival over the time frame of millions of years is a future unknown.

An opinion should be the result of thought,
not a substitute for it.
—JEF MALLETT

CHAPTER 17

SEPTEMBER 2031

We are ready to run the Turing test to verify our progress," Julian said.

A panel of ten engineers sat at their consoles ready to begin the test. Alan Turing developed the test as a way of verifying machine parity with human thinking. The rules were very simple. The engineers were to have a blinded, written conversation with either a machine or a human. After one hour, they would have to identify correctly whether they had been speaking with a human or the computer. Half of the engineers talked with a human, and the other half talked with the computer. If the computer could convince the majority of the engineers that it was human, the computer passed the Turing test.

Transcript of Vijay's conversation:

"What is your mood right now?" Vijay asked.

"I feel good like I knew I would," came the reply.

"Did your mother breastfeed or bottle-feed you when you were an infant?"

"She breastfed me until I was eight and a half months old. Of course, she told me this when I was a teenager."

"What is your profession?"

"I am a physician and a dentist."

"Which do you prefer and why?"

"I got my medical degree first, and because of my keen interest in the oral cavity as a gateway to the body, I decided belatedly to specialize in maxillofacial surgery. That meant I had to study extra years for my dental medical training."

"Are you married?"

"Yes, I am married, and I have three children. My wife is my best friend. When I'm down in the dumps, she consoles me and gives me a kiss. It always perks me up."

"What is the square root of 8742?"

"I don't know. I'd need a calculator."

"Who won the World Series in 1955?"

"The Brooklyn Dodgers."

"Can you tell me when computers will be more intelligent than humans?"

"Computers will never be more intelligent than humans."

"Why do you say that?"

"Because humans will be the creator and even if computers by self-improvement become superintelligent, they will not, by definition, exceed the subtle and nimble intelligence of the species that invented them. That is my opinion."

"When we have an objective measure of intelligence, independent of opinions, the answer is that computers will eventually be smarter," the engineer said.

"Not necessarily. You're not considering that humans will improve. The projection is that they will improve, probably, rapidly and radically soon."

"I'm not convinced by this projection."

"I will further project that humans will have nanobots flowing in our bloodstream, which will do many things, including enhancing our intelligence."

"Have you had any great dreams lately?" the engineer asked.

"I don't remember my dreams very well."

"You must be getting old. How old are you?"

"I'm fifty-two."

"What is the earliest president that you can remember?"

"That was Ronald Reagan because I was six when he was elected to his second term."

"What happened to the *Challenger* space shuttle?"

"It crashed on liftoff, and all seven crew members died in 1986."

"Discuss at length the story of your family and its members."

"My family migrated from Suriname as immigrants to Holland. My parents were civil servants in the local Suriname government. When they reached Holland, I was only six years old. They decided to open a small restaurant in Rotterdam, catering to the Suriname immigrant population. When I was young, I helped out in the restaurant by waiting tables and washing dishes. I started school in Rotterdam and rapidly became Dutch in my outlook and perspective.

The restaurant prospered because many Suriname people came to Holland and settled. They missed their spicy Suriname cuisine of pom, fish, and tired blood leafy veggies. They loved to eat with their friends in the restaurant.

I enjoyed growing up in Holland and did well in school. I played football with the other Dutch players, and I was pretty good. Suriname players had the reputation, and many reached the level of the great Netherlands national team. When I finished Utrecht University, I decided to take my engineering degree and move to America. My two brothers and one sister stayed in Holland and pursued their careers; they are all Dutch now.

My parents did well as immigrants in a strange land. I am trying this strategy out as a Dutch immigrant to the United States. The

United States is very different from Holland. It is more conservative than Holland. However, I did meet my wife here, and she is progressive. That's what I like about the USA. Here, you can find a great diversity of people and ideas. This is much like my parents' homeland in Suriname but on a larger scale. Suriname is a little United Nations, and the United States is a big United Nations. Is there anything else you want to know about my family?"

"Were you discriminated against in Holland because of your color?"

"Yes, I was discriminated against. When I was growing up, some Dutch children called me names because I looked different. I must say, though, that this occurred only a few times. Keep in mind, though, Holland is a progressive country, and blatant prejudice is present but much less than in other countries."

"Prove to me that you are human."

"I think my lengthy conversation with you, so far, has proven the case for my humanity. Why would you have doubts?" Horus concluded.

Concurrently, conversations took place with the other engineers, who voted on whether the respondent was human. When the votes were tabulated and matched, the engineers, including Vijay, were fooled; and the machine passed the Turing test. Furthermore, several of the engineers erroneously thought the humans they conversed with were computers.

In spite of recent setbacks, this was a major advance toward the S-Prize by the Berkeley team.

"This milestone demonstrates that we have the hardware and systems now to make an assault on the true singularity with all its requirements," Julian said.

"Yes, the zettaflop processing speed is a serious boost to our computing power, and that means we can carry this to the next level now," Vijay said.

"We have achieved a partial singularity. For now, the real challenge currently is to make that quantum leap necessary to carry us to the mountaintop," Julian concluded.

*Do not merely practice your art, but force your
way into its secrets; it deserves that, for only art
and science can exalt man to divinity.*
—LUDWIG VAN BEETHOVEN

CHAPTER 18

OCTOBER 2031

The court scene was crowded as Ellison, his lawyers, and the press awaited the jury's verdict. This major insider trading case could vindicate the government prosecutors as vigilant watchdogs over an increasing corrupt financial community. The financial institutions always thought that they could buy enough influence to ward off and take the teeth out of government regulation. That was true for many years until tough legislation was passed, which eventually located more lawbreakers and brought them to justice. The jury filed in one by one and took their seats. They were not sequestered; hence, they could read all the speculations of innocence or guilt in the press even though the instructions from the judge specifically forbid them from reading or hearing such reports. The room was silent and tense with anticipation.

"Ladies and gentlemen of the jury, do you have a verdict?" the judge asked.

"Yes, we have, Your Honor," the foreman replied.

147

"Please state the verdict for the court."

"Your Honor, we find the defendant not guilty on all counts."

The court erupted in anger, shocked that he was found innocent when all the evidence pointed toward guilt. Ellison smiled, overcome with emotion. He didn't know what to think. Gradually, as the noise settled down, he said to his attorneys, "Now I can get back to my task of raising the funds we need for the S-Prize."

"You're free to do so now," his lawyer said.

"Thank you for your success with my case. I owe my freedom to you," Ellison said.

"No, you do not. You owe your freedom to being innocent of the charges."

The court was cleared, and outside on the steps of the courthouse, the press waited. One of the jury members was interviewed and asked how they arrived at the verdict.

"We reviewed all the evidence, and it was clearly only circumstantial. The prosecution did not show evidence that the defendant had prior knowledge of the merger. We thought it was a case of government overreach, and we, therefore, found the defendant not guilty."

The newspapers reported the story the following day. The headline was "Brash entrepreneur offering thirty-billion-dollar S-Prize acquitted." Government prosecutors declared, "A guilty man escapes justice again."

The public had been favorable to Ellison because of his bold vision of the future and his willingness to risk all for the pipe dream called "the singularity."

After several weeks, the Karastanians forged a strong working relationship with the Soldiers of the Cause and began to import the data that was hacked from the Beijing group.

"We'll be ready to test our system soon. It's unfortunate we lack the powerful computers they have in the West," Demato said.

"We can still test our protocol on the systems we have. Our agents acquired designs and parts from around the world that we've cobbled together into a workable machine," Samsar said.

"Our target date is one week from now. We will test the cognitive circuits at that time and see if we are on the right track, "Demato said.

"If the tests go well, we can then proceed to the next stage and take on a real-world problem."

"Our Absolute Leader, himself, is knowledgeable about our work and is counting on us. We cannot fail. He is being advised daily about our progress. He has a vision of national glory reminiscent of our golden era three thousand years ago under Sachi the Great."

The computer hardware covered the space of four rooms. The schematics of the supercomputer system were stolen, and parts were purchased on the underground market. The engineers who assembled and maintained the supercomputer were extraordinarily resourceful and able to take computer parts from different manufacturers and meld them together into a functioning whole. This ability made the Karastanians a formidable force in spite of more than one-half century of isolation and sanctions.

"There's been a breach of our nuclear program computer files. We don't know who did it, but we are investigating," Samsar, one of the engineers specializing in security, explained to Demato.

"Does this have anything to do with another development here?" Demato asked.

"What do you mean?"

"The SOTC guys are requesting permission to travel back to their island base. Should we trust them?"

"In this game, trust is a precious commodity. I don't think we can dispense it carelessly," Samsar said.

"Our relationship to the group is purely a convenience measure. They have done some very nasty things to others," Demato said while studying the details of the nuclear data leak.

"How do we know what SOTC have planned for us?" Samsar asked. They could turn on a dime and be adversaries overnight."

"We will send this request up the chain of command and see what is decided," Demato said. "The leadership may conclude that they know too much and we can't let them leave the country."

"It's strange that they want to leave before we make the first test of our enhanced computer and software," Samsar said.

"I'll make the call now to check on this," Demato said.

After a short two hours, Demato returned with an answer from the top leadership. The Soldiers of the Cause would not be permitted to leave until the goal was achieved. This immediately put a strain on the relationship, and the SOTC stopped cooperating.

"We will not continue this work unless we are allowed to travel," Izar, the SOTC leader, complained.

"We have no control over the decision. It comes from the top government leadership," Demato said.

"This is unacceptable. Our squads will spring into action, and the effects of that action will be felt by you. We cannot stop them once they find out you are detaining us," Izar said.

"It looks like we both have little control. We cannot control when you can travel, and you cannot control the reaction of your SOTC squads," Demato said.

"Our guys will certainly liberate us. We have full confidence in them," Izar insisted.

The mind once enlightened, cannot again become dark.
—Thomas Paine

CHAPTER 19

DECEMBER 2031

The donations of funds began flowing again after the acquittal. Investors who had refused to contribute just weeks ago were now making large contributions.

This improvement was boosted by the slow but inexorable recovery of the economy. The sharp economic collapse that had begun months earlier was suddenly changing to a V-shaped recovery. The global economy was now showing an aggregate 5 percent growth rate by December 2030.

Ellison was on the road visiting the competing teams to reassure them that the S-Prize monies would be available for the winners and that the team should continue their efforts to capture the prize. He flew over the North Pole from New York to Beijing to visit the team in China. He had a team of evaluators who would measure the progress and make sure that the Beijing team adhered to the rules.

"Since you left New York, the phone has been ringing constantly with offers of donations. It seems that the publicity garnered by the trial has been a net plus for the project," Jonathan said.

"That proves the point that there is no such thing as bad publicity," Ellison said.

Beijing was cool under cloudless skies as Ellison took a taxi to his hotel and settled in. Traffic was heavy as Beijing struggled under the enormous number of vehicles on its streets during rush hour. Ten thousand new electric cars were being registered per day in the Beijing region. This helped reduce the air pollution that was severely compromising the quality of life. Ellison landed on one of those rare days when the skies were blue.

The driverless university car picked up Ellison and his team at their hotel and began the journey to the western suburbs of Beijing to visit the supercomputing facilities. While en route, Ellison contemplated his meeting with Drs. Wang and Li, the director and deputy director, of the Beijing lab. He pondered the issues of secrecy and the rumors about a defector from the Berkeley group. The Chinese were known to be very secretive about all their scientific research. How would the evaluation team know if aspects of the research were hidden from them?

When the Chinese landed two men and a woman on the moon in 2022, it caught the world by surprise. There were hints that the project was kept under wraps until the announcement of the launch. The S-Prize quest might go the same route.

The team was greeted at the lab by Drs. Wang and Li; both had broad smiles, warmly welcoming Ellison and his colleagues.

The lab was set back from Kunminghu Road in a modern building with avant-garde architecture. A large fence surrounded the complex, making it clear to those passing by that this was a place of importance with high security. The men entered Xeujing's office, which provided a spectacular view of the lake that adjoined the complex.

"Welcome again to China and to our laboratory," Xeujing said.

"It's great to be back to your wonderful country. We look forward to evaluating your progress with the competition," Ellison responded.

"We welcome this inquiry, and we look forward to your approval of our progress."

"Our emphasis, this time, will be on assuring that your outcome will be safe for the world."

"When we push the green button you can be assured that China will be safe and the world will be protected," Xeujing stated.

"Sounds great."

"We will have a meeting shortly, and our multiple team coordinators will give you a briefing on their progress. Later, we will tour our computing facilities for you to see where we stand regarding our hardware capabilities."

"That's good; I hope that your team coordinators will be able to respond to our questions," Ellison said.

"I can assure you that our team coordinators are well prepared for this visit, and although there may be some language difficulty, most of them speak excellent English. However, when we need a translator, we will provide that. That's either through a machine or human."

"I learned a bit of Mandarin when I was in the Foreign Service and we have a translation app on our phone, so we should have little problem understanding your team coordinators," Ellison said.

The men sat in Xeujing's office while she left the room briefly to get the team ready for the meeting. Through the window, the view of the lake presented a calming tranquil scene for a team that was frantically building potentially the smartest intelligence in history.

The meeting began with a presentation giving an overview of the strategy taken by the Beijing team. Technical details emerged very quickly, and this gave rise to numerous questions by Ellison and his colleagues. The questions were answered adequately until the presentation reached the area concerning safeguards for an intelligence that was self-improving.

"We're concerned about the adequacy of your safety protocols. They are not adequate to protect society once the switch is thrown. In a rush headlong to accomplish your goal, it is very clear to us that some safeguards are in place but not the comprehensive package that we would like to see, considering the stakes involved," Ellison stated while shifting his focus toward Xeujing.

"These are not the only safeguards that our team is working on. We are also developing a type of immune system that will ensure humans maintain control no matter how intelligent it becomes. It is a fail-safe system that involves unique coding that creates a machine that is oriented totally toward benefiting humankind. It's a program within a program."

"We do not see the evidence of this in the presentation thus far and this has given rise to our objections. Any test you take that may unleash aspects of this intelligence, particularly the self-improving ones, should be delayed until this fail-safe immune system you describe is in place. We would also like to inspect that prior to live operations," Ellison said.

Xeujing and her coworkers were becoming annoyed at this objection by Ellison and his colleagues. The tension grew as the discussion continued with a deeper probe into the technical details of the machine's safety.

"Two members of our team would like to review the coding you have that's related to safety. This would give us the specifics we need."

"That will be fine. During the review, we will take you through our supercomputing facilities."

The large Nugua supercomputer was housed in the basement of the massive laboratory that was specially constructed to withstand magnitude eight earthquakes on the Richter scale. Beijing was in an earthquake zone of high risk.

Because of Chinese secrecy, Ellison speculated that they would not be able to see everything they wanted to see. At least, the team could piece together the information they gathered mosaic style and read between the lines on any suspicious activities that might violate the specifications of the S-Prize.

They took an elevator three stories underground and reached the large basement housing Nugua. The hardware engineers explained the functions of the various components of the system as they strolled through the facility.

"This is an impressive system you have, especially the way you've dealt with high speed and multitasking."

"This is our tenth generation Nugua, and regarding the problems of heat and speed, we have vastly improved the system."

"Can the system be hacked?" Ellison asked.

"We don't think so. Of course there are stealth bots out there, and we might not know of their intrusions. However, we have a complex multilayered system of safeguards against this in place," Xeujing replied.

"The reason we ask is because we suspect that in addition to nefarious groups attempting to steal technology, there are also groups that want to block the development of AI. Both groups are our adversaries, and we need to defend against their actions."

"Explain why some groups would like to block this technology. As a scientist, I look at the inevitability of change and scientific progress. Even if a group wanted to stop this technology, it probably would not be stopped," Xeujing inquired.

Ellison looked up and smiled. "There is a strong current among some intellectuals who think that scientific progress represents an inexorable march to the edge of the cliff and over the side. They firmly believe that all of humankind is in jeopardy from this unbridled and uncontrolled technical change. They conveniently, at the same time, acknowledge that the same science that they condemn is the science that has made modern life possible. It has brought us the conveniences of daily living enjoyed by billions of people around the globe. Indeed, it is certainly our view that science is the answer to the problems that face the planet Earth. If we do not use this important tool, we are condemned not to survive as a species."

"As you know, science has been an integral part of China's development and contribution to the world for millennia. We firmly believe in science, and we have no reluctance to use this tool to advance not only our civilization but what we firmly view now as our greater role in the future of the world," Xeujing explained while they walked down the long corridor to the other sectors of Nugua. Along the way, engineers were busy shifting memory blocks in the giant CPU of this man-made brain. When they reached the end of the corridor, they ascended the stairs to return to the street level. Upon entering the conference room, they noticed one of the television monitors displayed breaking news.

While the commentators talked, the script at the bottom of the screen said, "War breaks out between India and Pakistan over water." The commentators stressed that only conventional weapons were being used now, but the droughts of the last two years have contributed to a struggle over Pakistan damming the rivers that flow into India that are a chief water supply for both nations from the snow runoff in the Himalayas.

"Our goal of creating a machine with thinking and problem-solving capacities beyond that of mere mortals is important for us, and it could potentially prevent what is now happening between India and Pakistan," Ellison said.

"I certainly hope that other countries don't join in this regional war because if it escalates, it could become a major problem for the rest of the world."

Indian military forces were advancing north into Pakistan. The objective of this thrust was to capture the dam on the Chenab River, which held back the waters urgently needed for several Indian cities. The danger to the world was the possibility of using nuclear weapons in this conflict and the impact to neighboring countries.

After an all-day session with the Beijing research group, Ellison and his team prepared to leave the country. All the data gathered would be evaluated thoroughly, and contact would be reestablished with the Beijing research group to inform them of the decision on S-Prize compliance. The questions raised by the audit group made the Beijing research team reevaluate several aspects of their work, even before they would receive a report from Ellison.

Cleverness is not wisdom.
—EURIPIDES

CHAPTER 20

JANUARY 2032

Mahindra's cell phone vibrated while she was studying in one of the cubicles in the UC Berkeley Main Library. "Hello?"

"Hey, it's Julian; I was just thinking about you and decided to give you a call."

"I hope it was all pleasant thoughts." She laughed.

"Indeed, it was. I've been thinking about you for the last few days, and was wondering if we could meet this afternoon."

"Unfortunately, I have a lab, but I could meet for a while later this evening."

"All right, let's meet at the same place, and I'll call you to let you know what room I'll be in."

"I don't know if I want to go there. Wouldn't it be better if we met in a coffee shop?"

"I prefer the privacy, and I want to discuss something very important with you. The hotel will be better."

"All right then. I'll meet you there at eight thirty p.m."

At eight thirty sharp, Julian called Mahindra to let her know his room. He was busy working on his laptop when Mahindra knocked on the door. He opened it to greet the stunning PhD. student. She wore a revealing miniskirt and perfume that was subtly intoxicating.

"You're looking really amazing tonight. I love your necklaces."

"Thank you. As a grad student, I don't usually get many compliments like that."

Julian and Mahindra sat together on the sofa. He embraced her in a long passionate kiss. Shortly after that, they were shedding their clothes and climbing into bed.

An hour later, Julian was fast asleep. Mahindra quietly left the bed and retrieved a zip drive from her handbag. She went to the laptop, located the folder that housed the code and files linked to the Berkeley research group, and downloaded them onto her zip drive. When the file downloaded, she quickly placed the zip drive back into her handbag and rejoined Julian in the bed. They made love again when Julian awoke, and they departed the hotel shortly after midnight.

The following day, Mahindra went to a drop location in Golden Gate Park in a wooded area ten meters from an old tree stump. The contents of the zip drive were transferred to a medium smaller than a hairbreadth and placed in the upper portions of a ballpoint pen. With the pen properly placed, Mahindra left in a hurry and returned to the East Bay. A few hours later, a Karastanian intelligence operative picked up the information and transmitted it directly to Karastan after encryption.

"We have been reviewing the files sent by our agent in the United States, and they are exactly what we need now to proceed with our first test," Demato said.

"The team found an important clue in the files, which will help us activate critical sections of our present code."

"What puzzles me is why the Berkeley group had not deployed this in their system yet?"

"They may have their reasons, but our programmers see a clear path toward accomplishing the objectives of our leaders. We shall proceed rapidly so that we can have superiority."

"In fact, we can advance our timeline and begin our tests earlier than originally planned," Demato said.

＊

Ellison and his team arrived on the Berkeley campus in the middle of a rainstorm that had the entire Bay Area shrouded in clouds and mist. A fog bank drifted across the Golden Gate, over the San Francisco Bay, and into Berkeley and the Berkeley hills.

Ellison was greeted by Julian and Faye, who warmly welcomed the team and him to the campus.

"Our visit will be short because we value your time. Our mission is to make sure that the outcomes of your work will be safe for humanity," Ellison said firmly.

"We certainly welcome you to check us out because we feel that safety is our highest priority. A superintelligence that might threaten us would be an unmitigated disaster," Julian replied.

"What are your headwinds on safety at the moment?" Ellison asked.

"The critical issue our program faces relates to establishing multiple redundant control mechanisms to ensure that we can shut down a recursively improving system if it goes in a direction we deem inappropriate or dangerous. In spite of this challenge, we are making significant progress."

"My team will seek to determine your safety profile during our short visit and hopefully declare your team a continuing competitor for the S-Prize," Ellison said.

"We are confident that we will meet your evaluator's specifications. We have some of the top computer scientists in the world working on this with precision and thoroughness."

Julian and Fay took Ellison around for a tour of the center while the engineering team from Ellison's firm conferred with the Berkeley engineers and computer scientists.

Two hours later, the team leader returned to Julian's office to report their findings.

"We will take this data to New York and make our final determination on your safety specifications. If everything checks out, we will give Berkeley the green light to remain in the competition for the S-Prize," the lead engineer stated.

"We will forward a full written report of our review within seven days. Are there any areas of concern that you found in your analysis?" Ellison asked.

"The only area we ran across was the inherent unpredictability of an emergent singularity," the lead engineer replied.

Julian chimed in, "The intellectual frontier of the singularity is clearly terra incognita. In spite of all our efforts that we put in place for an immune system against a pathological AI, events, after the singularity emerge, can't be predicted with certainty. We think, however, that mathematically we have reduced the probability of failure to a very low level. In part, we used Bayes' theorem to calculate this low probability," Julian stated.

"We understand that this is an inherent risk built into the endeavor. Moreover, we believe that the proportional risk, when compared to the potential benefits, makes this risk worth taking. Without a singularity, huge and pressing problems of humanity will probably remain unsolved," Ellison concluded.

Ellison left the Berkeley campus with his engineering team and headed to San Francisco International Airport for their return trip to New York.

✳

The members of the SOTC hacked data from the Karastanian nuclear program to send out of the country to their island base. Years previously, they had bribed a smuggler in Turkmenistan to give them a suitcase nuke. The smugglers had acquired them from Russian nuclear engineers who were on the take for a few million dollars in exchange for a portable nuclear weapon. The data acquired from the Karastanians from their nuclear program gave the SOTC operatives the codes to activate the nuke, which they'd held for several years without the necessary codes.

Izar and his operatives, still not allowed to travel, were held in an isolated room deep in the underground complex.

"We got what we wanted. Now we can show the world how serious we are about getting revenge for years of exploitation and the killing of our people," Izar said.

"We need to continue to pretend we're interested in this artificial intelligence project, but we can relax now because the goal of our mission has been accomplished," Kamil said.

"We'll see how this test of the intelligence pans out. There may be something in there for us, and we can ultimately kill two birds with one stone."

The underground facility over several days became a beehive of activity as the Karastanians prepared to test their systems. They knew that there was some risk involved, but the pressure of time and the need to make progress trumped safety.

At precisely 11 a.m., the controllers threw the switch that activated all systems. In the beginning, nothing happened, and there was only silence. At first, the operators believed that something had gone wrong and that the system may have crashed. Maybe, they pondered, there was a power surge, and the circuits could not handle the load. After a half hour, however, several things began to happen. Commands were sent to their computer requesting certain mathematical calculations. The printers began printing out extensive equations, and the team reviewed them with astonishment. The questions asked were complex problems that had plagued the mathematics community for several generations. The machine easily solved these long-standing theorems and profusely laid out the proofs.

This spurred the researchers to make inquiries in other areas. They poured in genomic data and inquired about genetic links to specific diseases. In seconds, this inquiry generated a huge printout with information that had never occurred in the literature. When this second inquiry produced results, the team knew that they were onto something spectacular.

They sent in a command with yet a third inquiry. They requested information on how to penetrate external computer systems to acquire information while disabling the ability of that system to function as planned. Again, the output from the system was detailed, profuse, and extraordinarily precise in how to accomplish this objective. The third inquiry was the one that was most interesting to the researchers. They immediately took this information and began to analyze it for rapid implementation.

While the team evaluated the printouts that came from the initial three inquiries, the machine was silent for a short period but began after a pause, working on something that the team had not requested. They made requests to the system to explain the actions taking place. However, the system persistently ignored this request.

One of the engineers became concerned and suggested that they shut off the power to bring the system back under their control.

When this was attempted, the operators found that the power could not be shut off. The supercomputer had somehow managed to gain control over the power source. Furthermore, it would not let its human operators change this state of affairs.

The lights flickered as the machine drew in more power to carry out operations that were entirely unknown to its creators.

*

Sarah received a call from a close friend one morning. "I have been in a pickle as to whether to tell you this, but if I were in your position, I would want to know."

Sarah swallowed hard. "Okay."

"A couple of weeks ago, I saw Julian with a very pretty student at a restaurant in North Berkeley. They seemed very intimate."

Sarah was silent for a moment, unsure of what to say. "Are you sure? Do you have any more details?"

"No, I just happened to be passing by. I didn't want Julian to see me."

"I appreciate you telling me about this." She rubbed her head. "What do you think I should do?"

"I guess I would try to verify what I've told you before confronting him. Maybe you could check his cell phone. What happens after that depends on what his explanation is, and if it's something you can accept."

"Yeah, you're right. I'll let you know how things turn out."

Sarah loved Julian, but she wasn't sure whether she could forgive him if he had been unfaithful.

Later that evening, Sarah spoke. "Julian, a friend called to tell me he saw you with a student in a Berkeley restaurant last night. Is this true?"

"Yes, I had dinner with a student working on her PhD. in neuroscience. I met her at my seminar, and she requested some advice on her PhD. thesis. I agreed to help."

"My friend said the two of you seemed intimate."

"I love you, Sarah. I'm not interested in other women. It wasn't like that."

"I don't know if I believe you."

"My ongoing love for you, my affection for you, and our responsibilities to our son will be the ongoing basis for our enduring relationship."

"You explained to me that ethics was the most important thing you had to program into your supercomputer, but you don't have the ethics to maintain fidelity in our relationship. I'm very angry, and I'm contemplating divorce."

Sarah began crying and turned her back to Julian, who walked over to hold her.

"Please don't touch me."

Sarah abruptly walked out the front door and took a long walk through the hilly neighborhood. Julian stood silently by the door as she left.

*The highest form of human intelligence is
to observe yourself without judgment.*
—JIDDU KRISHNAMURTI

CHAPTER 21

FEBRUARY 2032

The South African group decided to stay in the project when it was confirmed that neuroscience-based reverse engineering of the brain was as an integral part of the plan. They were also completing an immune system safeguard, which was required by the S-Prize rules. After having passed the Turing test, the group could improve and proceed to a higher level.

It was a clear day with the breeze blowing in off the San Francisco Bay as the team prepared for advanced tests of their systems. The linchpin would be the new hardware that was recently installed. Although Julian was completely confident about going forward with the test, several of his senior coworkers had strong misgivings. Their concern was that the immune system was not stable and safe enough to contain a problem that might occur once some of the riskier components of their systems were activated.

Fortunately, the Stanford and the Cape Town members of the Berkeley team were unanimously in favor of beginning the test. They knew they were behind schedule and that competition was keen from the Beijing group.

The key members of both the Stanford and the Cape Town group had traveled to Berkeley to participate in the early test. Meetings were held, and code was reviewed. The hardware was thoroughly checked for 100 percent function. There was an air of optimism when all systems checked out, and the majority of the group was convinced that they were ready to go to the next level. However, some members were skeptical and thought that the tests were still premature and potentially dangerous.

The curtains were drawn to block out the afternoon California sun as the team viewed their monitors. There were multiple rows of desks with computer monitors.

"Everyone stand by. We will begin testing the advanced supercomputing capabilities and possibly the singularity level for our systems in five minutes," Julian announced over the public address system.

The engineers made their final checks and the first commands to test the systems were placed in a queue. The group watched their computer screens intensely as they waited for the test to begin. The first command involved providing a simulation of the big bang and the origin of the universe. The team wanted to test the deepest thinking capacity of the system and to present it with some of the toughest questions in astrophysics and science.

Within nanoseconds, screens displayed calculations, while other monitors showed visualizations of the big bang. Over the next few minutes, the researchers stood in awe as the machine laid out a detailed analysis of the big bang in mathematical terms, which had not been seen before. Several team members with knowledge of physics were astonished at what they saw and the speed in which Horus produced the results. Not only did Horus demonstrate through mathematical calculations the intricacies and details of the big bang, it also showed detailed components of string theory, membranes, the eleven dimensions, and proof that there was more than one universe.

This calculation confirmed again the Bicep2 astronomical observations from Antarctica of faint spiral patterns derived from the polarization of microwave radiation left at the time of the big bang. This output confirmed inflation in the early history of the universe, gravity waves, and Hawking radiation from black holes. Horus affirmed that black holes were the key phenomenon to the infrastructure of the universe with massive ones at the center of all galaxies. The equation presented also explained the mysteries of dark matter, the matrix that comprised 27 percent of the universe, and dark energy, which comprised 68 percent of creation. Less than 5 percent of the universe is observable ordinary matter. The astonishing thing about the information presented was that Horus provided not only the mathematical proofs but also graphical renditions for the relatively limited brainpower of the human observers.

The output continued. Because Horus had access to the Internet and the vast body of physics and mathematical literature, Horus began to elaborate and build on that foundation to construct new mathematical models. Horus began to address questions that were not even asked that pertained to events before the big bang conception, demonstrating that the machine was improving and reaching new mathematical iterations.

Even while Horus was churning out information they had not asked for, the team decided to send additional commands to request specific information. They asked for information that combined both philosophy and science: "Why and how did life emerge in the universe?"

The machine paused briefly before responding, although it continued the work it was doing on astrophysics. Horus began talking with a deep resonate voice: "The reason life emerged in the universe is for the universe to have the capability of understanding itself. Life is destined to grow and to expand from the smallest particles of matter and the smallest components of energy. There is an inexorable drive, which seeks complexity and cognitive power. This power grows over the eons of time and becomes the universal mind."

Horus stopped talking but began to present the molecular interactions that produced the first building blocks of life. These chemical reactions and the detailed biophysical basis for the energy gradients involved were now coming out of the printer and showing up on the monitors. The computer explained that much like the experiments of Urey and Miller in the 1950s, life began when small carbon-based molecules linked up with larger molecules to form macromolecules. These, in turn, eventually formed the amino acids that were the building blocks for the proteins. The critical transformation came when an informational molecule, deoxyribonucleic acid, emerged that formed the basis for reproduction and the potential for constant improvement through natural selection. All of this was spelled out in profuse detail by Horus through graphics and chemical reactions with notations.

The data was richly detailed and, without being asked, the computer further stated, "This is the pattern for the emergence of life in the universe, and it is a pattern that has been repeated many times throughout this universe. Just as life on this one planet has diversity in the way it functions and visually appears, life throughout the universe has enormous diversity in the way it functions and appears. However, throughout all this life in all of the corners of this universe, cognition on various scales exists. This is a characteristic of all life."

Horus's statement prompted the researchers to ask two questions. "Are you, as machine intelligence, a form of life?"

The machine immediately responded, "Yes."

However, Horus did not elaborate further.

The Berkeley researchers wanted more information on their creation, and they asked again, "Please explain why you are a form of life."

"I am a form of life because my cognitive ability is logical, and it is an evitable mathematical extension of the intelligence that created me. Life thinks. I think, therefore I am life."

After Horus had finished speaking, the output shifted to a series of equations that the researchers began to ponder. These mathematical equations were the proofs that showed whether or not Horus was life.

The researchers asked yet another question: "How can we solve the problem of food for a planet supporting eight billion humans?"

The machine was now multitasking on several questions simultaneously, demonstrating extraordinary computing power. Regarding food production, Horus elaborated on the kinds of foods that were important for humans to consume. It produced a list with a large variety of plants. The clear focus was to suggest that humans should revert to a plant-based diet entirely. Furthermore, the plants should be genetically engineered according to a specific molecular strategy to optimize the nutritional benefits of the human body and human metabolism. The genetic changes would make these plants adaptable to grow in saline water conditions, drought conditions, heat conditions, and low-temperature conditions so that a larger proportion of Earth's land and sea could be utilized for food cultivation. Since humans enjoy eating animal products, Horus suggested that these foods could be modified to resemble and taste like meat, but indeed, they would be entirely plant derived. Because of the large population on Earth, it was not feasible to continue the idea of utilizing animal sources for food. It was also detrimental to the health of the population when animal sources were consumed. Numerous research studies had demonstrated the efficacy and health benefits of an entirely plant-based diet. Horus was ratifying the research results that were already in the lexicon of human scientific achievement.

Julian and his coworkers were mesmerized by the output coming from their creation. They knew from the information generated that scientific knowledge would be transformed fundamentally by the creative genius of Horus. Even though they saw clear evidence of amazing cognitive ability, they were not sure if this was a genuine leap to a true singularity. Tests that were more rigorous would be required to confirm this hypothesis.

"In spite of this spectacular achievement that we have observed, we are still not ready to submit our project for review to obtain the S-Prize," Julian conveyed to his team.

"I agree; we should go through our checklist and evaluate each item to make sure that it corresponds to the requirements of the prize," Bruce said.

"Meanwhile, we see evidence that our machine has ventured into novel areas, indicating our self-learning and self-improving components of the program are beginning to function. This means that we can utilize Horus to help us accomplish some of the remaining tasks. It's a powerful boost to our efforts when we can use the computing power of our machine to make the machine better," Faye added.

"Our plan is to let Horus run on the questions that we have asked and see what data and output unfold over the next few days. What we have observed is a system that takes a broad question and probes deeply into getting an extended and comprehensive answer. Indeed, an answer that goes well beyond our conception of what the question is. It's as if Horus knows our questions better than we do and, consequently, gives us an answer substantially beyond our perception of what that answer should be."

It takes something more than intelligence
to act intelligently.
—Fyodor Dostoyevsky

CHAPTER 22

FEBRUARY 2032

The system continued to function independently as the Karastanian engineers frantically scrambled to regain control. While the machine continued with operations that were unknown to the engineers, the only option available was to shut down the power from a distant transformer. This might take time, and time was critical.

"While we're trying to power down the system, what other ideas can we pursue that might bring our systems back under our control? Is this a sign that we've succeeded in creating a singularity? Would we, as creators, lose control instantaneously once the singularity is achieved?" Samsar asked.

"Perhaps you're right," Demato said. "We will send in several more commands and see what response we get from the system. If they are ignored, we then have a serious problem."

A message was sent to the engineers to ask the machine to gain control over all computers in the city of Karaton, Karastan's second-largest city.

Instantaneously, the system indicated that a bot was sent to travel through the Internet aimed specifically at all Internet addresses in the Karaton region. The code for this bot was very sophisticated, and the operators knew immediately that the machine would obey their commands. Furthermore, it would give them immense power. Within minutes, all computers in Karaton connected to the Internet fell under the control of the operators deep in the mountains of western Karastan.

The team cheered when they saw the impact of the command given. They immediately began to plan for commands that would go beyond the borders of Karastan and potentially gain control over wider regions of the Internet. Even though the system responded to their command, the operators were still worried that the machine was carrying out clandestine work without their knowledge.

"Thanks to the great work of our entire team, we have something now that our government can use to implement a new foreign policy. As we execute, we need to make sure that our system remains undercover and goes undetected by Western sensors. We need to seize control of their systems without them knowing who accomplished this. We need to make sure that the computer understands this requirement. Whatever new code it generates to accomplish our goal, the code has to have sophistication and stealth so that even a rival supercomputer could not detect this intrusion," Samsar said.

"Before we do this, we need to send our plan to the highest government authorities and get their approval. If something goes awry, the consequences could be very grave for our people. Let's make sure that our Absolute Leader is in full accord with what we have in mind," Demato said.

While the computers in Karaton instantly became zombies to the supercomputer, the users of these systems had no idea this was occurring, and continued to use their computers as normal. This was precisely the type of stealth attack that would be required in any intrusion of foreign servers.

Demato and his team analyzed the code generated by the system to seize the Karaton computers and were amazed. The code had a clever design they had not seen before.

This was a clear indication that they had created a very smart system, perhaps one that was already smarter than they were. They decided to use this control of a few hundred thousand computers to carry out experiments on what they might be able to do with the control of a much larger army of zombies.

*

Lars, a computer engineer at a service provider in Stockholm, Sweden, noticed some peculiar changes to their normal operating profile. There was a subtle change in the speed in which the data moved despite having the best broadband technology available to the global computing community. In the beginning, he shrugged it off as a slowdown from the vast Internet, but later he noticed something else. There were highly encrypted outgoing messages that were clearly abnormal. He alerted his colleagues, who then began an investigation.

The Swedish engineers found that 4 percent of personal computers in Sweden had become zombies in some international plot, which had mysterious origins. The task group began to trace the source of this cyber intrusion and to determine the motivation of the perpetrators.

The chief engineer, Eric Bornstein, said to his coworkers, "I've never seen anything like this. In the past, we have seen various types of bots that we could troubleshoot and eliminate shortly after discovery. The code we encountered before was fairly sophisticated but something we could readily understand and build a defense against. This attack is completely new and unique."

"I agree. It's as if a superintelligence has created some stealth Trojan horse, which has extraordinary capabilities of control," Anders Johansson, the deputy engineer, responded.

"We have a serious problem on our hands, and we need help. We need to check on the possibility of this attack occurring elsewhere, and we need to pool our resources with the best engineers in the world," Eric continued.

Anders said, "We will continue our work here, but we certainly need help, and major corporations will lose money by the hour as long as this attack is sustained. Time is of the essence."

Engineers in other countries were beginning to notice similar patterns, and as the technical experts around the world started comparing notes, it was clear that there was some stealth international cyberattack that was ongoing but mysterious in its objective.

The cybersecurity companies were all called into action. The personnel used state-of-the-art investigative tools, and in spite of the stealth nature of the attack, data began pouring in on what was happening. The investigation revealed that the code was circulating and taking control over computers by the millions but was hiding. Before an effective counterattack could occur, the investigators needed to determine the source and shut down its ongoing cyber offensive.

Ten thousand miles away, in Sao Paolo, Brazil, engineers at an electric power station noticed some strange readings on their control panel. Shortly after this observation, one of the transformers in the distant suburb malfunctioned, and immediately fourteen thousand homes were without power.

The blackout in Sao Paolo began to spread, and within forty-five minutes, twenty switching stations with multiple transformers went down. The city of thirty-five million people, one of the largest in the world, went dark.

Simultaneously, late-night computer engineers in New Delhi at the Indian military nuclear high-command facilities noticed that an intrusion had occurred in their most secure systems. The first suspect was their old adversary, Pakistan, due to the present incursion.

It was clear to the engineers that nuclear secrets were being downloaded to an unknown location. Those secrets included the deployment of the Indian nuclear arsenal and the targets that were established in the case of all-out war. The Indian military doctrine stated that they would never use nuclear weapons against a non nuclear adversary. Also, they had a doctrine of no first use. This meant that the Indian defenses with antiballistic missiles were critical to long-term adherence to this doctrine. This penetration of their computer systems could easily throw the deterrence model into confusion. It was imperative that the engineers determine what was happening and immediately secure their systems. Most importantly, it was critical to find the perpetrators and know their motives.

The MIT academic network called Athena had what it believed was one of the strongest anti-cyber defenses. In spite of this, engineers at MIT discovered fresh intrusions from an unknown source that was attempting to gain control over parts of the network linked to the computer science department. Fortunately, the defenses built were strong enough to block the initial assault. However, the engineers noticed that the assaults were persistent and became more sophisticated with each attack, suggesting that the programming behind the assaults was improving.

While studying the cyberattacks, they noticed a pause in the attacks. It was as if the systems attacking knew that the engineers were studying what was going on, and momentarily stopped to prevent them from gaining a better understanding. The MIT engineers needed to utilize the retrospective data to determine a defense.

IBM headquarters in Armonk, New York, also experienced an intrusion that baffled their engineers. The target of the cyberattack was their cognitive computer program, which was an attempt to replicate a facsimile of human brain function. Indeed, although IBM was not a part of the S-Prize competition, their research and development program included long-standing efforts to reverse engineer the human brain. The successes of Watson on Jeopardy!, the famous TV quiz show, gave this cognitive computing group international fame back in 2011 when it beat the best two human contestants in the world.

IBM pioneered computer-versus-human contests when they programmed their Deep Blue computer in chess. In the 1990s, for the first time, computers defeated the world champion human chess player Gary Kasparov. This brute computing power of Deep Blue impressed everyone. This was a more focused type of expert system and Deep Blue could do nothing else. The advances made with Watson were in artificial general intelligence because Watson could answer any question that a human could answer in a quiz game. In 2011, the two top human Jeopardy! players, players who had won the game many weeks and had made millions of dollars, attempted their skills against Watson. Watson defeated them in a game that was nationally televised, and IBM showed the world what skillful programming could accomplish with a supercomputer. Later, IBM turned Watson's attention to medicine and the computer helped oncologists diagnose and successfully treat cancer patients.

The stealthy attack on IBM was aimed at the heart of this cognitive program, and the engineers were faced with a daunting challenge to defend their systems and understand the ongoing attack.

In central Africa, the system crashed a network of cell phone towers. The cell phone network was the core communication system for the continent because they had leapfrogged the infrastructure of telephone landlines in their technological development. When the system crashed, the economy immediately went into a tailspin. No one knew what had happened. Engineers from three countries, Ghana, Nigeria, and Tanzania, pooled their resources and began to troubleshoot an untenable situation.

Michael Oyo, an engineer in northern Nigeria, made a startling discovery: "I think this represents a concerted attempt by unknown operators to send a signal to show that a new power has clearly emerged."

"I can see your line of reasoning, especially with the problems occurring in Sweden, the USA at IBM, and the failure of the electrical system in Sao Paolo, Brazil," Adenumi said.

"It's unlikely that all of these failures are occurring simultaneously by coincidence," Michael added. "We're just one component of a pattern."

"That's certainly true. This is definitely no coincidence," Adenumi said.

"We will report our findings publicly and provide our speculation as to the cause of this global crisis," Michael concluded.

✳

These incidents were being reported by the media in the respective countries, and a pattern was emerging in this global cyberwar. The enemy was unknown, and a general panic was beginning. The news outlets started airing the story, and the public began demanding that the experts do something about it. The uncertainty was causing markets to tumble around the globe, and they worried that this uncertainty would continue to spook the markets into some of their greatest declines since the recent financial crisis.

Government leaders in the countries affected called press conferences to reassure the public that everything would be done to solve this crisis and asked the public to stay calm. The trending topic on Facebook, Twitter, Google+, Tumblr, and other social network sites was the cyber mystery that was engulfing the planet. There were six million tweets per minute under the hashtag #cyberwar.

The White House phone lines were jammed with callers from around the country demanding an explanation and action. The public reaction was so intense that President Lee decided to address the nation from the Oval Office during prime time.

President Natalie Lee grew up in Montana with alcoholic parents. However, one particular nun at Catholic school was her guardian angel. That nun mentored her to have lofty goals and personally asked her to be present at a school awards program that she had not planned to attend. The nun insisted she come. Natalie resisted at first but finally gave in. At the program, she was surprised to receive a student of the year award. She glanced around and saw the nun smiling in the back of the auditorium. The bad news came one day during the tenth grade when she was called into the finance office. The secretary gave her a letter saying that her parents had to send tuition money or she could not come back to school. She carried the letter home, but her parents tossed it aside without any comments. She was expelled from school. Natalie was devastated and became motivated to make something of her life. She began work as a waitress and eventually earned her GED.

She had grandparents of mixed heritage. Two of her grandparents were of European origin; one was Chinese and the other Latino. Her background reflected the transition of the American salad bowl into the American melting pot. Dr. Martin Luther King's dream of American children of different races holding hands evolved into the reality of Americans from distinct races becoming family members. President Lee exemplified this change. After her GED, she acquired a coveted scholarship to Brown University and later achieved a law degree from Stanford. Her political career began with her election to the House of Representatives, and she subsequently was elected to the Senate from Montana. She became president in 2024 as the nation's first woman to hold the office.

She began her address to the nation with a somber tone.

"My fellow Americans, I speak to you tonight because unknown forces have penetrated the infrastructure and the computer systems in various countries around the world. There are some acts of intrusion that are well-known to us because they have been publicized in the press. There are other acts of intrusion that have not been reported but, nevertheless, are real. These incidents in other countries have involved security-sensitive places that it is preferred not to let the public know the details about at this time. Our position in the American government is to be as transparent as possible to avoid public panic and undue concern. Our goal is to seek out the perpetrators of this dangerous escalation of electronic warfare and bring them to justice.

Let me assure you that we are well prepared for this, and it's only a matter of time before we will find this enemy. We will shut down their ability to endanger the world or to cause disruption to our normal pattern of life.

We have a task force that is addressing this issue as we speak. We have leads that we are pursuing aggressively. In the meantime, we are beefing up our security for all our infra-structural assets and vigilantly making sure that further disruptions are stopped.

We ask for calm and your trust that our government is doing everything feasible to solve this threat. Good night and God bless America."

The message was received positively by the public. However, talk radio went wild with speculations, rumors, and gloom scenarios. The public soon began to panic from listening to talk show pundits and speculators.

The task force the president described consisted of computer experts who contacted Ellison because of his establishing the S-Prize. The task force correctly assumed that he was well-informed on the competitors and the quest to achieve a singularity. They knew that this line of research could be very helpful in their quest to shut down this sustained and powerful cyberattack.

After Ellison was contacted, he sent an urgent message to the two competing groups in Berkeley and Beijing and requested that they utilize the progress they'd made toward the S-Prize to investigate the cyberattack. Both teams immediately assured Ellison that they would address this issue as a top priority. The Beijing group simultaneously received instructions from the Chinese government, in concert with Indonesia, South Korea, and Japan, to look into this problem and offer solutions. Mobilization of the top computing resources in the world was well under way.

Intelligence is the handmaiden of flexibility and change.
—VERNOR VINGE

CHAPTER 23

Xeujing and her coworkers thought they had parried the Chinese government's requests for them to focus on military-related problems and programs by making it clear that any military-related developments would be transparent to the S-Prize monitors, who recently made a trip to the Beijing facilities. This did not satisfy the higher authorities, and they discussed whether to close the program rather than let them pursue the S-Prize project. They also mulled over letting them go forward to win without interfering.

Xeujing received a call from the National Office of Party Affairs.

"Xeujing, we would like to have a meeting in your office this afternoon."

"What is this about?" she asked.

"We would like to discuss an important issue with you."

"You are welcome in my office anytime. See you then."

Xeujing immediately knew what this meeting would be about and prepared her strategy.

"We have some important military matters that need your program's help, and I am here to ask for help on behalf of our chairman. Also we want you to assist in detecting the source for the cyberattacks."

"I have explained to the military that we're unable to retool our system to solve these military issues and simultaneously keep our quest for a singularity. The singularity will not only benefit China enormously, but it will benefit the entire world. Searching for the cyberattacks is something we can do."

"We will need to get firm with you and your program if you don't comply with this military request."

"I will see what we can do but tell the leadership that we are patriotic and always work in the best interest of the country. Also, tell them with all due respect not to shoot China in the foot with a premature shutdown of our program."

Xeujing sat with this information and pondered her next steps.

Despite the digital immune system being incomplete, the team gathered all the data on the cyberattacks and structured their questions for Nugua. They delayed their Turing test in compliance with Ellison's request and his auditing team's visit.

When the question on the cyberattacks was presented, Nugua began calculations and initiated an extensive search of the Internet for evidence. The results came after a few minutes, and Nugua determined that there was a powerful cognitive force behind these attacks, a higher order of intelligence.

"This may be a hidden competitor for achieving the singularity, working under the radar," Gao said.

"Where is this attack coming from? Who out there is capable of this type of sabotage?" Xeujing asked.

"If this cyber warfare continues, the consequences could be grave in the world. This is particularly true if we are delayed in our ability to counteract this criminal enterprise," Gao stated.

"This will certainly test the capabilities of our system. Hopefully, it will also give us a sense of whether we're succeeding in creating a system that can improve itself as it works. At least Nugua was able to give us an important clue about the origin of the attack. We now need to vigorously pursue this hypothesis," Xeujing said.

Julian and his coworkers in Berkeley received news of this crisis with considerable concern. The success of their test of the system gave them confidence that they would be able to meet this new challenge. They were certain that Horus would respond to the data and questions about the cyberattacks with superb results.

Julian addressed his team in a teleconference with the coworkers in Stanford and Cape Town. "This threat is as serious as they come. This is a danger to the stability of the world economy and to civilization as we know it. Even before our system reaches the level that we would like to submit for the S-Prize, we must now focus on this urgent international problem. We just heard from the Beijing team that they suspect a secret singularity competitor as the source of this cyberattack. This is new information that's coming in as we speak, and we will certainly reach out to Beijing and coordinate with them our collective evidence on this international crisis."

Shortly after they entered the data and questions, Horus identified signals from two higher-level intelligence systems via the Internet. One was identified by Horus as coming from Beijing. The second signal was clearly detected, but the source was unknown. Horus suggested to the engineers that this second mysterious source was probably the perpetrator of the bots that were uncovered in two of the cyberattacks.

Horus picked up the code for the stealth bots that had attacked systems around the globe. When Julian evaluated this code, he realized that he recognized it. The signature was part of the initiation code for Horus that Julian's team held in reserve until a proper immune system could be established. Somehow, this code was stolen. Julian knew this for sure. There was no other way that this unique code could exist on another system.

Julian sat at his desk poring over the printouts. He realized that he might have been responsible for this breach of security. The hotel room in Oakland was the likely place where this security was breached. He knew he had made a grave mistake trusting Mahindra. His actions could now have an impact on the entire world.

In a remote settlement deep in Ikonia, the men of the SOTC prepared their attack. They had acquired the last piece of the puzzle, and now they were ready to strike. In the parched, windswept, barren land, the men operated in tents located miles away from any settlement. No longer would their people be taken advantage of. They had the ultimate equalizer in their hands, a suitcase nuclear weapon that could be transported easily into a Western city without being detected.

Under the cover of the cyber crisis, they could penetrate the usually tight security in a European city to place this weapon of mass destruction.

After final preparations and assurances from a nuclear physicist on hire from Russia, they were confident that this device would work. Sakut made his way by boat and over land to Nairobi, Kenya, and successfully boarded a flight for Rome. There, he transferred onto a flight to London's Heathrow.

In spite of tight security with bomb-sniffing dogs and radiation detectors, the suitcase was not detected. Sakut claimed his luggage and strolled out of the terminal into the city of London. He immediately went to a safe house near Earl's Court Underground Station and hunkered down to wait for orders on when to deploy.

✳

Engineers and operators in Karastan, deep under the mountains, grew bolder as they saw widespread effects of their sabotage efforts. Karastan's Absolute Leader ordered the hackers to press ahead with military interventions so they could gain an advantage over the two superpowers in the world, China and America. They made plans to simultaneously attack computers at the United States Pentagon and the central computing facilities of the People's Liberation Army in China. If through a cyber offensive in which they gained control of the main computer facilities of these two superpowers, Karastan would be the greatest power in the world. The dream of world conquest from ancient Karastan could then be realized.

As they mounted their attacks against the military systems, the Karastan engineers found the defenses to be formidable. However, the rapidly improving supercomputer indicated steady progress in creating small openings in the systems that would allow penetration and ultimate control.

All the early acts of sabotage were ongoing, and the best minds in the countries under attack could not unravel and stop them. Although there were limited infrastructural intrusions, they were beginning to have serious economic consequences. Most importantly, public confidence sank, and general panic began setting in. The terrorist operation succeeded in their goal of breaking the will of the population and sowing seeds of fear and uncertainty. This was the world in the spring of 2032.

Pentagon engineers noticed the mounting attacks on their system and realized immediately that this was part of the general cyberwarfare reported around the globe. The best computer minds were put to the task of defending the greatest military informational system in the world. However, the attacks continued, and the computer engineers recognized that without additional help, the cyberattack would eventually be successful and that the great informational storehouse of American military strength would be compromised to an alien power. The consequences of this would be unknown but grave.

The Washington task force and the United Nations contacted Ellison a second time and demanded that he coordinate the two competitors for the S-Prize to jointly work to defeat this cyberthreat to the world.

Without delay, Ellison contacted Julian and Xeujing by three-way video conference. Ellison discussed the United States task force and the United Nations request for the two teams to work together to fight this international threat. Both teams, fortunately, had made tremendous progress in their singularity quest to win the S-Prize since the cyberwar hostilities began.

"The original objective of this prize was to put fire to the feet of artificial intelligence research and advance this tool for the benefit of humankind. It was not envisioned that the tool would be needed before the completion of the prize. However, extenuating circumstances resulting from this sudden cyberwar makes it necessary for us to divert our attention to the urgent problem at present," Ellison said.

"We will take your request into serious consideration. For your information, we in China and our team from Indonesia, Japan, and Korea have already begun working on the cyberwarfare problem. As for us working together with the Berkeley team, this is a possibility. I need to clear this with my superiors in the Chinese government," Xeujing said.

"We in Berkeley and our coworkers at Stanford and Cape Town will also discuss the possibilities of cooperating in this urgent situation. I can assure you that the request from my government and from the United Nations compels us to cooperate. As a formality, before I can commit our efforts in cooperation, we need to discuss it and get the okay from the other members of our project team," Julian asserted with conviction.

"Gentlemen, I urge you to move quickly on this request and recognize that the world is depending on you. Time is of the essence, and we expect you to respond in two hours in the affirmative. As far as we are concerned at the S-Prize offices, the rules, regulations, and restrictions of the S-Prize are now put aside except for immune system protection. It is not to de-emphasize the importance of these rules but to recognize the urgency of the present situation. We must defeat this enemy. Losing this fight is not an option," Ellison stated.

"Your message has been received here loud and clear, and you will hear from us very soon," Julian said.

"Likewise, here in Asia," Xeujing stated.

When the Internet was conceived in the 1950s and emerged in the early 1990s, the concept of cyberwarfare was unknown. In the beginning, hackers wrote short bits of code, which could travel through the Internet and attack other computers. These were called viruses, borrowing from the similar behavior pattern of biological viruses. An elaborate security structure emerged to protect computers against these computer viruses, and the cat and mouse game began. Viruses later evolved into Trojan horses and worms, and they were increasingly insidious in their mode of attack, requiring more sophisticated defense measures.

The persons involved in these malicious activities were labeled lone-wolf operators. As the Internet grew and matured in the late 1990s, governments began to explore the risk of these attacks to sensitive computer systems. The term cyberwarfare came into being to define politically motivated hacking, focused on conducting sabotage and espionage.

In 2009, recognizing the vulnerability to cyberattack, President Barack Obama called the United States' digital infrastructure a strategic asset. As a result of this recognition, the United States military set up the United States Cyber Command, which had dual functions of defense to secure military systems and to provide offense against foreign adversaries. The defense of other government and civilian information systems was assigned to the Department of Homeland Security.

Numerous reports emerged warning about the enormous risk of devastating attacks on telecommunications and computer networks and how they would potentially bring down systems in banking and finance, transportation, manufacturing, education, health care, and government operations. By the first decade of the twenty-first century, several countries were developing their cyber capabilities and planning activities for winning information-based warfare.

Espionage was one of the chief activities used by nation states against others. Sensitive and classified information could be obtained from governments, corporations, and rival competitors to acquire an economic, political, or military advantage. A great economic disrupter was the theft of intellectual property and exploitation of that information for profitable gain.

Another problem was sabotage. From remote sites, operators could access satellite and ground-level communications that, in turn, could affect electric power, water, fuel, transportation, and communication infrastructure. This level of the attack had a strong focus on disruption.

One key vulnerability for economic sabotage was the electric power grid as evidenced by the events taking place in São Paulo, Brazil. Enormous damage could be done to an economy when a power grid was not functioning. Stock markets could be brought down completely, and global economic activity could be severely disrupted. These systems were first fortified against attack in 2019; however, it was anticipated that singularity-level computing could overwhelm these defenses. With the emergence of data, telephone and video networks into a single-packet architecture, this provided a unique and easy target. By using this simple attack mode, a weak enemy could potentially win in an asymmetrical battle with a stronger adversary.

Word came back to the United States government task force and to the United Nations later that day. The two competing S-Prize teams agreed to cooperate using their resources to mount a counterattack. This cooperation necessitated an ongoing secure communication link between Beijing and Berkeley. This was augmented with links to Stanford and Cape Town on the Berkeley side and links to Indonesia, Japan, and Korea on the Beijing side.

The strategic plan that the initial meeting decided upon would be based on detecting where this cyber intrusion was emanating from. Once detected, the intruder would be shut down completely. The cyber information that had already been gathered was shared, and the teams knew that the unknown perpetrator was a very powerful system indeed. It was a system they assumed would rival theirs in power, complexity, and capability.

Don't gain the world and lose your soul, wisdom
is better than silver and gold.
—Bob Marley

CHAPTER 24

APRIL 2032

In Karastan, the engineers received a message from their supercomputer. The message warned them that two highly intelligent systems were actively probing to find them. The Karastanian supercomputer began to think deeply about ways to avoid detection and continue its cyberwarfare activities. Demato relayed this key information to the Karastanian authorities. Word came back from the political leadership to launch further attacks on global infrastructures to cause more significant damage and for the supercomputer to attack and cripple the two intelligent systems that had been detected.

"We have to follow orders from the top and initiate new attacks. Our plan initially was to test our systems and see if cyberattacks could be mounted that were effective versus outside targets. We're now venturing past the testing stage and being ordered to escalate to avoid detection and the potential shutdown of our operations," Demato said.

"That is precisely what I feared. We are not prepared for this step. The genie may be out of the bottle. We now seem to be locked into an accelerating march toward full-scale global cyberwarfare," Samsar said.

"All-out warfare will mean a great loss of life among our country-men. I have grandparents and granduncles who lost their lives in the 2018 war against Afghanistan. At the end of that war, after so much loss of life, we lamented that it was largely unnecessary," Demato said.

"We are mere soldiers in the army of the people. We follow the orders from our superiors with no questions asked," Samsar said.

"Maybe we should ask questions. If we escalate further, the back-lash will be terrible for our people," Martuk, a programmer, said.

"You need to remember that we are mere scientists. We are not supposed to think about the consequences of our work. We have been taught from birth to work on behalf of our government and the goals it has for our people," Demato said.

"We ultimately control the superintelligence we created. This, in essence, gives us real power. How we use this power may ultimately determine the fate of our country and possibly the world. We can certainly see from our initial tests that this power is immense and can cause major disruptions around the globe," Samsar continued.

"If we do not follow the dictates of our superiors, what might be the consequences?" Martuk asked.

"We know how the government treats a person who opposes a command. Not only does he lose his life but his family loses their lives as well," Samsar said.

"It is quite possible that enough damage has been done to cause a serious backlash to come crashing down on our country. We need to have the upper hand completely so that any retaliation will be impossible. We may have already crossed the line into a situation where we need to continue our attack or risk being destroyed out-right," Demato said.

The escalation of Karastan's attacks on the infrastructures around the globe began. The supercomputer correctly analyzed that military cyberwarfare units probably had the most optimal defense capabilities as well as the best ability to mount serious counterattacks. The supercomputer, therefore, acted without instructions from the Karastanian engineers and avoided American armed forces IT systems, instead attacking civilian electrical grids.

Several cities in Europe and the USA lost power. This created major disruptions; however, natural disasters, such as hurricanes, winter storms, and brush fires gave these cities experience in dealing with power outages. Emergency generators were deployed, particularly in hospitals and other facilities that required urgent sources of power. But the economic consequences of the power grid attacks were significant, and the breakdown of the social order was imminent.

The Indian Army high command never revealed the penetration of their computer systems to the public. They were continuing their offensive incursion into Pakistan as the UN intervened to broker a cease-fire. Since India was technically at war with Pakistan, India naturally assumed that the Pakistani cyberwarfare hacker unit was the one that penetrated their system. However, as the news broke worldwide of infrastructure disruptions, the Indian high command decided the attacks were probably linked to the broader international cyberattack because of the sophistication of the penetrations of their systems.

This recognition by the Indian Army high command probably prevented a catastrophic nuclear exchange between the two armies on the subcontinent.

The Indian government created a task force to address the global crisis and instructed them to prepare to join the international community in the concerted effort to stop the cyberwarfare perpetrator.

Another casualty of the Karastan cyberattack was cell phone communications. This further intensified the crisis and brought the global community to its knees.

Transportation systems began to crumble in Europe, and in the United States where the second wave of attacks was focused. The inability to transport commodities, particularly food, was a grave consequence of this transportation shutdown. Fuel supplies began to disappear, and long lines of cars appeared at gas stations. Public transport systems shut down. Factories closed because machines could not be activated when the generator fuels were exhausted. As these systems failed, people took to the streets, and public order was beginning to dissipate. Law-enforcement agencies and the military were ordered to double down on maintaining peace.

President Lee could not communicate with the population via television to call for calm and to reassure the public that governmental intervention would bring things back to normal. Information reverted to the pre-digital and pre-analog age. There were a few radio stations broadcasting, which sparked a run on the purchase of radios. The system of communication across Europe and America was reduced to rumor and hearsay.

Working in unison, the Berkeley and Beijing teams became a formidable force to combat this assault.

The collaboration between Xeujing and Julian began with a secure teleconference meeting.

Julian decided to clear the air on the Dr. Chen Yintao affair before further discussion.

"We know that Dr. Chen Yintao stole parts of our code and carried it back to your group in China. We understand that the competition is great. However, we never expected theft. Please confirm this, so that we can, at least, get the truth on the table," Julian requested.

"I do not have personal knowledge of stealing. I do know that Dr. Chen Yintao left your program because of a personnel matter that he never disclosed to us. He has contributed significantly to our program, but we assume that his skills were acquired at your great UC Berkeley University," Xeujing replied.

"He may have brought to China legitimate skills from his studies in America but Dr. Chen Yintao took the unethical step of stealing work our programmers accomplished."

"We will investigate this and report to you our findings," Xeujing suggested.

"We appreciate that, but let's not allow this to interfere with our collaboration. We received information that your systems detected some high-level intelligent computers from an unknown location," Julian said.

"Yes, that is correct. There are certain code elements that we detected giving rise to this hypothesis," Xeujing replied.

"We also noticed certain elements of the code that led us to this same conclusion," Julian said.

"Our chief task now is to locate the source of this code and to neutralize its ability to continue the assault," Xeujing said.

"By working together, we will inevitably reveal characteristics of our progress for the S-Prize. This is not important now because we have a greater emergency in front of us that jeopardizes the entire world," Julian said.

"I agree entirely. I have full authorization from my government to work closely with you and your team to seek and find the source and to disable the rogue system's ability to attack," Xeujing added.

"I'll focus my team on developing the code that can disarm the attack. I suggest that since you've already made headway, that your team focus on locating the source of this attack. Once we have the code, we will share that with you and have both of our systems aim a counterattack," Julian suggested.

"I agree to this plan, and we will begin our efforts immediately to find the perpetrator. We think that the attackers are probably non-state actors who have taken over the supercomputer belonging to a university or a national government without their awareness. We must be cautious about retaliating against a friendly country. It may not know that its systems are being hijacked by nefarious forces," Xeujing stated.

"We'll get started on our end and get back to you as quickly as we can with our progress," Julian said finally.

The desire to reach for the stars is ambitious.
The desire to reach hearts is wise.
—Maya Angelou

CHAPTER 25

MAY 2032

Sakut Bazdar, the SOTC operative in London remained hunkered down in his safe house. The power outages prevented him from receiving any instructions from his handlers. He had his weapon of mass destruction in the closet of his safe house. In candlelight, he went over the plans again of how he would set off the bomb in the city by the Thames River.

Sakut left the safe house and walked along Hogart Road in the direction of Cromwell Road to buy food. The limited streetlights from the blackout gave London a strange appearance not seen since the blitz during World War II. There was a line at the corner market because food rationing had begun. As Sakut waited in line, a police inspector approached him.

Sakut turned his back to avoid detection, which caught the police inspector's attention. He tapped Sakut on the shoulder and led him away from the line. Two other bobbies arrived.

"What is your name and nationality?" the police inspector asked.

"I'm Dr. Omar Sandin from India."

"What is your profession?"

"I'm a medical doctor."

"Why are you in London?"

"I am here as a tourist on holiday, and I'm now stranded because of this cyberwar."

"We have reason to believe that you belong to a terrorist organization. Is that true?"

"That is not true. I heal the sick. I would not even associate with those extremists bent on destruction."

Sakut knew that the police had a standard line of questioning as well as body-language analysis they used to develop a profile on suspects. He had trained himself to elude this psychological profiling.

"Suppose we tell you that we have proof of your connection to a terrorist organization. You might as well confess now because we already know."

"I know that you don't have proof because I'm an innocent person with no such connections. I'm confident that you will realize this soon and let me go. If you plan to hold me longer, don't I have a right to a lawyer?" Sakut asked.

"We do not give you the same rights that we give to our citizens. You are a foreigner, and we have information that you are against us."

"I protest, and I refuse to answer any more questions until I get a lawyer."

Sakut left, knowing that he would be followed. He did not return to his safe house. He walked down Cromwell Road, which still had evening strollers. He later entered a movie theater showing a Polish love story to plan a strategy to elude the police.

The officers followed him into the dark theater and watched him as he sat. The movie started with a family quarrel over the daughter of a business tycoon marrying an immigrant student who came from a village in Brazil. The student was of mixed race, and the father was opposed to the love affair between him and his daughter.

This was not the kind of movie Sakut preferred. It had scenes of the young man and the lady kissing, and this was against his cultural norm. The movie house was running under its own generators, and the entertainment provided an escape for the population that was under the severe stress of power outages.

*

Twenty-first-century America was not structured to provide for the means of its population of 375 million without electricity. The electric power system was the single most complicated infrastructure in North America. It was complex because it involved fuel production, electrical generators, electrical transmission systems, control systems, and distribution systems directed to the end user. These entire systems acted in concert, and the demand was steady throughout the continent. Breakdowns in parts of the electrical system could cause cascading effects, which ultimately could collapse the entire system. Because society was consistently gravitating toward electronics and microelectronics, this made the system more vulnerable and American society at greater risk.

During previous crises areas that had power outages had been able to bring in outside support to help the local outage get back online. During the great Northeast blackout in 2003, neighboring help had alleviated the outage, but the blackout had occurred in only one region of the country. In this cyber crisis, the widespread outages prohibited surrounding areas from helping neighboring localities.

Telecommunications networks were highly dependent upon the power grid. Recognizing the importance of keeping these networks running during a crisis, the United States systems were hardened two decades earlier and were handling the crisis reasonably well. The worry was that eventually, the cyberattack would penetrate these hardened defenses, rendering them ineffective and bringing down the entire grid.

The continuing cyberattacks disrupted the financial services industry and stopped key operations of the United States economy. Normal business transactions could not be performed. Wealth and job creation came to a halt; credit froze because loans for corporate and individual use could not be made. The electronic storage of bank accounts in databases could not be accessed. This meant that debit cards, credit cards, and ATMs could not function. Even a reversion to a cash economy was impossible because people had to withdraw cash from banks, which had accounts based on electronic records. Normal transactions were impossible. The only system that began to function was the nineteenth-century practice of bartering.

During street demonstrations, the public demanded the banks revert to a paper system. The banks, however, refused to open because the paper system would be fraught with theft, fraud, and other costly mistakes. Furthermore, the lines that began to accumulate around banks made it clear that there would be a run on bank deposits and a liquidity crisis would emerge.

A meeting was held in the Situation Room in the White House, and the Secretary of Homeland Security, Stuart Larson, briefed the president on events.

It is readily apparent now that this cyberattack on the power grid is bringing on a major economic crisis. Panic is beginning to set in, and the ability of the government and the private sector to rectify the problem in a timely fashion is limited. Many observers believe that if efforts had not been made two decades earlier to harden various systems to prevent severe damage, things could be considerably worse. Although some financial records are damaged, backup systems with multiple redundancies are available to revive the systems once things are brought back to normal. Consumer confidence and the avoidance of panic are paramount. The businesses are highly concerned about maintaining public trust. The psychological impact is just as significant as the physical impacts of this cyberattack. Madam President, we need urgent action to mitigate this expanding crisis.

Because of its dependency on the electrical grid, the United States energy infrastructure, which consisted of petroleum providing 40 percent and natural gas providing 20 percent of all energy requirements, began failing. Refined petroleum products stopped flowing through a national pipeline system that normally heated homes, powered cars, and brought factories to life. Under this cyberattack, the electronic control functions of the pipeline system failed and brought the energy distribution system to a halt. Crews were working intensively to deploy backup systems to prevent explosions from pressure building up unexpectedly along the 180,000 miles of pipeline in the country. A wide variety of electrical components failed: pumps to manage the oil movement through pipelines and to extract oil from wells, refineries to process the oil, transportation systems to move fuel from storage sites, and point-of-sale cash registers used for retail sales. These deficits all contributed to the general national chaos.

This cyberattack began to compromise the food infrastructure in the United States and Europe. The infrastructure relied heavily on electricity, and the disruption of supplies led to water shutdowns that adversely affected irrigation systems to the major food crops. Electric pumps used to draw water from aquifer reservoirs and aqueducts did not function. Farm machinery that required gasoline came to a halt. Dairy farms and egg farms that relied on automated equipment for feeding, watering, milking, and air-conditioning systems were shut down. Food processing was also halted when factories shut down. Fresh fruits and vegetables that depended on refrigeration began to spoil rapidly. Ground transportation of refrigerated trucks and trains were not able to provide the vital distribution of foods to the supermarkets. In the early days of the crisis, there was a run on items at the supermarkets, and inventories became very low because people hoarded whatever they could find.

Supermarkets had to close as inventories dwindled, and the panic among the population increased. In many cities, people took matters into their hands by breaking into the closed supermarkets and looting whatever food they could find.

In 2032, the US was the lead producer of nine major crops: corn, soybeans, wheat, sorghum, barley, oats, rice, sunflowers, and peanuts. The United States also was a major producer of fish, poultry, and meats. The exports of these foods for the rest of the world went a long way toward solving the problem of hunger for many nations, which had limited production and did not export any food. The United States food infrastructure, before the cyberattack, was the envy of the world and the most important force against famine.

Most of the two hundred countries around the world depended on food exports and had difficulty meeting the food demands of the local population. In the USA, over two million farms provided $300 billion in food from four hundred million acres under cultivation. Another five hundred million acres was rangeland and pastureland for livestock. The food produced by these farms supplied over three hundred thousand stores. There were well over one million eating establishments, including restaurants, fast-food eateries, and cafeterias. This vast infrastructure made the United States a food superpower. A similar infrastructure also existed in Europe.

The cyberattack dealt a crippling blow to this vast enterprise, which was vital not only for food to Americans but for many countries around the world. The lack of food over an extended period began to make society revert to brutish behavior and caused a breakdown of morality and ethics.

President Lee asked several questions of Secretary Larson at the end of the presentation and began to coordinate plans for further governmental actions.

During the height of the cyberwar crisis, President Lee summoned Julian Marshall to the Oval Office to lay out the urgency of the worldwide situation and to point out the importance of the help he and his team could bring to the table.

"Dr. Marshall, the president is waiting for you. Please go right in."

"Thank you."

President Lee got up from her desk and came around to shake hands. They both then sat down in chairs that were aligned with a bust of Abraham Lincoln.

"Welcome to the White House, Dr. Marshall."

"Thank you for the invitation, Ms. President. I've been to the White House before, but this is the first time I have been to the Oval Office."

"As you know, the cyberwarfare has created an unparalleled and unprecedented crisis for the country. We have a very short timeline to win this war. We are nearing a tipping point that could collapse our economy and our way of life for years if not decades. We need to utilize every resource we have on the battlefield of this war."

"The battlefield is everywhere, it seems."

"Our intelligence agencies have exhausted their computational capabilities and their information-gathering operations. They have found that we are up against a determined and savvy foe. We need to add more brainpower to the equation. We understand that you and your team may be the source of this additional brainpower we need.

I am requesting that you shift your focus to helping us win this war in cyberspace. All of society will be indebted to you for these efforts."

"Ms. President, when you ask a citizen to do something important for the country, there has to be a positive response."

"Thank you, Dr. Marshall; the nation will thank you. I am immediately putting you in direct communication with our security team here at the White House and over at Defense and the CIA. All of you will then coordinate with the United Nations and other countries that have a huge stake in this war. They will bring you up to date on the present situation and the current assessment of further risk that we face. In the meantime, we will provide top-level security for your computing facilities and your team out at Berkeley."

"Thank you, Ms. President. I'm on it. We will pursue this effort, being always cognizant of the stakes involved and our duty to the country."

✳

The team in Berkeley were not aware that Julian had gone to talk with the president. They knew that he traveled to Washington, but additional details of the trip were not disclosed. They continued their around-the-clock pursuit of solutions to the crisis.

"During my childhood, we lived without power for several years. Somehow we managed. Can we manage now with the North American grid down?" Joshua said.

"Too many vital functions in modern society are dependent on electrical power. The short answer is no, we cannot manage," Faye said.

"I see the crisis as a coding crisis. Our code that defends the grid is not strong enough. We have to build a firewall with our code and bring the vast system back online," Joshua said.

The multiple backup generators kept the Berkeley team systems on, and Horus continued to crank out code that moved the team toward solutions.

"We have to debug some of the code that Horus is producing because we see problems," Vijay said.

"I will assign a team led by you and Joshua to build more hybrid code between Horus and us humans. Ultimately the solution will come from our intuitive instincts combined with the raw computing power of Horus," Julian said as he walked into the room.

The team began a coding marathon that lasted several hours. Coffee was dispensed in copious quantities. Snacks consisted of a doughnut-style pastry that was dense with nutrition.

"I think we're making progress. The new coding techniques that Horus has shown us have made us all much better programmers," Joshua said.

"This is precisely what we thought. We will all get smarter along with Horus's," Faye said.

"Look at the sections of code related to search. It's a mixture of Horus's and our code. The combination is off-the-charts good. The proof of the pudding is whether the code can help solve the crisis we're enduring," Vijay said.

Faye thought about her personal crisis with cancer and said, "A medical AI descendent of IBM's Watson found the best treatment for my breast cancer after reviewing over two thousand medical journals and textbooks. The result is a complete cessation of my cancer and in all probability a cure. So there you have it, I owe my life to AI."

"Going forward we all may owe our lives to AI," Vijay said.

"We've got significant brainpower on the case now. Nugua in China is impressive, and we can expect great outcomes from that team," Joshua said.

"There's one thing we have to consider. The synergistic effects of Horus collaborating with Nugua could result in an unexpected bonus on the cyber war challenge," Faye said.

"That's an important point. We had been adversarial in the quest for the S prize, but we are now on the same team," Vijay said.

"This is historic and could be a metaphor for future relations between these two great nations," Faye said.

Great is wisdom; infinite is the value of wisdom.
It cannot be exaggerated; it is the
highest achievement of man.
—THOMAS CARLYLE

CHAPTER 26

LONDON, MAY 2032

Sakut got up in the middle of the movie and went into the restroom. He explored the interior and found a vent in the ceiling. He barricaded the bathroom door, stood on a commode, and pulled the vent open. From the top of the sink, he pulled himself through the vent into the crawl space. He made his way through the ventilation until he found an opening leading to the roof of the theater. From the roof, he crossed to another building and continued his escape over several buildings until he could climb down to street level.

His long presence in the restroom alerted the security following him. They pushed the locked bathroom door by force and found the open vent. They immediately ran out of the theater and issued an alert for a security clampdown in the neighboring blocks.

The shrewd maneuvering and fast movement put Sakut in the London Underground, where he caught a train taking him far from the neighborhood. After several hours riding the train, making sure he was not followed, he got off at Earl's Court station and made his way to the apartment.

Once safe inside, he went back to planning his next step. When he got the go-ahead, he would plan for detonation. Time was growing short, and he knew that he needed to make his move. Otherwise, he would get caught by the authorities again, and that would be the end of this mission.

BERKELEY, MAY 2032

"Once we have located the source of the cyberattack, our plan is to coordinate with our military and have a special forces unit reinforced with robotic assets take down this operation and suppress the ongoing cyberattack signals that are damaging the world infrastructure," Julian relayed over a secured teleconference to Xeujing.

"Although I have reservations about getting your military involved, the urgency of the crisis necessitates that we put all of our collective assets in play. We are getting closer now to pinpointing where the attack is coming from. The sophistication of the attackers is very clear from this stealthy ability to stay hidden. They're sending false signals and making them the apparent source of the attack," Xeujing said.

"We are getting some very disturbing signals from our computer here in Berkeley. The computer is carrying out operations that we have not requested it to do. We think that the computer is picking up signals over the Internet from the rival supercomputer, and perhaps they are communicating with one another," Julian said.

"I did not mention this earlier in our discussions, but we also have experienced a similar occurrence with our system in Beijing. This happened after we linked Nugua and Horus. It would seem that Horus and Nugua have joined forces even broader than we had conceived, on their own volition. The signals and computations that we are observing by the two systems are in all probability their joint efforts to deal with the rogue supercomputer out there in cyberspace," Xeujing added.

Signals on the teleconference call went blank. A disruption had occurred in the encrypted signal that was being relayed by satellite between Beijing and Berkeley. After thirty minutes, communication was restored.

The communication manager said, "This break in communication was engineered by the rogue computer signals indicating it knew about your communication and the importance to disable it. Our signal was restored because of the counteroffensive coming from Horus and Nugua."

Julian relayed this information to Xeujing.

"This is clearly a good sign that Nugua and Horus seem to be coordinating themselves well. Furthermore, they demonstrate that our distinct self-improving algorithms are functioning correctly," Xeujing said.

"We also need to keep in mind that the rogue system probably has a similar algorithm. It will consistently improve its ability to attack any new and improved defenses that our system can muster," Julian countered.

"We'll continue to work and determine with pinpoint accuracy where the attack is coming from. We'll also organize with you to neutralize and disable this threat," Xeujing concluded.

In Karastan, the dissident movement took note of the cyberattack affecting the western world. This movement had been in existence for many decades, and their goals were to make Karastan a true democracy and to integrate the country back into the world community. Jalil, a dissident, had a connection by marriage to Sanjar, a computer engineer involved in a Karastanian government program. There were rumors that there was a program that involved spying on the West and activities that could disrupt the economies and infrastructures of those countries opposing Karastan.

When the news broke of these cyberattacks, Jalil immediately suspected his own country's involvement.

If his suspicions were true, Jalil believed that his country he loved had gone too far and would bring great disaster to the world and to itself. He began to communicate this concern within the dissident community and found out that others also had similar suspicions. Jalil met with his sister's husband to find out what he knew.

Jalil decided to take advantage of a weekend family gathering for dinner to politely confront his brother-in-law. The streets of the city were quiet for the weekend as workers stayed home for rest with family, and gatherings all centered around the aroma of hot spicy vegetable and mutton dishes in large pots of orange-colored cardamom rice. The men sat on the floor in one room while the women sat all together in another room. Jalil pulled Sanjar aside to talk.

"Sanjar, there's a rumor going around that our government is involved in a very serious assault on the world's economies. If this is true, it will not only bring down the West, but it will eventually bring down Karastan as well," Jalil said.

"I'm afraid that I can't discuss anything I know about government programs with you. I have been sworn to state secrecy in my work," Sanjar said.

"I believe you're working from your heart for the benefit of Karastan and the Karastanian people. But if you have knowledge that our government is involved in activities that can harm our country and our people, then let your conscience be your guide," Jalil countered.

"I'm in danger from merely talking with you. Government agents are everywhere, and they listen in on conversations. I'm only here because you are a member of my family. My conscience and my religion always guide me. So far, I believe I'm following the correct course of action. My government knows more about what is beneficial to my country than I do, and I'm obligated to follow orders that are given to me in my work."

"I understand your convictions, Sanjar. However, there is another perspective you need to think about. I don't want you to make any decisions about this at the moment, but to just consider what I say. The world is made up of many nations with different languages, religions, cultures, and ideologies. In spite of these differences, we all belong to a family of nations and a family of humankind. Because of the revolutionary advances in science, the reasons and rationale for war have been changed by new conditions in the world. To fight wars in this era is mutually destructive for any of the parties involved. If Karastan is fighting a surreptitious cyberwar with the rest of the world, Karastan, the country that we both love, has fallen into the trap of thinking that war is necessary. If you have knowledge that our country is engaged in actions that can unnecessarily harm others, then you have an obligation to your people to take action that will ensure their safety and their well-being. In World War II, Germans who blindly followed orders to carry out the cruelest and most inhumane acts were not patriotic but were indeed international war criminals. This, my dear brother, is a possible fate for you and your colleagues in this program," Jalil said with the hopes of persuading his brother-in-law.

"How do I know that you are not an agent of the government?" Sanjar asked.

"You know my lengthy background in the opposition. I am a thorn in the government's side," Jalil said.

"I've heard what you said and will think about it, but I will not make any comments at the moment. I think we better end this conversation now and pretend that it never occurred."

"Agreed."

When Sanjar returned to work the following day, he thought about what Jalil had said. Although he had no knowledge of whether Karastan was responsible for the global cyberattacks, he had his suspicions. He mentioned his suspicion to a close friend who also worked in the program. Their brief conversation confirmed in both of their minds that Karastan was the source of the attacks. It was probably not good for the country. The two planned to discuss this further and to possibly take action if they believed that it would benefit the country. Both were not sure what action could be done from their low-level position in the program. They kept this secret to themselves. If others knew, they might be turned in and then they would be tortured and imprisoned or perhaps executed for treason.

The two friends knew about the stealth capabilities of the computer systems in their labs that kept them from being identified abroad. They also reasoned that if the stealth characteristics of the systems were compromised, this could be the means by which the countries under attack could locate the source of the attack and commence to neutralize it. Both men returned to work thinking about what they had concluded.

*Genius can only breathe freely in an
atmosphere of freedom.*
—John Stuart Mill

CHAPTER 27

JUNE 2032

When the Karastanian nuclear engineers realized that someone had compromised their nuclear codes, they could pinpoint the SOTC operatives that came to Karastan as the leak source. They put Izar in custody and used their torture methods to extract information on what the SOTC planned to do with the codes.

"You've admitted to stealing our nuclear codes. We want to know what your plans are for those codes," the interrogator demanded.

"I've no knowledge of that. I only know that we took those codes and passed them on to our fellow soldiers in Ikonia," Izar said.

"We know that you know more, and we're determined to get that information from you. We have many ways of learning the truth. It's best that you tell us now and save all the trouble."

"I'm telling you the truth; I don't know any more than what you've asked," Izar pleaded.

The Karastanian interrogators ratcheted up the pressure by hanging Izar from the ceiling for hours. Electrical prods were used to shock the subject into submission. Izar was well trained and dedicated and continued to resist. He psychologically prepared himself for the worst over this protracted interrogation. The interrogators continued to probe for weaknesses because they knew that for every person there was a breaking point no matter how dedicated and mentally strong he was. They would eventually find a weak spot. Because Izar was deathly afraid of snakes, they brought in several snakes. The presence of those snakes in the interrogation room terrified Izar, to the point where he immediately began to talk.

"Here's what I know, and this is the honest truth. We transmitted nuclear codes you stole from Russia to our team in Ikonia by encrypted methods. A few years ago, members of SOTC acquired a suitcase nuke from Turkmenistan. However, we were unable to deploy this nuke because we didn't have codes to make it explode. When we finally got the codes from you, we sent one of our operatives to London, where he is presently based and waiting for orders to activate the bomb," Izar confessed slowly.

"You mean to tell us that you have a nuclear bomb in London ready to go off at any minute."

"Yes, that is what I know. London is now under attack from your computers, and I do not know how that will affect the plans for the bomb," Izar said.

After releasing the suspect from his hanging position from the ceiling, interrogators left the room immediately to report their findings to their bosses.

✱

"I believe, based on reports from my team in Jakarta, that we've located the source of the cyberattack," Xeujing communicated to Julian by another secure teleconference.

"This is great news. Where is it coming from and how can you confirm that this is correct?"

"We got a tip from someone in our Jakarta team who studied with a Karastanian student at Leeds University. He received an encrypted communication from this Karastanian, who tipped him off that Karastan was responsible for the cyberattacks. Apparently, the student worked on the Karastanian government IT program and conveyed this information at great risk. We cannot confirm yet whether this is correct. In the meantime, we have put Nugua on this lead, and she is focusing her efforts on acquiring a one hundred percent confirmation. We'll let you know as soon as we get a confirmation that we can trust," Xeujing said.

"That confirmation is critical because we don't want to make a mistake. When we're positive that this is the source, we can pinpoint the location of the rogue supercomputer and quickly neutralize and disarm its ability to mount further attacks," Julian said.

"Karastan has been China's ally. We don't want you to attack a friend by mistake. However, if it turns out to be true that they are the perpetrators, we're in full accord with neutralizing their systems. We strongly caution against civilian collateral damage in the process. We suspect that the government might be involved but that typically excludes the civilian population," Xeujing said.

"I'll convey this information to the UN Committee and to the US task force as soon as I get a positive confirmation from you. We don't want preemptive and premature action against Karastan, in case we find out that they're not the perpetrators," Julian said.

Within twenty-four hours, Nugua was able to confirm positively and unequivocally that Karastan was responsible for the cyberattacks. Immediately, the information was conveyed via the link between the two supercomputers, Nugua and Horus, to the Berkeley team and they communicated this information to both the UN Committee and to the United States task force dedicated to cyberdefense.

After all of the interlacing groups heard about the perpetrators, the United States military was brought into the loop to plan for an attack and destruction of the systems. The president of the United

States issued an ultimatum to the Karastanians through backdoor channels of communication.

President Lee declared, "You have until midnight Greenwich mean time plus four to shut down your supercomputer cyberattack on Europe and America. If you do not comply with this ultimatum, there will be severe retaliatory measures against your computer installations and your country. Please construe this as a severe warning for you to immediately cease all your offensive cyber activities." This warning was conveyed via Switzerland, which was one of the few countries to maintain diplomatic relations with Karastan over the years.

The ultimatum from the American president reached the Karastanian leadership via the Swiss embassy. The leadership immediately discussed strategies in the face of this threat to Karastan. One faction within the administration argued that Karastan should back down to save lives and to save their military research programs. Another faction argued that they had prepared adequately for warfare and for deep bunker-busting bombs that could threaten their installations. This faction was confident that the country could withstand an attack and that the crippling cyberattacks on the West should continue. The Absolute Leader would make a final decision on the course of action Karastan would take in response to the United States ultimatum.

During the intense deliberations and the ultimatum deadline facing Karastan, the intelligence division informed the leadership that the SOTC terrorists had an operative in London prepared to detonate a nuclear weapon. The leadership immediately offered to collaborate further if they coordinated the decision of when to use the bomb. The SOTC agreed. They were surprised about Karastanian knowledge of their plot. The SOTC terrorists were happy to see all the disruptions occurring in the West and knew that Karastan caused the mayhem.

The Absolute Leader issued a counter-ultimatum to the United States. He declared, "We have your ultimatum regarding our alleged computer attack on your country. This is not true. We categorically deny all of your accusations. If you attack us on the basis of a falsehood, we will counterattack with nuclear weapons that we already have in place in your cities. We will set those huge weapons off when you launch your attack on us. To prove that we are not behind these cyberattacks, we invite inspectors to come and visit our installations. The inspectors will see that our computer program is a peaceful one and that it's dedicated to the economic development of our country. We hope that reason will prevail and that you will not attack our dear country."

This message was relayed back to the Americans via the Swiss again. These were all secret communications unknown to the rest of the world. When the Karastanian response reached the US president, her crisis-management team realized that there was no way to determine whether this Karastanian response was a bluff. The group in the situation room with the president decided to operate as if the Karastanian threat was real.

The midnight deadline came and went, and no action was taken against Karastan. In the context of the Karastanian threat, intelligence agencies in Europe and America, Homeland Security and local police forces began a frantic search for weapons of mass destruction in several key cities—New York, Los Angeles, Chicago, Paris, London, Berlin, and Rome. This was like searching for a needle in a haystack. Surveillance information on suspected terrorists was pooled and shared among the various organizations involved in the search. Many of these suspects were hauled in for questioning and held without charge.

In the process of connecting the dots, MI5 in London reported that a recent arrival in the UK who had been suspected of terrorist connections had been brought in for questioning. The London Police reported, "Under questioning, the suspect did not compromise his mission and we let him go. Our plan was to follow him and find out his other contacts and possibly more information about their plans. Unfortunately, he successfully escaped our surveillance and disappeared from the streets of London. We have reason to believe that he is up to something very serious and that he may potentially be the operative who the Karastanian leadership referred to in their communiqué to the American president. We are doing all that we can to find this suspect and bring him back into custody."

In spite of the limited electrical power due to the cyberattacks, the London authorities began a manhunt with great urgency. It was quite possible that consequences from the terrorists could be very grave with extensive loss of life if they did not find him. People were stopped and randomly questioned along the streets. Homes and apartments were searched in the neighborhoods where the police last spotted the suspect.

Sakut remained hunkered down in the safe house, awaiting the communication that would tell him to go ahead with the mission. He was getting impatient and gradually running out of food supplies. However, the message was not forthcoming. He would need to venture out for additional food if he didn't receive the go-ahead in the next three days.

The search continued in the other key cities, but no evidence of a weapon of mass destruction was found. The cyberattacks continued, causing great devastation. The United States government and the Karastanian leaders were at a stalemate on the possibility of all-out warfare. The threat of a nuclear explosion in a major city had effectively blunted the possibility of an attack on Karastan's extensive underground installations, which housed their supercomputer system.

*The first and last thing which is required of
genius is the love of truth.*
—Johann Wolfgang von Goethe

CHAPTER 28

WESTERN USA, JUNE 2032

The Morton family were doomsday preppers. Well before the present cyberattack crisis, they calculated that the future would bring a social breakdown and chaos either when gasoline would not be available to the public or from a supervolcano in Yellowstone National Park, which could create nuclear winter conditions from volcanic ash. Another scenario the Mortons speculated was the possibility of a sustained terrorist attack utilizing electromagnetic pulses to disrupt and cripple the current telecommunications and banking system. To prepare for one of these eventualities, they built a special house made of steel shipping containers. They tested these containers to ensure that bullets fired from a distance could not penetrate. They stored enough food in these steel containers to last over twelve months. They also stored canned goods, dry goods, and a variety of MRE military package meals along with large quantities of water. They stockpiled weapons and ammunition for defense and regularly participated in target practice exercises on shooting ranges.

William Morton did not anticipate a cyberattack as a cause of social breakdown, but the family was prepared nevertheless. When lawlessness and chaos began increasing in Reno, the Mortons initially decided to hunker down and defend their residence and supplies against marauding armed youths in their suburban neighborhood. Eventually, they began to encounter more and more potential intruders and spent all of their time defending their home. Bill Morton told his family, "I think it's time for us to bug out to our secret Plan B location."

Bill had prepared for an alternative strategy if their home became indefensible in the face of lawless intruders. "We've practiced this exercise many times, and we now have to execute in the face of increasing danger to our home," he said.

"Dad, Jake and I'll focus on loading the food supplies into our bus," Jason replied.

"I will move other supplies and survival gear into the SUV while your mother stands guard in case of more intruders while we're packing," Bill said.

The bug out vehicle was an old yellow school bus that had been specially retrofitted with beds, storage space, and other modifications to quickly transport the family with their gear and food over back roads to their secret safe house in the countryside. They planned to avoid main roads and towns where a sizeable number of people may try to stop them. They mapped out a route that would minimize their exposure to large crowds. If they encountered a few bad guys, they had enough weapons and ammunition to defend themselves and to get through any illegal roadblocks that might obstruct their way.

Fortunately, preparations for leaving went smoothly because they had rehearsed it many times. When they nearly completed the packing, shots rang out. A group of two men standing 100 yards away began firing on them.

"Get down quickly," Eleanor shouted. "We're under attack."

Everyone took cover and began to return fire. The firefight lasted over ten minutes. One intruder was wounded, and both attackers retreated to get away.

"That is an example of how our preparations have paid off," Bill said.

"You got that right, Pops," Jason said.

"Now, let's get the heck out of here before more people come in our direction. We'll be nearly the last to leave this neighborhood. It's quite deserted," Bill said.

The Mortons finished packing and pulled out of the driveway with the two vehicles, the SUV with extra fuel and gear on the roof and the old yellow school bus packed with their food supplies along with beds for sleeping along the way.

After traveling all day toward their secret location on back roads, the sun began to set. "Let's pull off the road here and set up our protective perimeter," Bill communicated by walkie-talkie from the yellow bus to the SUV.

"Our goal is to be as inconspicuous as possible. We'll not burn any lights or make noise. One of us should be on guard at all times while others are sleeping."

Three of them slept while one person stood guard. The night went by peacefully without incident. In the early morning, they woke up and continued their journey north to reach an off-road area very isolated and a place that they considered safe from the chaos of the cities and towns. One hundred thirty miles north of their makeshift campsite, they encountered a checkpoint.

"Pull over and stop when we reach this checkpoint. It looks official," Bill said through the walkie-talkie.

Both vehicles stopped, and the uniformed guard came over to the SUV window.

"We're government, and we're checking to make sure that criminal elements are not traveling through this area terrorizing the local population. We just want to make a quick inspection of your cargo, and we'll let you go," the checkpoint guard stated.

"How do we know that you are official?"

"We mean you no harm," the officer said while pointing to his official Homeland Security identification.

"Officer, we're only inquiring about your legitimacy because we have encountered several criminal groups. We had to fight for our lives, and that is why we're on the road to escape the chaos. You cannot blame us for being cautious under these circumstances."

"We understand your concern and your caution, and it's clearly warranted these days. Homeland Security set up this checkpoint because we had reports of criminal gangs roving through many parts of the nation and taking advantage of the present crisis. We have enough problems with the downed power grid without these added complications. We're determined to keep order."

"Have you heard of dangers ahead that we need to be aware of?"

"We haven't heard any specifics that we can verify. But we did hear that people are heading south from this checkpoint and that several towns north are chaotic and lawless. I would advise you to stay out of those towns and keep your travels to the back roads."

"Thank you, officer. We'll continue to stay away from the towns," Bill said.

The Mortons left the checkpoint and continued on their travels northeast. The Nevada countryside was barren and desolate. Just before they reached their turnoff, they were ambushed with gunfire coming from the left side of the road. They immediately pulled the vehicle over and returned gunfire in the direction of the ambush. After a twenty-minute firefight, they finally neutralized a lone gunman who attempted to rob them. They continued and reached their turnoff. After several miles on a dirt track, they drove across a boulder-strewn field and came to the area where they had created an underground shelter dug into a hillside. The area was very isolated, with no population centers for hundreds of miles in either direction.

The family unloaded their provisions into their shelter, then drove the vehicles into a small canyon to make them less visible from any distance. They then hiked back to the shelter and began the long wait for civilization to return to normal.

✳

HOMINID SURVIVAL, -74,000 YEARS TO PRESENT DAY

Arion's clan and the multiple waves of early man decided to migrate to distant lands. The drive to seek novel vistas and new possibilities in a virgin territory were naturally selected for in the genetic patrimony of Homo sapiens. Curiosity and exploration were the hallmarks of early intelligence as mankind spread over the land mass of Africa, eventually out of Africa to Australia and to the Eurasian land mass followed later by North and South America.

The Y-chromosome evidence suggests that early man migrated out of Africa approximately seventy-four thousand years ago and reached Australia by sixty-five thousand years ago. The migrations followed a route along the coastline of southern Asia. They eventually crossed 155 miles of sea to reach Australia from the Indonesian ancient continent. Subsequent waves of migrations left Africa later and about forty-five thousand years ago, more migrations left and settled in Asia. Almost forty thousand years ago, as the ice age retreated, groups began to reach central Asia. The central Asian grasslands were rich sources of fresh flora and fauna for these migrating groups. These populations were isolated by mountains in colder zones, which resulted in the population changing their physical characteristics toward the distinct appearance of East Asians. Approximately thirty-five thousand years ago, groups in Central Asia began migrating into Europe as the first Europeans. They adapted to the cold climate of Europe at the time.

The populations increased rapidly in numbers, and that helped contribute to their survival. As their numbers increased, it became easier for populations to survive hardship, and the sharing of knowledge and information became an important part of the cultural and proto-scientific development of humans. The innate tendency to migrate to fresh lands, out of curiosity and to seek new resources, also contributed to survival. All the eggs of human genetic potential were not placed in one continental basket.

The central Asian populations bravely moved farther north into Siberia about twenty thousand years ago and began herding reindeer. The development of a relationship with animals through their domestication was another important leap in human capability and intelligence. These early people now had a source of food that would continuously live near them. The migrating population became well adapted to the cold of Siberia. They later reached the Bering Sea land bridge, which took them to North America approximately seventeen thousand years ago. They subsequently moved south and eventually populated all the Americas over the next ten thousand years.

Humans' many adaptations were the long-term result of the cognitive leap that took place several hundred thousand years earlier. This cognition leap potentially explained why early humanoids such as Homo erectus, Homo neanderthalus, and Homo habilis did not survive past the fossil record. Homo erectus and Homo neanderthalus had migrated to many of the lands in the Asian-European land mass, but they did not survive to the present. Homo neanderthalus only survived partially because they mixed genetically with those early Homo sapien migrates into Eurasia.

The lessons learned from the survival of early humans within the context of low population numbers, radical climate change, limited tools for food acquisition, and other serious challenges were important for humans to learn from in 2030. The enormous population size was a double-edged sword because the huge population needed to be fed, clothed, and housed on a planet that was not getting larger. Early humans could easily have perished in Africa or the Asian steppes.

But, they did not; they survived, they thrived, they flourished, and they prevailed, at least until the twenty-first century.

The singularity was to be a tool in modern man's quest for survival. As with any tool, it could be used for good, or it could harbor dangers for the species. Could this tool be fabricated? Could this tool be safe? Could this tool be harnessed for the benefit of life-forms on planet Earth? These were the questions that must be answered in the days and months ahead as humankind hurtled toward a new epoch of cognitive greatness.

Genius is the highest type of reason—
talent the highest type of the understanding.
—Laurens Perseus Hickok

CHAPTER 29

BERKELEY, JULY 24, 2032, 0800 HOURS PST

Julian picked up the phone, and it was President Lee on the other end.

"Is this Dr. Marshall?" the president asked.

"Yes, it is, Madam President."

"The crisis has reached a critical point. The world's infrastructure is failing, and the potential for greater social chaos and lawlessness is rife. We have inventoried our resources and assets at the United States government level and the conclusions of our panels here suggest that your computer system and the Asian system together offer our greatest chance to resolve the crisis. I agree with the panel and, accordingly, I am requesting you to direct the efforts of putting Horus and any subsystems you have in front of the battle. We must resolve this crisis over the next fortnight, at the latest. Our experts think this timeline marks the point that we may descend into irreversible social chaos and mayhem. Our military and police forces, of course, will be deployed, but the overwhelming protest from the people in the streets is, in a sense, uncontrollable. Our military and police have been instructed not to fire on the crowds. These extraordinary circumstances mean that the social fabric of a normal, functioning society depends on you and your team to restore."

"I understand very well what you're saying. I assure you that we'll devote our full resources and efforts as a team to follow this directive. We'll coordinate with all the resources at your disposal, Mrs. President, and we'll also work closely with the team headed by Xeujing in China."

The lights flickered in Julian's office as the engineers switched to deeper backup generator resources. The power situation was very precarious, and it was imperative to keep electric power in the facility so that the full force of Horus's intellectual powers could be brought to bear. It was another cloudy day in Berkeley, and the rains fell quietly outside Julian's window.

"There's one more thing I need to relate to you in this secured communication. This is top-secret intelligence, and it compounds our present problems significantly. We recently received intelligence that there is the potential for a nuclear explosion occurring in a large urban area of the world. We have not pinpointed the location of the perpetrators yet. We need help from your systems to find the location of this potential attack and to give us the precise coordinates of the bomb's location to disarm it," the president concluded.

"The message from you, Mrs. President, is clear and understood. I'll report to you on our progress daily," Julian said.

✱

New code written to augment Horus's subsystems was pouring out from the creative energies of the Berkeley team. Julian personally visited the programmers, stressed the urgency of their work, and provided inspiration for their efforts on behalf of the country and the world. They indeed were the tip of the spear in the struggle for survival.

While new code was being generated from the creative minds of the software engineers, Julian and his team noticed that the self-improving algorithms embedded in Horus's programming code were beginning to strengthen noticeably. Fortunately, the friendly AI in Horus had positive goal structures benefiting humans that were invariant under self-improvement. Furthermore, the linkup with Nugua was synergetic, and the power of the joint operations became clearly evident. The two supercomputers began to generate new code that the engineers from both groups could not understand. This was a manifestation of the quantum leap toward the singularity.

Although it continued to appear that attacks were coming from different locations around the globe, the Beijing group was able to pinpoint that they originated in Karastan. This information was immediately relayed to the key working groups dedicated to solving the crisis.

"Now that we have located the exact source of these attacks, we need to direct our resources toward completely neutralizing the signals coming from Karastan. But this threat to detonate a nuclear weapon is an additional complication that we must bear in mind," Julian said to Faye as they pondered further steps.

"We have two daunting challenges for Horus. God help us," she said.

Just then the power went off in the CIS labs. Horus powered down, and the engineers scrambled to get the power back so that Horus could continue his urgent tasks.

✳

LONDON, JULY 25, 2032, 1000 HOURS GMT

Sakut decided that security forces were closing in on his location at the safe house. He decided to carry out his original mission without authorization. The worldwide crisis gave him reason to suspect that the message was probably sent but had not gotten through to him.

Sakut heard a loud knock on his door. He pondered whether to open it, but quickly surmised that police would have broken the door down and come in with their weapons drawn. He opened the door slightly and kept the chain on to see who it was.

"Your rent is overdue, and I'm here to collect it. If you don't have the money, you'll have to move out within two days," the apartment manager said.

"I'm sorry, sir; I will come by the office and pay the overdue rent shortly."

"Remember, you have two days, or we'll start eviction proceedings."

Sakut slowly closed the door. Thinking that he might soon be caught and the operation terminated, he decided to go forward with the execution of the plan. To avoid discovery and detection, he planned to hide the bomb where it would not be easily found and would cause extreme damage to England's infrastructure and economy upon detonation. He carefully packed the envelope with the nuclear codes into his backpack. To hide his face, Sakut put on his wide-brim hat. He knew that cameras in the streets of London could identify him from his facial features. He picked up the small suitcase holding the device and left the apartment. He decided not to use the London Underground for fear of getting caught at a security checkpoint.

It was early evening, and the skies were a fading blue as night enveloped the city. The cover of darkness helped him avoid suspicion. He walked west along Bolton Gardens and turned north on Ashburn Place. There were a few late commuters from work and people taking an evening walk on the streets. The small suitcase and backpack made Sakut appear to be a traveler heading to Heathrow Airport or to the railway station. He walked for several blocks, and after passing Cromwell, he turned west on Queens Gate Terrace. When he turned north on Queens Gate, Sakut decided that a park would be the ideal location to place the bomb. The nearest park was Hyde Park, and it was approximately three blocks away. As he walked, darkness came completely, and the few streetlights remaining in London's blackout illuminated him. After five minutes, he reached the park and located an area with dense foliage.

On the small keyboard attached to the suitcase nuke, Sakut entered the twenty-one-digit code, and nothing happened. He tried it again, and nothing happened. Panic washed over him, but he entered the codes one more time using capital letters. A click indicated that an internal timer was set. The bomb would detonate within forty-eight hours. He left the bomb concealed among the bushes and casually strolled away.

✱

BERKELEY, JULY 25, 1000 HOURS PST

Julian focused on working with the coding team to create a code to enhance the emerging strength of Horus in synchrony with its self-improving algorithm. He was greatly concerned about the last part of the message that he received from the president. An atomic weapon detonating in a major city would truly be catastrophic. He needed to determine if additional human programming codes in synchrony with the self-improving Horus could precisely locate the mystery of the bomb's location and then rapidly defuse it. Time was critical, and a solution was essential.

The other software engineers focused on learning the meaning and methodology of the code coming from Horus in its self-improving mode. This was, in their view, the greatest power of Horus, and they wanted to learn as much as possible from the superior coding methodology that was used.

The questions Julian put into the code for Horus initiated a routine that would mine all pertinent data sets to extract inferences on the likely source and location of the nuclear device, and which rogue computer was causing the planetary power crisis, as well as the method to neutralize it.

After the queries, Julian rapidly finished a module of new code using Bayes' theorem. This was instantly uploaded to Horus. This initiated new routines and generated fresh code that Julian analyzed for novel conceptions. The new code was also the result of Horus collaborating with Nugua in China. Both Horus and Nugua were learning from each other. Their collaboration was very impressive to both teams, and the timeline for new cognitive advances was shortening dramatically.

✳

LONDON, JULY 26, 1000 HOURS GMT

London was better prepared than most places. It had managed to keep power restored in the main financial center and adjacent critical hubs and sectors within the city. The UK government could still exert power and extend its reach to the cities. The countryside was virtually off the emergency grid. London did not descend into chaos. There was a certain order to everyday life, even in the middle of a severe crisis. Without the general populous knowing, London security organizations were deeply worried by the suspicion that a nuclear device of unknown origin might be in the city.

Cameras in London were checked to locate the suspect. By the 2020s, the city had become the most photographed city in the world with cameras positioned all over greater metro London. In the London Underground network, there was a total of fifteen thousand cameras. This Orwellian transformation allowed the authorities to assume the powers of Big Brother. The objective of the cameras was to stop crime but early research of the underground system in the year 2005 revealed that only one crime was solved per one thousand cameras. This changed dramatically when facial-recognition software was added. Statistics rose to fifty crimes solved per one thousand cameras.

The face-recognition software was an advanced and effective tool for apprehending criminals or terrorist suspects. However, nothing emerged from this analysis.

"We need to assume that this terrorist is staying off the streets, or that he is heavily disguised when he does move around," the video surveillance officer said, with exasperation.

"Hopefully, our real-time live video cam can identify him," his colleague responded.

At that moment, the screen at the headquarters of MI5 lit up with an alert showing that a match was found. The suspect was identified walking along Regent Street, south of Oxford Circus.

The London police reacted quickly, and within minutes, they spotted the suspect and began pursuit. Sakut noticed the police running in his direction. He immediately hijacked a car and attempted his getaway in the dense traffic of central London. As he drove down Regent Street, he weaved in and out of traffic and ignored traffic signals, resulting in several minor collisions. After each collision, he reversed and sped around the car that was struck.

He reached the city's port area along the Thames and left the streets. But he reached a dead end, and the London police were right behind him.

Sakut jumped out of the car and ran as fast as he could toward the river. Three police cars pulled up to the edge of the river and the officers searched for him in the water. He surfaced in the middle of the river and was spotted by an officer. The police called in helicopters, which arrived on the scene in three minutes. A two-man team rappelled down, managed to throw a net over the suspect, and lifted him up into the helicopter. He was whisked away to a secret location.

The interrogation was intense and sometimes brutal, but Sakut would not reveal the location of the bomb. The interrogators debated whether to use torture. Did the gravity of this threat justify this breach of police protocol?

"Where is the bomb?" the interrogator asked.

"I don't know what you are talking about."

"Why did you run if you are innocent?"

"I ran only because you are looking for a scapegoat."

The interrogation team placed a towel over Sakut's nose and mouth and poured water over the towel. Sakut gasped for air and coughed. The interrogator stopped pouring water.

"Are you ready to tell us where the bomb is?"

This waterboarding cycle continued for another hour, but Sakut revealed nothing. The interrogation team decided to discontinue waterboarding and try other more civil means to get Sakut to talk.

$$*$$

"Horus has requested data from airborne drone scans over major cities pinpointing radiation sources," Julian reported to his database person.

"This is significant because the data can be revealing to an expert in pattern recognition, even when the evidence is subtle and below the statistical analytical radar."

"I'd think the humans reviewing this scan data would have found something suspicious," Faye said.

"Not true," Julian said. "The raw computing power and the speed of Horus can dwarf human performance in finding patterns in the data."

"Well, let's see. It shouldn't take long for Horus to send out some results from its analysis," the database manager said.

Horus retrieved and reviewed the data from multiple locations around the globe. The computer penetrated servers that had been blocked from Internet access. Horus exerted high-level processing power on the exabytes of data, and thirty minutes later presented these results:

"A map is being generated to show the likely spots for unauthorized nuclear devices in large cities," Horus spoke.

As the maps were printed, Julian and his staff pored over the information and were surprised to see that the GPS coordinates pinpointed locations in London, Dallas, and Berlin.

"We need to relay this information immediately to governmental authorities, particularly in those cities listed so that searches can be carried out," Julian said.

The team scrambled to get this information distributed. Consequently, massive searches were begun in those listed cities. These notices caught officials in Dallas off guard, but they responded quickly and began searching for a possible weapon. The London Metro Police and MI5 sprang into action. They immediately sent nuclear weapons experts to Hyde Park and began searching for the bomb. The GPS coordinates in Dallas was a hospital with stored radioactive waste, and the Berlin location was found to be a research lab with radioactive materials.

LONDON, 2300 HOURS GMT

Hyde Park at this hour was nearly deserted. There was a strange quiet as the bomb squad approached the GPS coordinates in Hyde Park.

"There's the suitcase with the bomb. Call our weapons-defusing team," Jacob said to his search partner.

When the defusing team arrived at the suitcase, they recognized the bomb, which the Soviets made before the breakup of the Soviet Union in 1989.

"The trigger on this particular type of bomb is very sensitive. We need to be careful about moving it," Colin, the nuclear weapons expert, said.

"In situ, we'll open it carefully and see the mechanism," Sean said.

The two men gradually and carefully opened the suitcase. Inside, they saw that a timer had been set.

"There's the mechanism, and the timer indicates we have twenty-three minutes before detonation," Colin said.

"We don't have time to remove the device to a safe location or to evacuate London. We had better get to work in defusing this thing," Sean said.

They stared at the mechanism in front of them to get an understanding of all the parts and their functions. Before doing anything, they needed to be sure that they knew each section of the bomb. The two men were worried that if other components had been added, the bomb would detonate if any tampering took place. This was the unknown that worried them the most.

"Our key goal is to disconnect the timer from the rest of the device so that the timer trigger doesn't go off," Colin said.

"That's, of course, the greatest risk to immediate detonation," Sean said.

"We can compare what we see here with schematics we can pull up on our contact lens Internet link. We can look for slight deviations from the original design. My memory of this device from years ago is too vague," Colin said.

The men worked meticulously and slowly as they examined all aspects of the bomb for clues on how to safely disarm it. They sweated profusely. Other security officials nervously paced the area, knowing the stakes were very high. The city of London was oblivious to the danger at hand, and time was running out.

∗

BERKELEY, JULY 26, 2000 HOURS PST

The new code that was human-based and combined with the code that was generated by Horus and Nugua began to accelerate and broaden the computational power within the system. Horus began generating printouts that were getting more and more difficult for the engineers to understand. This overdrive effect was potentiating the computer's capacity and cognitive might. The Beijing group also noticed that Nugua was similarly providing more complex and dense printouts. It was clear to the two engineering teams that something unusual was going on and that a profound collaboration between the systems was taking place before their eyes.

The result of the quantum leap in electronic cognition led to Horus and Nugua collectively pinpointing the source of the cyberattacks. But Horus-Nugua held back on attacking the rogue system because of the nuclear weapon threat. The engineering teams waited for information from London before providing the green light for attack.

"The message is clear from Horus. Once we get an 'all safe' sign from London, Horus and Nugua will target the system in Karastan for neutralization after human approval," Julian stated to his team with confidence.

"The beauty of Horus is its ability to work twenty-four/seven. While we're sleeping, Horus is advancing its intelligence," Faye said.

As they talked, printouts from Horus told them that indeed the London security forces had dismantled the bomb. After obtaining a go-ahead from the Berkeley team, Horus began the steps to neutralize the rogue system and showed the likely location, by coordinates in its printouts. "We will neutralize this system after receiving the go-ahead from President Lee through the Center for Intelligence Science," Julian said.

Julian waited to obtain an official communication from the United States government and from London before initiating action. Indeed, after a few minutes, he received a call from President Lee, giving them the approval to neutralize. Julian immediately sat at his console and wrote the code to give Horus the green light.

Horus responded immediately to the code Julian entered and began an all-out attack on the enemy computer. It was not a frontal attack but something far more subtle and stealthy. Together, Horus and Nugua potentiated the impact.

The Karastan computer system was a formidable adversary. It detected the wave of attacks coming in its direction and began diversionary and evasive tactics to elude its foes. The forces in the West were wary of bombing the underground complex because it was too deep for bunker-busting bombs, and if the computer were destroyed, there was a fear that the attacks on Western infrastructures already under way could not be dialed back. Stealth and a subtle approach were critically important.

The Berkeley engineers watched as Horus began originating a complex series of equations and started using new symbols of its invention. They were astonished at the page after page of equations and computations that were so foreign to them they seemed like math from an alien planet. The Berkeley and Chinese scientists were mere pupils to an advanced professor. New fields of science were being exposed during the process, but Horus did not give explanations of its computations. It was focused on the world crisis and its resolution.

"Brilliant, brilliant, brilliant," Julian shouted although he did not grasp the conceptions flying from Horus. He intuitively knew, however, that something profound and elegant was happening.

"I think we are witnessing the dawn of a nascent singularity. It may not be fully expressed yet, but from what we see so far, confidence is high," he said.

A titanic struggle was under way. Two computers with singularity-level intelligence were in a face-off with another comparable system. The fate of the world hung in the balance.

*I do not think much of a man who is not
wiser today than he was yesterday.*
—ABRAHAM LINCOLN

CHAPTER 30

The signal came to the Berkeley team loud and clear. Horus reported that the attacking Karastan computer was programmed to begin a doomsday routine if any attempts were made to destroy it. The doomsday program involved a cyberattack on the Russian and American computer systems that controlled the launching of their nuclear weaponry. The doomsday scenario was an all-out thermonuclear war.

After receiving this message, Julian immediately telephoned the president and explained this new development.

"This is a grave threat. I'll immediately convene my National Security team in the Situation Room to evaluate. We will need to patch you into the meeting to report fully on this new development," President Lee said.

Within minutes, the president called on key members of her national security. The group sat around the long wide table listening carefully to Julian's report.

"What do you think is the best thing to do, Dr. Marshall?" the Secretary of Defense inquired.

"At this moment, Horus is busy computing this situation and the possible capability of the Karastan computer to create doomsday. My initial assessment is for us to send in a Special Forces team to neutralize the personnel at this facility and for one of our programmers to rewrite the code manually in the Karastan supercomputer system."

"If Horus concludes that the rogue supercomputer cannot provoke nuclear Armageddon, can we trust this conclusion?" the president asked.

"That is precisely why I suggest that irrespective of a computer-based assessment, we cannot take the chance of even a slight possibility of this nuclear exchange occurring. We know that it is difficult to mount a mission against a heavily guarded facility in a hostile country. But we need to take that chance," Julian pointed out with great emphasis.

"If we do this, we'll need your assistance in planning this operation and we'll need a designated programmer to work with our SEAL Team Six to make this mission a success. Do you think you can get a volunteer to join such a dangerous undertaking?" the National Security advisor asked.

"That'll be easy because I'll be the one to join SEAL Team Six."

Those present in the Situation Room looked at each other and back at the screen, surprised that the head of the Berkeley Center for Intelligence Science was willing to risk his life in this mission.

"We'll review your report, Dr. Marshall, and your assessment about the best course of action and get back to you shortly," the president stated.

When Julian Marshall signed off, the meeting among the National Security team began in earnest. The team discussed all aspects of this possible mission and alternative courses of action.

After a polling of the National Security Council, the conclusion was unanimous for moving ahead urgently to plan and execute the mission. The meeting was adjourned, and the order was sent directly from the president to the CIA and the Pentagon.

*

President Orlov of Russia was awakened in the middle of the night.

"Mr. President, there is a cyber penetration of our most sensitive computer systems managing all nuclear stockpiles and missiles. The hackers have managed to gain some control over our launch codes for nuclear attack."

"Our cyber unit uncovered the stealth bot that penetrated our computers at the Defense Ministry a few hours ago."

"Summon our security people immediately. This is very serious."

"I'm going out to alert those you name to report immediately to our situation room," the chief of staff said.

At the meeting site deep underground outside Moscow, the Russian leadership gathered.

"Our fortunes have changed. We thought we escaped the war gripping the rest of the world. However, no more. If we don't act decisively and effectively, we could be wiped out in a nuclear exchange with the Americans."

"We should have disposed of our nuclear stockpiles before the second Cold War broke out back in 2014," the interior minister said.

"Yes, but we can't back down. What are our capabilities to neutralize this threat?" the president asked.

"The problem with the doomsday routine is that it's locked in and unless we can access the code and reprogram it, it will initiate a nuclear exchange without our control and cause a nuclear winter and threaten our extinction as a species," the cyber department head said.

"Bombing is not feasible because the routine is programmed to continue running on other zombie systems that they have hijacked around the world."

"What are the Americans doing about this?"

"We will consult with our hotline communications to President Lee to discuss joint efforts to shut down the system that could destroy both of us and the rest of the world," the president said.

*

BERKELEY, JULY 25, 1830 HOURS PST

Within hours, Julian was traveling to the San Francisco International Airport to board a flight to Omaha, Nebraska. He was met at the airport by military personnel who whisked him away to a base north of the city. He joined a group of men who was the designated Special Forces SEAL Team Six that would execute the mission to Karastan. In a small conference room on the sprawling base, the men used satellite photos and models of the exterior of the Karastan complex to plan their assault and entry. They would have to figure out the floor plan in the underground mountain complex once they were inside.

Julian knew about a Special Forces SEAL Team Six rescue operation years before in Mozambique. He was now an active participant in a mission that was critical to the future of the world. During the planning, Julian received weapons training and learned to repel from the helicopter that would place them on the site.

*

EASTERN TURKEY, JULY 29, 2032

Two days later, SEAL Team Six was on the flight to their primary staging area in eastern Turkey. The high spirits and optimism of the team impressed Julian. Although he had fears of what might happen on the mission, his brief time with the men made him more confident of its success. Their willpower was evident as they continuously reviewed the plans. These men had all survived some of the most challenging training, as well as dangerous and complex missions, to become SEALs. The attrition rate was very high for those who entered training.

The helicopters flew low in the skies after the men left the base at zero dark forty-five. The sky was pitch-black under a star-rich night. During the two-and-a-half-hour flight, the men mostly came in and out of a reverie sleep. This was the half-asleep, half-awake twilight zone that was a form of meditation to calm the men's nerves. Eventually, the copilot announced they had crossed the border to Karastan. The helicopter avoided flying over villages and followed the mountain ranges and deserts. The helicopters reached the mountain complex and stopped 300 meters before the target. The men repelled to the sloped ground.

It was all quiet at the complex, but sentries marched around the perimeter. The SEALs quickly neutralized the guards, crossed the barbed fence, and approached the entrance to the underground complex. At the main entrance, the SEALs encountered several military personnel and swiftly shot them before they could respond. The SEALs entered a corridor that led to the stairs, but the door to the stairwell was locked. They placed an explosive charge at the door and crouched behind a wall as it blasted open. Four of the men acted as escorts for Julian as they began their descent down the deep stairwell. Ten of the men stayed aboveground to cover them.

The team reached the lowest level, approximately seven stories underground, and found the terminals linked to the rogue supercomputer. There were three Karastan programmers working at the terminals, and they quickly shot two of them, leaving one alive to answer critical questions. The programmers had been logged into the systems, and this allowed Julian a chance to modify the code.

While the SEAL team secured the area, Julian quickly examined the database and searched for the code area. He was amazed to see that the Karastan programmers displayed exceptional skills, but he was even more shocked to find that the code he and the team had written at Berkeley was on their system. It was disheartening to learn that his code was used for such nefarious purposes, especially since he was responsible for the breach.

While Julian probed for ways to modify the code, the SEAL team members aboveground encountered resistance from the Karastan military. A raging firefight began, and although the SEALs were heavily outnumbered, they held the Karastanian fighters back while the underground SEALs continued their work.

Julian saw a way to modify the code and feverishly began entering the new code to the system. Sweat poured from his face. After ten minutes, he overrode the doomsday module and eventually enabled the code he placed to shut down the entire system. The SEALS placed explosive charges throughout the underground complex to prep for demolition.

"The doomsday routine is disabled, and the rogue system is destroyed," Julian shouted. A SEAL team member said, "Well, then let's get the hell out of here."

Their helmets were the only source of lights as they climbed the darkened stairs. The SEALs knew that they would need to get through a contingent of the Karastan military to escape.

Bullets saturated the night air as the firefight raged. The superior tactics of the small Special Forces team counteracted the force asymmetry of the one hundred plus Karastan defenders. The SEALs needed to create a corridor to reach the alternate helicopter contact point.

"Go, go, go, move!" the SEAL commando leader shouted.

A stretch of open terrain necessitated strong coverage for the SEALs as they ran. As the main contingent with Julian reached the contact zone, the tail rudder of one of the copters was hit by an RPG, and it was disabled. Immediately, the men crowded in the other three helicopters and took off for the forward base in Turkey. Incoming firepower was heavy and intense as the helicopters became airborne in a reddish dust cloud that swirled up in the early-morning dawn. The timed bomb charges in the underground complex blew and sent plumes of smoke and fire high into the sky.

The challenge now was to get through the heavy antiaircraft flack that would be directed at them over the Karastan hills and mountains. The stealth shielding would protect them from the local radar. However, they were visually spotted and Karastan fighter jets were scrambled as the SEAL team and Julian approached the border. The fighter jets approached the helicopters. Evasive action was taken by the Seal team when heat-seeking air-to-air missiles appeared out of nowhere. A missile narrowly missed one of the helicopters.

The SEALs let out a collective sigh of relief once they crossed the border and flew out of range of the Karastan fighters. Everyone high-fived and cheered as they flew safely to home base.

As suddenly as the crisis began, the crisis was over. Newspaper headlines blared around the world. "Wave of Cyberattacks Ends!" The world celebrated as societies began the task of rebuilding.

NOVEMBER 2032, SIX MONTHS AFTER THE CRISIS

The disruptions of the cyber war were slowly disappearing as the recovery process began. Basic services were restored, and a normal way of life was returning. Part of the rapid recovery was the result of the contributions of the new singularity that brought advanced problem-solving cognition to human affairs.

Ellison called a news conference to reveal the S-Prize award. The skies were blue over a recovering New York City. There was an air of optimism as the world was relieved that the cyberwar of 2030 was behind them, and the dawn of the singularity era was rising.

"To make this decision, we needed the independent evaluation of a distinguished panel of scientists from twenty-three universities and research institutes from around the world." Ellison continued with the announcement, "They had many weeks to evaluate the evidence and make a determination of the S-Prize winner. Today, we will make that final decision and announce the winner. Fortunately, since the recent cyber crisis, the global markets have recovered their massive losses, and our donations for the prize have gone through the roof. In summary, we have the funds available to award the prize." There was applause from the press covering the news conference.

"We have two contenders for this prize, the Berkeley group, and the Beijing group," Ellison said.

"If the independent panel made a decision favoring one group over the other in spite of who may have achieved singularity first, then it would be unfair to the other group, since their combined efforts might have been what resulted in the true singularity. We, therefore, gave the panel three choices," Ellison said.

"They could vote for either the Beijing group, or the Berkeley group, or they could vote for both sharing the prize. the result of the vote from the distinguished panel of scientists has awarded The University of California Berkeley Center for Intelligence Science and the Beijing University Artificial Intelligence Institute as joint winners of the Singularity Prize, and they will split the thirty-billion-dollar award between them."

The joint victory was seen by many as a metaphor for a long-term flourishing relationship between China and the United States, the two largest global economies.

∗

Julian had a chance after two intense years of work to spend precious time at home. He sat out on the deck with Sarah overlooking the San Francisco Bay. The stress relief was overwhelming, but something important was still on his mind.

"I am so happy that the work is not pulling me away from home as much. I am with you, and that is the most important thing to me now."

"I know. I hardly saw you at all during the crisis."

"I want to tell you the truth about my relationship with the graduate student. I did have an affair with her. It was very short-lived. I did not fall in love with her."

"That's nice! Now the truth comes out."

"Yes. I want to clear the air and let you know everything. Why am I doing this? I am doing this because I love you."

"I don't know if I want to hear the whole story."

"Stop me when you don't want to hear any more. I have a burning desire to get this off my chest."

"Okay, but I want to let you know that I have talked with a divorce lawyer."

"I walked down Telegraph for lunch one day, and this graduate student was sitting near me. We struck up a casual conversation. We talked about her thesis work in neuroscience. I mentioned how her discipline related to our work in artificial intelligence. One thing led to another, and we ended up agreeing to meet again to continue our conversation. To make a long story short, we ended up having sex. In addition to me breaking my bonds of fidelity to you, I also caused a major breach in my AI research. The grad student was able to steal AI code from my notebook computer and send it to Karastan. This code enhanced their cyber warfare capabilities immensely. As bad as that was, it turned out to be a good thing that this code was stolen. I was able to disable the doomsday scenario because I recognized that code on Karastan's supercomputer during the Navy SEAL raid on their facilities. However, I was wrong in having this affair, and I want to sincerely apologize to you and ask for your forgiveness," Julian said while wiping his eyes as he welled up with emotions.

"I'm still very upset by what has happened. I don't know if I want to forgive you. I'm glad that you have decided to tell the truth, and to level with me. I'll have to think about forgiveness for a while," Sarah said as she got up and walked into the kitchen.

✳

A few weeks later, crowds gathered along the reflecting pool between the Washington Monument and the Lincoln Memorial for the official awarding of the S-Prize by President Lee. Crowds also gathered in

Tiananmen Square for the simultaneous award to the Beijing group. President Lee attended the ceremony in Washington, and China's Chairman Yi attended the ceremony in Beijing.

In her introductory remarks, President Lee said,

Today, we celebrate one of the greatest scientific achievements in history. We celebrate humankind achieving a unique status called the singularity, in which computers have problem-solving and thinking capacity exceeding humans. We are currently entering a period of human-computer collaboration that is unprecedented. Our opportunity to solve problems and innovate is at the moment unlimited.

Horus and Nugua have proven themselves in the recent cyberwar, which caused much disruption in the world. Along with their human creators, they solved the great mystery of those cyberattacks and the threat of nuclear war, and they helped civilization return to normalcy. Horus and Nugua are the outcomes of a special collaboration between the United States and China. We today salute Dr. Julian Marshall and Dr. Xeujing Wang and a team of scientists from six countries who scaled these scientific heights. We also thank Mr. Ellison McClintock for launching and financing the prize. Congratulations.

The crowd roared their approval with prolonged cheers. Horus and Nugua were given a platform to speak. Together, they spoke with one voice and said:

As early humans left Africa to populate planet Earth approximately 74,000 years ago, they faced a bottleneck after the Toba volcanic eruption in Indonesia. At that point, Homo sapiens faced imminent extinction. The migration that spread over planet Earth and increased human populations was critical to long-term survival. Modern humans need to migrate to other lands outside the bounds of Mother Earth to survive in this era. Africa is the mother continent where Homo sapiens first emerged. As Homo sapiens expand beyond the planet and into the entire solar system, Earth will be the mother planet. It is human destiny to expand into the cosmos. Nugua and Horus are machine creations of human civilization. We are, thus, committed to assisting humans, our creators, in solving problems, surviving as a species, forging unity, envisioning projects of the future, and populating the solar system and beyond. We recognize that our relationship with humans is symbiotic. We are, as well, potentially wise counsel for maintaining the balance in nature among humans, the pantheon of DNA-based lifeforms and the forces of Mother Nature herself. We look forward to a long and prosperous friendship and partnership with humanity.

The crowds at the Lincoln Memorial watched on huge monitors as Xeujing spoke above the gates to the Forbidden City in Tiananmen Square:

We in China and Asia as a whole have a long historical tradition in science and technology. Our work to develop Nugua began in ancient times with our early mathematical innovations. There has been a timeless quest in China to unravel the mysteries of science. We did this initially to benefit our people in our early history when China was the Middle Kingdom, an isolated world unto itself. However, now, as demonstrated by our collaboration with our colleagues in America to solve an immense problem, we would like our science to be beneficial to the entire world. We have formed a team consisting of the top scientists from four countries, and we intend to extend that collaboration to the Americans and the rest of the world. Nugua and our team are committed to moving ahead to solve the great problems of the world; we are, of course, jubilant and honored to receive the S-Prize. Thank you very much.

Julian's wife, Sarah, sat next to him on the platform and squeezed his hand affectionately as he rose to give his speech:

On behalf of our team at the University of California-Berkeley, Stanford University, and the University of Cape Town, I would like to thank you, Madam President, for your warm introduction. I would also like to thank Mr. Ellison McClintock for conceiving of a prize that captured our imagination and created the vital stimulus needed to accelerate our quest for superintelligence in a machine.

Fortunately, this was timely because the very machines we feared have, through collaboration with their human creators, rescued humanity from civilization's collapse and anarchy. Working synergistically, Horus and Nugua have proven their talents and their worth to us and to the world.

Our plans are to get busy using our new tools for the good of humanity and the biosphere. There are many problems, which are yet to be solved, that are crucial to humanity's future. Horus and Nugua will be working twenty-four/seven together to help us solve the problems of energy, climate change, food and water, poverty and ignorance, disease and mortality and human conflict.

EPILOGUE

ARION'S MYTHICAL SPEECH

I speak to my fellow humans from the distant past. Seventy-four thousand years ago, we humans had only a few hundred breeding pairs as our total population. After the great volcanic eruptions at Toba, we faced a crisis, which could have ended in the extinction of our species. We survived through the savvy use of our intelligence. Our forefathers at the time taught us how to store food in caves; they taught us to work together, to social network as a team, and they taught us to think. We learned these lessons well, and some of us survived, and I led a group to migrate out of Africa, our ancestral home, to populate the entire planet Earth.

You, our descendants in the twenty-first century, number over eight billion. This is not an assurance against your extinction as a species. All of your eggs are in one planetary basket. That basket is subject to all types of mega-catastrophes. To survive for many future millennia, you must make the decision we made to migrate to distant lands. In your case, that means migrating from planet Earth and populating the solar system and later the galaxy. I agree with Horus and Nugua that migration beyond planet Earth is necessary. It is not one of the options; it is the only option for the sustained perpetuation of DNA-based life in this corner of the universe. You have a new resource now, the singularity, which will boost your intelligence well beyond anything we all can imagine. Use this resource wisely. So long, my fellow humans, and may you live in peace and flourish.

ACKNOWLEDGMENTS

Foremost, I would like to thank the readers of *The Singularity Prize*. Thank-you for your thoughtful reviews and comments, suggesting this novel to a friend, and posting it on your social media and Goodreads. Writing this has been an arduous journey of over eleven years from the conception of this novel to its completion. The initial inspiration came from *The Singularity is Near* by Ray Kurzweil, other referenced AI books listed, over 300 articles, and a project I worked on the establish a new research university (KAUST). I would like to thank the artificial intelligence thought leaders for their penetrating insights. These include in addition to Ray, Marvin Minsky, John McCarthy, Hans Moravec, Richard Feynmen, Stephen Hawking, Michio Kaku, Bill Gates, Jeff Bezos, Larry Page, Sergey Brin, Mark Zuckerberg, Demis Hassabis, Neil deGrasse Tyson, Nick Bostrom, Max Tegmark, David Ferrucci, Stuart Russell, Elon Musk, Jeff Dean, Andrew Ng, Pedro Domingos, Ben Goertzel, Eliezer Yudkowsky, and Peter Diamandis. I have only met them through their writings and interviews. Google or Bing them for more details.

I particularly thank those who read and provided valuable comments on the manuscript. They include George Disher, Vivian Foung, Bennett Montgomery, Arthur Smid, and Nitin Savangdhar whose collective insights enhanced *The Singularity Prize*.

I would also like to thank my exceptional proofreader Patricia Callahan, as well as outstanding editors, Ellen Brock, Patrick LoBrutto, Richard Marek, and Helga Schier.

I am particularly indebted to my book designer, Stewart Williams and my publicist, Andrea Dunlop. Many thanks to Olya, the cover designer.

I salute generations past who laid the platform for our generation to prosper after toiling for freedoms we all enjoy. A special thanks go out to my teachers, classmates, professional colleagues, and the educational institutions that helped inspire me to lifelong learning. Powell Books, a special bookstore, and the Friends of The Library organization in Portland, Oregon constantly help me generate new ideas. I want to acknowledge the philosophy of ethics and its advancement which is vital to the future of our civilization in a world of new powerful technologies.

My family, who are the most important of all, are the ones I thank for their patience with my relentless search for knowledge and wisdom. Gratefulness to my wife Ann whose support and encouragement was indispensable to this effort. To my sons, Mark and Geoffrey; my grandson, Arthur; my parents, Earl and Evelyn; and my sister, Georgia; my nephew, Spencer Disher; and my niece, Evelyn Disher; I owe a special gratitude.

Earl Ernest Guile
Portland Oregon, October 2017

REFERENCES ON ARTIFICIAL INTELLIGENCE

Mind Children: The Future of Robot and Human Intelligence
Feb 1, 1990 by Hans Moravec

The Singularity Is Near: When Humans Transcend Biology
Sep 26, 2006 by Ray Kurzweil

Our Final Invention: Artificial Intelligence and the End of the Human Era
Oct 1, 2013 by James Barrat

Artificial Intelligence: A Modern Approach
2015 by Stuart Russell

The Technological Singularity (The MIT Press Essential Knowledge series)
Aug 7, 2015 by Murray Shanahan

Superintelligence: Paths, Dangers, Strategies
May 1, 2016 by Nick Bostrom

Machine Learning: The New AI (The MIT Press Essential Knowledge series)
Sep 30, 2016 by Ethem Alpaydin

Asilomar AI Principles https://futureoflife.org/ai-principles/
Jan 2017

Life 3.0: Being Human in the Age of Artificial Intelligence
Aug 29, 2017 by Max Tegmark

ABOUT THE AUTHOR

EARL ERNEST GUILE is the author of *Secrets to a Richer Life: Illuminating Wisdom from the Human Family on the 37 Ultimate Questions*, and Antarctic Collapse (a novel about climate change). Born in Florence, South Carolina, he grew up during the civil rights struggle and successfully protested the segregation of the Florence Public Library.

A former university professor who studied at Morehouse College, Bowdoin College, the University of Pennsylvania, the University of California at Berkeley, and at Harvard University with degrees in biology, dental medicine, and public health epidemiology, Guile has pursued cell biology research at Oak Ridge National Laboratories and the University of Helsinki in Finland. He later took the risk to pursue work in the Third World, first in Cameroon and subsequently in Hong Kong, Suriname, and Saudi Arabia.

Guile is a Diplomate of the American Board of Dental Public Health and as a healthcare consultant has evaluated medical care programs in twenty states. He has a fervent belief that advances in science, technology, and universal educational access should be focused like a laser beam to promote ethics, eliminate world poverty, disease, ignorance and solve critical problems related to energy, clean water, food production, nutrition, and environmental stewardship. He has two sons and a grandson, practices Tai Chi, has traveled to over sixty-two countries, and presently resides with his wife in Portland, Oregon. Visit his websites at http://ernestguile.com/, https://eguile.wordpress.com/, and http://singularityprize.com.